About the Author

Tanya Rose is a graphic designer and photographer from Victoria, Australia. Living in the leafy outer suburbs of Melbourne, she fulfilled a lifelong dream with the release of her first novel, *The Wave*, and continues the journey with this follow-up book, *The Sun*. She loves to travel and is a passionate reader, especially when it comes to supporting local and independent authors. You can find her on TikTok and Facebook where she documents her current work and upcoming projects.

www.tanyarose.com.au

A HOUSTON HOTEL NOVEL

Tanya Rose

The Sun

Tanya Rose Author

"Be yourself; everyone else is already taken."
Oscar Wilde

This book is for the girls, *the Romance Lovers*.

In a world filled with uncertainty, political unrest, and judgment; find emotional support, passion, excitement and love within the pages of a good book. I'm truly humbled by your support, encouragement, laughter, and the time you spend reading my books.

Thank you once again to my family, and Merilyn, Rhondda, Katrina & Melinda. You have been the best 'hype girls' a debut author could only dream of. Thank you eternally.

To add, like last time, I'm still not embarrassed to write sex scenes. Enjoy!

Love, Tanya.

CHAPTER ONE

NEW YORK

I'm captivated. On stage, at the front of the room, is the most mesmerizing couple on planet Earth. I doubt I'll ever witness anything this beautiful again.

Bee and Jarrod just might be celestial beings, with their heavenly voices, her angelic golden-blond hair and emerald eyes, and his devilish dark features and midnight-blues. The pair is performing in front of a full house tonight. They're only here for the next six weeks, but word quickly spread that this spectacularly talented duo is playing at The Houston Hotel New York, and it didn't take long before we were reaching capacity every night they performed.

I'm essentially stuck with my back to the wall in this glorious and classy lounge, Le Soleil, whose name literally translates to 'The Sun'. Mrs. Houston likes to give her restaurants and cocktail venues names inspired by natural elements.

The room is decorated in classy and luxurious art deco style—with Italian marble flooring, black-and-gold-patterned geometric wallpaper, and lush golden chairs—like something from the pages of an interior design magazine. Mrs. Houston calls it her mix of neoclassical and art deco, two styles she fell in love with as a young girl.

I love to ask about her early life in Paris and listen to her describe all the places I wish I could visit. Unfortunately, I need to work my butt off to pay for all my student loans before I can afford to travel anywhere—and my bosses need me here.

I'm a self-professed workaholic. Even now, though I attempt to switch from work mode to, well, non-work mode, I can't help thinking about all the work waiting on my desk for tomorrow.

I focus on Bee's beautiful voice. I've only known her for a short time, but we have a lot in common, and she's already made such an impression on me. Though I'm slightly younger at twenty-four, we're both in our twenties, independent and with a lack of blood relations.

Bee and I might have bonded over our shared experience of being orphans, but now she describes her friends in London as her family, and she's so happy it radiates from her like a sunbeam. It all sounds like a dream to me.

I admire her bravery in building a chosen family and welcoming others into her life. I can't let anyone get so close. I throw myself into work because I barely know how to have a long-term friendship. My childhood was far from conventional, and as a result I find that trying to befriend people isn't worth the challenges that come with it.

So, I work and study, and I eat and sleep, then I work some more. I like it that way. The only responsibility I have is to myself.

A warm, delicate hand pats my hair, like my mother used to do when I was tired or sick. It's comforting, yet the nostalgia also feels like a stab to my heart reminding me what I'll never experience again.

"*L'été*, why are you hiding away at the back of the room?" I turn towards Mrs. Houston, my boss and one of the most stunningly vibrant and confident women I've ever known. I couldn't be more grateful for the opportunity she gave me two years ago when she hired me to help her run this hotel.

Tonight, a figure-hugging black dress cocoons her petite frame like a glove. How her giant of a son came out of her lithe body is still a mystery to me. She gazes at me with familiar coffee-colored eyes that emanate affection, almost like I mean something to her. We may be close, but I feel like she just has an extraordinary ability to make everyone feel accepted and important.

"I'm fine here, Mrs. Houston," I say, pushing off from the wall and standing up straighter. "I just want to listen to them again… They're so magical together." I sigh, and my eyes drift back into the Bee and Jarrod orbit once again.

"I know, *ma chérie*, they are, how you say, *stupéfiant*. Breathtaking, astounding." Her eyes well up a little as she looks toward the stage at her handsome, talented son, and his beautiful love. She told me Jarrod used to be very reserved before he met Bee, and she's overjoyed that he's chasing his dreams with such a strong and talented partner.

"They are almost finished. Join us at the family table? That's where you belong." I nod. "And, *L'été*…" She turns my chin towards her to get my full attention. "My name is Eléa. No more Mrs. Houston, yes?" She smiles, and warmth floats over me as I look into her eyes.

"Yes, I know, Eléa. I just like to maintain formality at work." Though my shift is over, she knows how committed I am to professionalism. She's the owner of this grandiose hotel and can do as she pleases, but I can't be friends with the staff. They won't respect a manager my age unless I distance myself. Eléa is my only exception to the 'no friends' rule.

"I know, dear, but I get bored with that name. It was my mother-in-law's name, and I am not so old yet!" She laughs, face glowing with youth even though she has smile lines from years of good humor. I think age only makes her more beautiful, like a fine wine—a Chateau Mouton Rothschild from Bordeaux. Expensive, exuberant, rare.

"Give me a minute to hear the last song, then I'll join you, I promise." I give her hand a squeeze.

"Good, good." She nods to herself. "I'll order the champagne, and you join the family and toast to my son and his *Petite Abeille*."

I love how she prefers her names in French over English. Mrs. Houston—Eléa—only uses French names for her family and close friends. Maybe that's what makes me feel a little special.

Bee has been '*Petite Abeille*', or Little Bee, since she arrived, and my name, '*L'été*', means Summer—or 'summertime', as Eléa tells me. I don't think I look very summery, truth be told. My hair is dark and long, and my eyes are a storm of charcoal gray. The only summery thing about me is the dusting of freckles across my nose and cheeks. They're inherited from my father's side—the Australian side.

I watch her as she saunters off into the crowd. Her glossy black hair is up in a French knot, diamonds dripping from her ears, yet for all her class, she never makes anyone feel any less. Even I feel less like an employee and more like her daughter.

There goes my heart again… Just a little more pain to endure.

I close my eyes and listen to Bee and Jarrod's last song. The lyrics are poetic and raw. I can hear how they complement each other; her bright, pure tone and his deep, dark timbre just work. I am not a jealous person; I never really had a reason to be jealous—no siblings, no long-term friends—but I feel a little envious deep down. Somewhere in my locked-up, key-gone-missing heart, I feel a longing to someday find that too.

The last strains of the song diffuse through the packed room, and I open my eyes. There is a collective silence. I suspect everyone in this elegant room needs a moment to absorb the incredible magic they just witnessed. Then, thunderous applause explodes from the audience. Jarrod takes Bee's hand, giving her a kiss before they both take a well-earned bow. I look over at Mr. and Mrs. Houston, their faces shining with pride as they clap along with the rest of us. I'm so lucky to be a part of this establishment; at my age, Mrs. Houston took a massive chance on me.

When I first applied to work for her, I was fresh out of college with no experience. She must have seen something in me that day, because here I am two years later, co-managing one of the most successful hotels in the city. Being a general manager at my age doesn't come without its challenges, but this is my home. I never want to leave. I've found my place in the world, and until I came here it was a pretty fucked up world. This is my paradise.

I make my way over to the family table, or *'table de famille'* as Mrs. Houston calls it, permanently reserved for her family and friends, the inner circle, and those special few she honors with an invite. Bee and Jarrod are sipping on chilled champagne; no doubt Jarrod's parents ordered the top shelf bubbly for this occasion.

"Summer!" Bee chimes in her musical voice, and suddenly I'm surrounded by her embrace, her golden hair flying around her shoulders like an angelic halo. I give her a squeeze back. I am still learning to be comfortable hugging people, especially those I've just met, but Bee makes it easy. She is so genuine, and I can see why Jarrod totally adores her. With a killer body, face of an angel, and voice of a sultry temptress, she effortlessly draws every eye in the room. Jarrod, aware of the danger that accompanies so many hungry eyes, keeps her close.

He himself is so intimidatingly hot, like magazine-underwear-model hot. But his stunning features also distance him, like he sits on a pedestal, immune to the effect of ordinary people. His demeanor sends a cautionary message to everyone nearby, wordlessly broadcasting his capability to annihilate someone who hurts Bee. He doesn't seem possessive; rather, he acts protective of her. I guess, being famous, Bee's had her share of stalkers. Jarrod seems more than able to keep them away, though, so I'm not worried about Bee's safety.

"Bee, I have no words. You were just perfection again tonight," I tell her while she holds my hands, excited to hear my review of their show.

"Really? Oh, I'm so happy you liked it, Summer. Jarrod and I haven't been performing together for very long, but it feels good, you know, like we've found our sweet spot," she exclaims, as her eyes glide over to her handsome boyfriend. He smiles at her with such force I have to look away, because *shit*. That smile unleashed is dangerous.

"Angel, I know exactly how to find your sweet spot," he murmurs, and I catch a blush rising to her cheeks like an overflow of hot lava. "And that's my cue to get a drink and leave you two lovebirds to burn up the place. Just do me a favor, don't set the fire alarms off. I don't want the clean up on my day off tomorrow." These two are hotter than an Australian summer, and I remember those days I lived in Sydney... No amount of swimming could tame the blazing heat when the Aussie sun beat down on us.

"Jarrod, my son, are you tormenting our best employee?" Mr. Houston—Max—arrives and hands me a crisp glass of Rosé Dom Pérignon gold edition.

"What, me? I'm always on my best behavior, Dad. It's Chris you have to worry about. That tosser gets himself into all kinds of strife. I wish Daniel well in babysitting him while I'm here." He laughs. Bee slaps him on the shoulder, and he leans down, giving her a kiss on the head.

"Christopher is not a tosser. I can attest to that personally. Well, aside from that one time, but otherwise he is a perfect gentleman," Bee states, standing up for her soon-to-be brother-in-law. Her British accent sounds so melodic compared to the constant vocal babble in the room.

"Bee, I know my second born can be a perfect gentleman when he so chooses, but let's be honest: he is more like his mother. And she can be as unpredictable as the weather," Max comments, a rosy glow on his face. His vivid blue eyes, the same eyes Jarrod inherited, sparkle in the dimly-lit room.

He is so thrilled to have Jarrod and Bee here in New York. Mr. and Mrs. Houston lose a part of themselves being so far away from their sons, but I know how immensely proud they are to have the boys run the London Hotel. Now they've got me, they return to the UK at least twice a year. They have complete faith in me, and can travel, confident that I've got everything covered. And I would never let them down.

"Here you are, my loves. Come and sit, hors d'oeuvres have been served." Eléa takes mine and Bee's arms and escorts us to her table.

The hour is late, but thankfully I have tomorrow off from work, so I can enjoy the company tonight.

As I take a seat, I look out the window and notice the delicate shapes of the raindrops falling around the buildings. Without any wind, the rain seems to float down at a leisurely pace, weightless as a feather. Thankfully, I can't feel the chill of the outdoors on account of the warmth in the room.

"*Ma chérie*… will you come to my suite tomorrow? I must talk to you about something."

I turn towards Eléa, a frown on my forehead as I grow concerned. "Of course, is everything OK?" I ask her, because I can't think of anything that's amiss with work or the hotel right now.

"Yes, yes, do not worry, *L'été*, all is well. I have some news I must discuss with you. It's *magnifique!*" she exclaims, and I release a bated breath. OK, it's some kind of good news.

"Yes, of course. I'm having lunch with Bee, then I can see you around… two p.m.?"

She nods, patting my arm like she always does.

"To Brooklyn and Jarrod, may they be as successful as they are happy." Mr. Houston holds up his drink in a toast, and we all do the same.

I look over to see the couple sharing a quick kiss. Jarrod's eyes don't leave Bee even as she turns away. His gaze never abandons her for more than a short time when she is nearby. That kind of love, that kind of devotion, is something I have only seen in movies. It can't be real, can it? I know what my eyes see, but this is surely just a one in a million bolt of lightning. Turning, I see Mr. Houston look at his wife, a woman who he has been married to for thirty-four years, and I realize he looks at her the same way Jarrod looks at Bee. It may be a few decades later, but that love still shines bright in his eyes.

I sip my champagne, tasting the bubbles as they burst on my tongue, and wish someone had loved my mother like that. Someone who could have looked at her the way these men look at their partners. However, she knew nothing but pain and sorrow. Despite that, she loved me with the fierceness of a lioness, and I will be forever grateful for the time we had together.

She passed while I was finishing college; I knew the cancer had spread, but she wouldn't let me defer my classes. Even so, I didn't know that it would only be a few short months from diagnosis to her leaving me for good.

Getting this job meant the world to me. Maybe that's why Mrs. Houston—Eléa—hired me. A fierce mother in her own right. Maybe she saw something in me—desperation, determination, who knows? But she took the chance, and I will do everything I can to show her I was the right choice.

Dinner is wonderful, and we all enjoy a few too many champagnes. Of course, the French can drink wine like it's water; I, unfortunately, will feel its effects tomorrow.

After dinner, I head to the twenty-ninth floor. The entire floor is private and reserved for the Houston family and their personal guests. I have my own apartment suite; it came with the GM position and is much more comfortable than the student accommodation I lived in previously. Thank God I don't have to share a bathroom with random strangers and exchange students any longer. Those days are nothing more than a terrible memory of the past.

My little space is my sanctuary. No guests can access the floor, and no random door knockers or strange men can follow me back here. I love the security, I love the peace, and I love that it's mine.

I swipe my card to open my door; it beeps as it unlocks, then I let myself in. I immediately kick my black pumps off into the corner; my feet are usually in slightly smaller heels during the working week, but tonight I dressed up for the performance. My apartment is a one-bedroom suite, with a luscious king bed and a bathroom with only the most amazing shower I've felt in my entire life—you know, the ones with the body sprays that massage you from head to toe. What else would they have in a five-star hotel? All the best fittings for The Houston Hotel in New York.

That's why we often have some of the world's most elite clientele staying here. Everyone from famous Hollywood actors to musicians, politicians, and even a regular old billionaire who thinks he can click his fingers and get whatever he wants. I try and keep him away from the attractive girls; he can be a little handsy when he's had a few drinks. One time he slid his hand up my skirt, only to be met with my hand across his face.

I'll never forget his look of pure and utter shock. I guess no woman has ever refused him, let alone slapped him—hard. To this day, I still smile at the thought of the red handprint on his cheek.

He developed a healthy dose of respect for me after that; he never did it again and has been nothing but polite and professional since. But I'm sure he hasn't changed his ways for everyone.

Such is the life of a GM running a humongous hotel and entertainment complex. We get a little of everything here; it keeps me on my toes, but I love it.

My space is tidy; I have a comfortable sitting area with a massive flat-screen TV—not that I watch much television. My time is dedicated to working, studying online for my master's degree in business, or contemplating work again. I like it that way. I do head over to the on-site gym every morning—it's not busy at that time of the day, as most guests are still sleeping.

I enjoy the quiet time while I work out and mentally prepare to start my day. Ten-hour shifts require me to be in good health; I must walk every corridor in this place five times over every shift. My legs are toned with obvious muscle definition like a professional athlete after nearly two years working here. This place keeps me fit and in top shape.

My apartment has a small kitchenette and full-sized fridge that holds all my weekly staples. Of course, the in-house restaurants will give me anything I like, but I've been on my own for a while now, and even when it was just myself and mom, the cooking fell to me most days while she worked to support us. I'm a decent cook; I'm not a master chef by any means, but I can whip up a healthy meal and make it taste good.

The Houston allows me to decorate my space any way I like. It still has the hotel furniture—comfortable, neutral-colored sofa and chairs, imported Italian marble benchtops, and floor-to-ceiling drapes, as you would expect for such an opulent hotel—but my walls are decorated with massive frames that hold my own black and white photographs. When I get time off, I love to wander New York and photograph the architecture and stunning skyline of this iconic urban jungle. I tend to be drawn to buildings and cityscapes, the contrast between dark and light. It's beautiful yet stark at the same time.

That's my hobby, if you could call it that. I just love to capture the city in a way no one else has. Mrs. Houston wants me to enter my images into a competition, but I don't feel the need to have a group of strangers analyzing and critiquing my photographs. I don't mind if they are only for me, because I see the beauty in them. I have my dream job; I don't need any distractions. We argue this point constantly, but I just nod my head and promise someday I will enter my work into an open competition. She only smiles and responds, "Yes, *L'été*, someday you will."

I look at my walls, swathed in beautiful wallpaper—a charcoal color, like my eyes, with a golden fan pattern spread across the surface. It sounds garish when I describe it to people, but in situ it looks perfect. The neutral furniture and dark gray drapes are very chic and in fashion right now. The modern features of the room's surfaces, linens, and furniture give the room a contemporary style, but the vintage accents, like they have downstairs in Le Soleil, are the perfect amount of yester-year. It's like Gatsby crossed with Neoclassicism. Eléa says she draws inspiration from the art and culture of classical antiquity.

I walk into the bathroom and inspect myself in the massive wall mirror. My long, dark hair flows gently down my back, not curly but not straight. It retains a natural kink no matter how much I brush it; I inherited that from my mother. My face is pale now. My summer tan has come and gone, yet those freckles still shine through my makeup, a reminder of my past never allowing themselves to be covered up. They remind me of my father, who was as fair and sun-kissed as the Australian beach near where I grew up. They are a memento I carry from him. My freckles make me look much younger than I am, and sometimes people mistake me for a teenager, but that doesn't bother me. I cherish this part of myself and the memories they elicit of the few short years I spent with my father, before he died in a boating accident when I was six.

My eyes, like a storm over the ocean, as my mother used to say, darken when I'm angry. She said she could always tell whether I was upset by the color of my eyes. My lips, a little too full and wide, smile back at me in the mirror. I usually prefer a nude lip color, but tonight I chose red, so they stand out more on my heart-shaped face. I don't like to wear bold colors, or draw too much attention to myself, especially at work, but Bee gave me this color the other day. She looks amazing in red lipstick; it suits her blond hair and pale skin. I wasn't sure if it would suit me, but looking at myself in the mirror… I don't know who this girl is.

My black strapless dress clings to all the right places on my athletic body, and tonight I have a modest amount of cleavage peeking above the low neckline. I'm a decent handful, but I'm not exactly a 'busty' girl. My winged eyeliner and red lips give me a young fifties movie star look tonight. The girl in the mirror is more grown up, more like a woman, than the one my mother left behind.

I strip off, throwing my dress and underwear in the clothes hamper, and turn on the shower. Hot water starts cascading out almost immediately, something for which I thank the hotel gods daily. My old student apartment never had hot water.

I step in and feel like I can relax for the first time today. As I wash my hair, I wonder what Eléa wants to talk to me about. I hope it's something to do with an important guest, or maybe they've decided to take a vacation and leave me to run the hotel for them—they deserve it. Yes, I think I know exactly what she is planning, and I'm happy.

I'm in the best time of my life, and even though I wish my mom were here to see all my hard work and achievements, I am still proud of myself.

I feel like I can be self-indulgent for a moment—I have a fantastic job, my employers treat me like family, I have a new girlfriend for the first time in a long time—Brooklyn, or *Bee*, as she insists I call her—and I have an amazing apartment to call home in the middle of one of the best cities in the world.

In the words of Carrie Bradshaw from *Sex and the City*: "That's another reason I love New York. Just like that, it can go from bad to cute."

She was right! I may not be getting the sex she did in New York—gosh, it's been six months since I even *sniffed* a man—but the city has my heart, body, and soul.

I'll never move; NYC is my only true love.

CHAPTER TWO

ONE-WAY TICKET

I wake with surprisingly little effort after staying up late and drinking too much expensive champagne. I pull on my black athletic shorts and crop top, grab my water bottle from the fridge, and head out. The hotel is still quiet at six a.m., but the staff I see give me a wave or say hello. I think most people like me around here.

Some may call me standoffish, boring, or even eremitic, but I'm not anti-social; I just like privacy and keeping my personal business separate from my work relationships. I don't gossip during break or eat lunch with the back-of-house crew. The only people I let through my guard are Mr. and Mrs. Houston—and now Jarrod and Bee. It's rare for my bosses to welcome outsiders into their Houston Corporation family, but I feel at ease with them, which is more than I can say for anyone else in my life—other than my mom, when she was alive.

I enter the top-floor gym. Of course, it's fitted with the best equipment money can buy. That's one perk of living and working here; I have full access to all the amenities, like this state-of-the-art gym, the lap pool, day spa, cocktail lounge and music venue, and four Michelin-star restaurants. With thirty-three floors of nineteen-thirties Beaux-Arts style blended with twenty-first-century elegance, it's truly a timeless beauty.

I can see a few hotel guests using the pool through the tinted windows of the gym. I spot a couple of men lifting weights in the back of the room as I head over to the treadmill area, grabbing a towel from the linen cupboard along the way. I approach one of the state-of-the-art machines and start my workout with a slow walk to warm up, when I hear someone say my name.

"Summer, I expected you to have a sleep-in on your day off." Jarrod hops onto the treadmill next to me and starts at a fast walk.

I still love hearing his British accent; although Mr. Houston himself is English born and bred, I feel he has lost a little of his accent since moving to the States. As a loyal citizen of the crown, I'm certain telling him that would horrify him!

I don't think I have an accent, but people ask me occasionally where I'm from, and when I say here, New York, they don't believe me. I think the ten years I lived on the east coast of Australia when I was a child still lingers in my voice.

My mom and I escaped a terrifying situation after my father died and ended up fleeing to her country of birth. She was a young backpacker in Sydney when she met my dad. A simple one-night-stand led to a child and ten years of trauma for her. She ran—*we* ran—and ended up here.

"I think it's a habit now. I don't need an alarm anymore; my body wakes up at the same time every day."

Jarrod is the definition of a perfect male specimen. I don't allow my gaze to linger too long, but when you have an objectively beautiful person right beside you, it's a little distracting. Jarrod has been hitting the gym early every morning since his arrival, and then he comes back with Bee later in the afternoon for another session. No wonder the guy's physique resembles an NFL player.

"I'm having lunch with Bee later; are you going to join us?" I ask, taking a drink of my chilled water, and speed up the pace on the treadmill.

"Don't you mean breakfast?" He smirks at me, jet-black hair pushed back off his face, as his blue eyes assess me with interest.

"Shit! Did I get the time wrong? I thought we were doing lunch at twelve," I reply, anxiety making the numbers on my treadmill's heart rate monitor skyrocket.

He barks out a laugh, running his hand through those thick black strands; he has hair just like his mother's.

"I'm just teasing, Summer. In case you haven't worked it out yet, my angel doesn't surface until noon." My heart stops racing. "So, for you it's lunch, but for Brooklyn it's breakfast."

I notice Jarrod is the only person who doesn't call her Bee; I've only ever heard him use her full name or call her an 'angel', like he did just then.

"Jarrod, you almost gave me a heart attack! I thought I was going to be late and keep her waiting. I *hate* being late; I'm a schedule maniac," I tell him, laughing but still feeling residual anxiety.

"I know, my mother told me you are the perfect human; she wants to clone you." My heart does a little skip at the mention of how much his mom appreciates me.

"Well, *she* is kind of wonderful—and so is your father, I might add. I would do anything for them," I say with all seriousness. I make eye contact to show him how much I mean that.

"Summer, from what I've been told, this hotel is nothing without you. I know the pressure that comes with running a corporation like this; I was doing the same job back in London with Chris…"

His tone surprises me. I know he's here to write and play music with Bee, and from what his parents have told me, they are thrilled for him; but he sounds… conflicted.

"Can I ask you something?" Hesitation fills me; I usually wouldn't do this, but Jarrod and I share common ground.

"Of course you can, Summer. You are family to us," he replies genuinely, and I detect a strange feeling in my chest.

I feel like an impostor. Do I deserve to be included in this extraordinary family?

"How do you feel about taking time off? Are you going back to London once you and Bee finish your contract here?"

He doesn't respond right away, so I look out the window, watching the guests swim laps in the pool. It's heated, of course—no one would be swimming in this frigid winter weather otherwise.

He takes a moment to look out through the glass too. I give him as much time as he needs. I'm curious to know what he's decided on—a life with Bee, singing and making music? Or returning home to his hotel and all the stability that comes with it? Does he plan on continuing to build the family empire with his brother—who is surely struggling on his own in the U.K.

I haven't met Christopher, but I've heard him on many phone calls with his parents; he speaks French with Eléa, so I don't know what he is saying, but it sounds musical to my ears. There's just something about a guy speaking another language that gets the tingles going—and I definitely mean the good tingles.

OK, mind out of the gutter, Summer. You are a professional! My self-pep-talk brings my attention back to Jarrod.

"I'm not sure yet, Summer. I worked hard for ten years in London, doing everything I could to learn about the family business and support my parents… but my passion has always been music. It's just a spark that's always been inside me, and when I met Brooklyn, it lit a fire." He looks over at me with a really serious expression, and for a second I'm worried—what's so important that he stopped walking?

My full attention is now on his handsome face, waiting for what comes next. I don't know why, but I have a feeling this is a critical moment.

"Whatever happens, regardless of the choice in front of you, do what your heart tells you to do, Summer. You are amazing at your job. I see how much work you have put in—not just the hotel, but the way you support my parents too.

"I'll be eternally grateful that they can trust you to take the reins and enjoy their lives, especially after thirty years of building this corporation," he says, prying my hand off the treadmill I'm clutching like a lifeline, because he makes it sound like I have a choice, too.

Why is he telling me to follow my heart? My heart is here!

"This business is not for everyone, but I can see how much you love it. Just don't lose yourself to it. Make sure you follow *your* heart, too, because that's the only way to be happy. Do you know what I'm saying?"

"Maybe?" I phrase it like a question, hoping he will give me more insight.

"You'll understand soon enough. Now, finish your session, and take care of my angel at breakfast. She had a rough night last night; she may need extra sustenance today." His bad boy smirk is back, which means our talk is over. Jarrod does not waste words.

"Breakfast, lunch, brunch, whatever," I say with a laugh. "I'll take care of her," I add to reassure him. "She must be exhausted after singing, and then all the drinking we did last night… I'll pack her a Tylenol and give her lots of coffee." I guess Bee isn't used to having so much French bubbly.

"It wasn't the singing and drinking that exhausted her, Summer." He takes off running, muscles rippling in his arms and legs as his feet impact the treadmill.

I look away, cheeks flaming as his innuendo hits me about ten seconds too late. And now I'm sweating for a different reason.

"Uh… thanks for the mental reference to your nightly shenanigans, Jarrod. I do not need to hear how much everyone else is getting."

I stop the treadmill, deciding I've warmed up enough, and head to the other side of the gym, pressing my ice-cold water bottle against my cheeks to cool myself down.

I can hear Jarrod laughing from behind me. Jerk-face.

I'm glad that they are happy, though. It really seems like they were made for each other.

I start doing leg extensions on one of the machines, trying to ignore the feeling of Jarrod watching me.

I'm not looking for a relationship right now, so I'll just have to work out my frustrations in the gym. If nothing else, I'll be too exhausted to think about a hot, sweaty hunk who might tire *me* out enough to sleep until noon. *Lucky* Bee.

I'm yet to even find a man that could make that happen— well, in my limited experience, anyway. I'm not a prude—I've had some fun—but I have little time for… shenanigans.

Unfortunately, that means unless I get on a dating app to look for a hookup—which I find unsettling and terrifying—it means I am currently celibate and frustrated as hell.

Oh, the joys of being a schedule-obsessed workaholic who is neither spontaneous nor adventurous.

It's been six months since I last had sex, and it was average at best. His name was Justin, and I met him while I was photographing the Chrysler building on the East Side of Manhattan. Metal ornaments protrude from the corners of the art deco skyscraper, like the gargoyles of a gothic-era cathedral—I like to say it's a masterpiece of gothic proportions. I keep going back to see if I can get a different shot.

This time, I was searching for the ideal angle to capture the spire against the cloudless blue sky.

Justin works in the building, and he struck up a conversation when he saw me, which led to him asking me to dinner. I had the night off and decided to take a chance, so I said yes.

He was intelligent and witty, but a little full of himself, to be honest. Even so, when he invited me back to his place for a drink, I said yes.

He seemed to have all the equipment; he just didn't know what to do with it. So, before the sun rose, I did a walk of shame from his apartment back to my place. I never gave him my number, so I avoided any uncomfortable follow-up situations. Let's face it, he probably wouldn't have called anyway.

Since then, I've barely even spoken to another person outside of work, let alone slept with them.

My lunch, or brunch rather, with Bee is just what I need. I didn't realize socializing with another like-minded girl could be so much fun.

Now *that's* a word I haven't used in forever, but I really do have fun. We enjoy a coffee-fueled banquet with all kinds of food, both savory and sweet. I, of course, overdo it with the French pastries that Mrs. Houston's chef—a Parisian pâtissier—made for us, and end up in a food coma. If I ate like this every day, I wouldn't be able to walk around the hotel like I do now.

Much of what I do is office-based—making phone calls and answering emails—but I also spend a lot of time attending to things in person and checking in with department managers, chefs, concierges and cleaning staff.

Working in a hotel that operates twenty-four-seven feels like a never-ending cycle. When I'm off, or in the evening, my night staff take over, but I'm always on call in case of an emergency. Thankfully, the staff are well-trained and don't often panic in hairy situations. They know the protocol and usually execute it perfectly.

Mr. and Mrs. Houston are just here for support. They make all the final decisions, but they don't run the day-to-day grind anymore. They have free time to watch a performance on Broadway, wine and dine with friends, and take in shows like Jarrod and Bee's performance last night. I'm happy they can finally take a step back and enjoy themselves. They are still young—in their late fifties—but already they have time to slow down and savor the thirty years of hard work they sacrificed to accomplish international success.

As I walk down the hallway to Mr. and Mrs. Houston's Premier Suite, I take a moment to breathe and collect my thoughts. Whatever the news is, I will take it with professional dignity and respect. I'm sure it's nothing major; I have a feeling that something may be happening here at the hotel.

Jarrod's cryptic comments this morning in the gym, followed by Bee gushing about the Hotel in London and how amazing it is, make me think they might be going back home. Maybe Bee was trying to tell me I'd be losing her friendship sooner than expected.

The thought makes me sad. I really connect with Bee. We've shared some personal stories, and her childhood sounds about as disturbing as mine was. It's not easy for me to open up like that, but Bee just makes me feel so at ease, so comfortable. Knowing that she lived through some really shitty times and came out the other end successful and smart, with a kick ass career and a hunk of a boyfriend, gives me hope. Maybe us orphaned adults *can* make it in this world after all.

I knock twice on the door and wait, looking at my watch. It's two p.m. on the dot. I am never late; I pride myself on being reliable and punctual. I'd rather be early and wait outside than be even five minutes late. I'm not sure why; perhaps rushing from place to place when I was young and never having a routine made me loathe any kind of disarray. All my staff know I run a tight ship. I don't like surprises, and this way I can see what's coming.

Mr. Houston opens the door, his spectacles resting on top of his light-brown hair. I assume he was probably reading the paper like he does every afternoon.

His smile is contagious, and I give him a grin in return. I've noticed he's put on a little weight since he and his wife started to slow down—nothing drastic, as they are both very active people— but I can tell Max has enjoyed having some free time to take his wife out and about over the last few months.

I wonder if they are about to announce going back to London for a while. I know I'm prepared for the challenge of managing this enormous hotel by myself.

"Summer, darling, come in. Eléa is in the study on a phone call. She won't be a minute." I follow him inside the family suite.

It has three bedrooms, two of which are always available for the boys if they visit; Jarrod and Bee are most likely occupying one of them. The master bedroom is on the other side of the gargantuan apartment, separated by a large sitting room, study, and full-sized kitchen. It's a convenient layout, allowing the family to have separate spaces but remain connected.

"That's OK! No rush. I have time," I say, as he walks over to the fridge and takes out my favorite brand of sparkling water. He's such a gentleman. I thank him and take a seat.

As he sits down opposite me, a loud thud comes through the open doorway of the study, and an angry voice hurls French out of a speakerphone.

Shit, that doesn't sound good. I know I don't understand a word of what is being said, but the person at the other end of the line is obviously not in a cheerful mood. Then I hear Eléa raise her own voice, and she lobs even more rapid-fire French back. Mr. Houston looks at me with an apologetic grin and hunched shoulders.

We can't even make conversation, because the angry vocal volleyball match seems like it's coming out of a surround sound system throughout the apartment.

"Should I come back later?" I ask, raising my voice a little over the noise.

"No, no, it's almost over... Just give them a few more minutes," he responds, and goes back to reading his paper. I envy him for being able to ignore the fiery, passionate communication happening in the other room.

At last, everything goes silent. A few minutes later, Eléa emerges from the study with rosy cheeks and a determined look on her face.

"*L'été*, my apologies…family business is…how you say… *passionné* at times." She must mean impassioned.

"It's fine, Eléa. Honestly, I can come back later if that suits you," I offer again, because clearly she has a lot going on. I doubt she wants to discuss hotel business right now.

"No, no, this is perfect, *ma chérie*… now, let us sit and talk. We have much to discuss."

My mouth goes a little dry in anticipation of the conversation, so I take a sip of my sparkling water. I don't know what's coming, and Eléa promised it was nothing bad, but I'm kind of getting nervous butterflies right now.

"*L'été*, you know we love you dearly. You have been a godsend to us since the very second you arrived on our doorstep." I'm looking into her coffee eyes, and as she takes my hand in hers, my stomach drops like a ride at Disney World.

I think I might puke right here on her carpet.

Are they about to fire me? Why else would she say that?

I can't force myself to speak, so I let her continue. But I can tell by the look on her face, I've turned a little green.

"We," she says, looking at Max, who nods in agreement, "have much to consider lately, with Jarrod's leave from London to travel with his *Petite Abeille*, Brooklyn. We want to give them time to discover their talent, their passion, yes?"

I nod in agreement. She is still clutching my hand; it's comforting and motherly, but I can feel the shoe about to drop.

"So, my son Christopher is… struggling right now. The staff in London—especially Daniel, the *exceptionnel* manager of The Wave—all do their best. But my Christopher, he needs help."

"Of course. I understand it can't be easy now that all his family is here in New York. I know you are worried for him," I say, and squeeze her hand.

I am genuinely concerned for Eléa. I notice she is unusually flustered and upset. Something must be going on London.

I decide it's a good idea to reassure them. It seems like they are worried about leaving me here alone, but I will be fine. They are only a phone call away.

"Mr. and Mrs. Houston." I regard them both. "Eléa." I look into her eyes and try to communicate my earnestness as best I can. "If you need to go, please do. Help your son, take all the time you need. I can manage here just fine. I have Frank in customer relations, Marta to manage all the housekeeping, and Walter in concierge. They're all very experienced and will support me. The restaurants practically run themselves. Go back to London and do what you need to do. I'll be here when you get back."

To comfort her and ease the guilt visible on her beautiful face, I embrace her. Returning my hug firmly, she gently cups my face and kisses my forehead.

"Ahh, *L'été*. You are special, do you know that?" she tells me. Love shines in her eyes, but what she says next floors me. "We are not going back to London. We should spend some time with Jarrod and Brooklyn."

I feel confused. Why would Eléa bring up Christopher if she doesn't want to visit him?

She continues. "We can run this hotel with Jarrod's help. We are sending *you* to London, to our Christopher. You will be his savior. You can help him manage the hotel now Jarrod has left. It is time my second born learns to take responsibility, and he can't do that with his *mère* looking over his shoulder."

I take a couple of minutes to let her words soak into my shocked and frazzled brain. Send me to London? What the heck?

"Do you mean, like, just for a month or so? Until Jarrod is ready to go back? Or until you hire more help?"

She looks at me with a combination of guilt and pride. In under two years, the inexperienced orphan girl she took in has blossomed into a top-tier hotel manager in New York.

"How long do you need me in London?" I ask, sure it must only be a few weeks, months at most.

"*Indéfiniment*," she replies, and I look to Max for clarification.

"What my wife means, kiddo, is permanently." My jaw drops. The word *permanently* echoes inside my head. "Jarrod and Bee may be about to accept a recording contract here in New York. They're meeting with Atlantic Records this afternoon to discuss possibilities. So..." He takes a breath and looks at his wife, who nods for him to continue.

"We can't give you a time frame. This may end up being permanent. Jarrod will be here to help us every other day, and we have the network you set up to run the New York hotel like a well-oiled machine.

"But London needs you, Summer. *We* need you to help our son. You are the only person we can trust from the other side of the world. We know you can do this," he says with conviction.

I know he said they trust me, but it doesn't stop me feeling like my life just upended itself. My work, my apartment, my sanctuary. My passion for walking the streets and taking photographs of the iconic, quintessential New York City I love. I'm heartbroken.

Tears well in my eyes. I'm not a crier—I rarely show emotion in front of people—but I can't help it. I'm shocked. Their words feel like a fifty-pound weight on my shoulders.

"Don't cry, *ma chérie*." She wipes my eyes with her thumbs, gently comforting me like I'm her own flesh and blood. I've missed that feeling of my mother comforting and consoling me. It hurts even more knowing I will be giving that up.

I know it's selfish, but she opened my broken heart, and I want to keep her close. But I also know I can never let her down. I can't refuse, and maybe that's what Jarrod was talking about. I need to do what I know in my heart is right.

"This is an enormous responsibility, kiddo, and a promotion for you. I know it's a big change, moving to London, but I also know it will be good for you, too. You'll even get to see the world a bit. You have given us two years, never once letting us down. What do you say, Summer? Will you go?"

I stare at him, stunned.

"That's a question, not a direction," he clarifies. "This decision is totally up to you, darling." I look at their faces. There's hope, pride, and something else there—maybe a little sorrow for losing me like this.

I'm not dying, for fuck's sake, I know that… but it feels like they are letting their last baby bird fly the nest. Although it's a monumental achievement, it also signifies their work is done. They're telling me it's time to fly away.

I take a moment to think, *really* think, and I know I have to accept their proposal. I can't stay where I am not needed; that's just not me.

Jarrod is here. He will assist them when they require it, and after ten years of hard work, plus his years of study, he has earned the right to spend time with Bee, to play music, and maybe even make an album of their own. I can't deny that for him—for them both. I just wish the solution wasn't me leaving this city.

I made my life here; I moved so much as a child I never felt safe or settled up 'til now. It'll be like starting all over again.

Mr. and Mrs. Houston are waiting for my answer. I can't hold them up any longer.

I take a huge breath, so I have the strength to speak the word they need me to say: "Yes. If you need me in London, then of course I will go…for you."

They both hug me like I'm the hot dog in the middle of a soft bun, squeezing me and thanking me all at once. Then Eléa pulls away and takes my face in her hands again.

"*L'été*, you are too good to us. Thank you. We are so happy."

My eyes sparkle with bittersweet tears again. I still feel sad, but it's nice being able to give them this gift. They have never asked me for anything personal, and this is one thing I can choose to do for their family.

"This will be an adventure, you will see, *L'été*. The best adventure."

Max pats my shoulder, giving it a little squeeze. "Darling, let Summer have some time alone to digest all this. We can talk more tomorrow." With a gentle touch, he pats her hands in an obvious gesture to release me.

After walking out of the Premier Suite and heading down the hallway towards my apartment, I begin to cry.

The floodgates open as I realize I just booked a one-way flight to London with no return in sight.

CHAPTER THREE

DOWN THE RABBIT HOLE

I wake to the sound of someone knocking on my door.

I panic for a second, worrying that I've slept through work. After a moment of disorientation, I realize it's still nighttime. The sun isn't shining outside my window, and my watch is telling me it's only nine thirty p.m.

I must have cried myself to sleep after I got back. I didn't even eat dinner.

The knocking continues, and I decide I should get up and open the door in case it's urgent. Other than a Houston family member, only certain staff or security can access this floor. I get off my plush sofa and pad over to my apartment door, feet sinking into the soft carpet.

Bee stands there with a worried look on her face, and when I look at her, she must see the emotional evidence of my mini breakdown because she exclaims, "Oh, babe, it's going to be alright," and launches herself at me. I grab hold of her to avoid falling backwards.

She hugs me fiercely for a minute—no words, just the tangible energy of her angelic aura. Bee is like a spellcaster. She bewitches people with her stunning eyes that are green one minute and amber the next. I soak up her warmth and hug her back. It's so strange to feel this familial comfort again.

We disengage, and I wipe my face with my hands, trying to clean any residual mascara streaks from my cheeks. "I'm OK. It just took me by surprise, that's all. Come in." I open the door to allow her to enter my little sanctuary.

"This is beautiful, Summer, and—holy shit, look at these pictures!" She walks over to my gallery wall where my work is displayed. "Who is the artist? I need something like this for my flat back in London. They are amazing." She takes in each picture one at a time, ending with the centerpiece—an abstract I took of this hotel, The Houston. It's one of my most precious images.

I feel a little embarrassed, not about the photographs, but because Bee is so talented and successful. Having someone like that admire my work feels surreal. I'm just regular old Summer Hart, solitary and boring.

I'm amazed when anyone likes my artwork. I know it's not for everyone. It can be a little sharp, with the horizontal, diagonal and vertical lines skewed in such a way that you can't tell which way is up. It's surrealism, created by using perspective to control the lines converging through the space.

"Actually, they are all mine. It's kind of a hobby," I tell her, my cheeks warming at her admiration.

"Wow, Summer! You're really talented. These are sensational. Have you thought about selling them?" she questions, still looking at the frames with interest.

"Don't let Eléa hear you say that. She has been riding my ass for over a year on this issue." I laugh as I walk over to the fridge and take out a nice, chilled rosé imported from Australia. This wine is one of my favorites, and when I tasted it at the international wine festival last year, I knew I had to order it for the hotel.

Kellybrook is a small boutique winery in the Yarra Valley, and they create some beautiful wines. My palate detects wonderful notes of fresh strawberry, blackcurrant and peach, with bursts of Turkish delight and violet tones.

Being educated in all aspects of guest services, from interior design, soft furnishings and linen quality to current trends of food innovation and wine pairing, is essential. Unfortunately, I have become a bit of a wine snob, and now I like to treat myself with a delicate glass of wine every so often.

I hand Bee a glass and sit down on the sofa with my own. It's slightly fuller than I would normally pour, but I'm in a state of shock and I feel the anxiety creeping up my chest. I need to numb the feelings before I unload all my junk onto Bee.

She sits down next to me and takes a sip. "Oh, this is nice. I'm normally a gin girl, but this is delicious." She kicks off her six-inch red heels and folds her feet under her. I like that we have this immediate connection where we feel comfortable with each other so soon. It's never happened to me before, and I feel disappointed knowing that not long from now, we will be oceans apart.

I'm not some stage five clinger, I've just never really opened up to anyone before Bee, and now I'm about to lose her.

"I know, I feel like I could drink a dozen right now," I tell her as I take a calming breath and relax back into my soft seat.

"Talk, girl, get it all out. Use lots of swear words, like 'motherfucker' and 'big, hairy balls'," she instructs, and we both crack up laughing. Who knew angelic-looking Bee had such a dirty vocabulary?

"All right, I'll unload. But I'm not sure I can use 'big, hairy balls' to describe my current situation. Unless we're talking about a certain aging actor who stayed here last month, and accidentally-on-purpose dropped his robe when I entered his room. Let me tell you, nothing can erase the image of his tiny dick hidden under all those folds from where it's been burned into my brain. I took three showers that night." I mimic a vomiting motion.

"Oh, fuck no!" She covers her eyes with one hand. "I don't really want details, *but*… the perverse side of me wants to know who it is." Her expression is a mix of disgust and curiosity.

"My employment contract states I may not comment on guest relations, but if you get a random text message from me one day with a photograph of a man and the eggplant emoji, you'll know." I hold up my thumb and forefinger, separating them by an inch.

Bee cracks up, which makes me laugh too, and next thing I know we are killing ourselves laughing. It feels good to laugh right now. If I don't laugh, I'll cry, and I much prefer this.

"Ah… But seriously, Bee, I'm kind of in shock right now. I thought my life was set. I thought I had found my place, and now… I don't know. I feel like I fell down the rabbit hole and haven't stopped spinning." I take another sip of my cool wine, willing it to flow through my veins and make me numb so I don't have to feel this inner conflict.

"I understand." She pats my knee, scooting a little closer to me. "Honestly, Summer, I experienced the same thing a few months ago, with Will. I told you about him?" I nod. She's mentioned her previous musical partner, Will, and everything that happened during her Houston hotel contract.

"I didn't know I was going to take the job at The Wave and have my life tipped upside down. And now I'm in New York, singing to a whole new audience, with a potential recording contract and the most amazing man by my side." Her eyes glow like a dozen emeralds reflecting the sun. Her entire face lights up when she mentions Jarrod.

"This move may intimidate you, Summer, even scare you badly, but it could also be the best thing that ever happens to you."

Her words hit me like a tidal wave.

I know she's right. I know I'm needed there, and it's the chance of a lifetime, but I'm still petrified. I'll be alone. The city and architecture will be alien to me, not my comfortable, steady NYC skyscrapers. It is literally an Alice in Wonderland moment, and let's be honest: not everything in that wonderland was good.

"Heck, Bee, I know. I just didn't expect it. It shocked me. I don't do well with surprises, you know? I'm a follow-a-schedule, prioritize-stability kind of girl. I don't like to mess with the set menu, if you know what I mean?" I sigh. "I need predictability."

"I know, babe, but sometimes life throws us curve balls, and you can either duck, or hit the fucker and—what's it called—make a home run." Her baseball reference is comical. It's clear she isn't a sport lover.

"And besides, Jarrod's brother Chris is amazing. Sweet, funny, so easy to deal with. He's not as introspective as Jarrod. Chris is the life of the party. You'll get along with him so well." She takes my hand, giving it a little squeeze. "We are just a phone call away. Call anytime—you know I'm always up late—just don't call me before eleven a.m. I may say things I'll regret at that ungodly hour of the morning." I laugh. Eleven is hardly early, but given what Jarrod tells me, Bee is on her own time. *Bee time*.

"Thank you," I tell her. "Thank you for checking in on me. I feel a little better." I think she understands how grateful I am for her concern. She knows I don't let many people in, so I really appreciate her taking the time for me.

Bee continues, her tone a little more light-hearted now. "The Houston in London is vibrant, multicultural, and cosmopolitan. I'll hook you up with Anton and Trey, my BFF and his BBF—they'll show you around the city and give you a true British welcome. Just be wary of Anton's Margaritas; they pack a punch!" I smile. I'm not as naturally friendly as Bee, but if they are her friends then I'll try.

"Oh! And Summer: go and find a hot guy to tango with—if you catch my drift. You're young, beautiful, and I would kill for your freckles. You have that girl-next-door vibe that guys love. Enjoy yourself! Have *mad-hot sex* and multiple orgasms!" I almost spit out my wine.

Bee's laughter is accompanied by a knowing look in her eyes that suggests I seriously need to get laid, A-S-A-P!

"'Mad-hot sex', huh?" I ask, and she nods. "Well, let's see if I can find a guy who's up for the job. I'm difficult to please in bed." I don't orgasm easily. It takes something special for me to get there—not that I don't enjoy the journey, it just doesn't happen often. My battery-operated-boyfriend is a faster and more efficient tool these days.

"I'm sure you will find a line of *gorgeous* men up for the challenge, girlfriend. Now, let's plan your wardrobe. Show me everything you have!"

We head to my bedroom, and Bee releases a little squeal of excitement as I turn the light on.

"Maybe we should go shopping before I leave. Just in case you think I need to update my wardrobe, you know? Fit in more?" I remark as I follow her into the walk-in.

Bee takes a second to look around the tiny room. Everything is perfectly neat and tidy, just how I like it. Order.

"Um, Summer…" Bee pauses, looking from left to right. "It's all black!"

"I know. It's my color," I answer, confused.

"OK, this *has* to change; I'm taking you shopping tomorrow, and we are going to fix this travesty. Don't get me wrong, black is a staple, but with your dark hair and sun kissed skin, you need pops of color. *Trust* me on this. I'm not letting you leave till we have this situation rectified."

She takes out several items of clothing and throws them on the bed.

"I'm a situation?" I ask, only half-joking.

"You're a temporary situation. One thing I know is shopping. I will cure you of your all-black affliction by this time tomorrow. Now, put some music on and let's see what you have to work with." I sip my wine, watching her go all Marie Kondo on my stuff, and that's pretty much how the rest of the night goes.

Over the next few hours, Bee and I order some food from room service and finish a full bottle of Australian rosé, and all the while Bee entertains herself by scouring my clothes and shoes for hidden gems. It's awesome. I've never had a girls' night like this before.

My heart does that little pain thing again. It'll hurt leaving here—leaving the people I care about—for the deep, dark unknown of the rabbit hole that is London. Was Alice this afraid when she fell? She was trapped, far away from home, in an absurd and unfamiliar land. She was confused, like I am; she cried, like I have; she even got angry at herself, at the world around her; but in the end, it was all just a dream.

I wish I was in a dream, too. I wish I could wake up tomorrow and have everything be back to normal—back to how I like it. But I know, deep down, *my* Wonderland is real.

The next two days are a whirlwind full of shopping with Bee, packing suitcases and arranging a hand over with Jarrod so he can help his parents run the hotel on the days when he's not busy performing or rehearsing.

Eléa has assured me she will ship the rest of my belongings separately, so I've only packed two cases of clothing, hair and makeup supplies, basic necessities, my work laptop, and a few other electronic devices. I stand back and admire the two suitcases, both full to bursting. I have no idea how I managed to close them, but I'm not going to touch the zips until I arrive in London.

There's a knock behind me, and barely a moment passes before Mrs. Houston breezes through my open door like a dandelion in the wind. She looks stunning as usual, dressed in a Camilla raglan-sleeved, silk button-up blouse. The blouse is decorated with ornate golden swirls, floral designs, and hand-embellished crystal adornments, and it might look gaudy on some women, but Eléa, as always, wears it perfectly.

"*L'été*, my love, the car is here. I have the porter outside ready to take your luggage down." She looks me up and down, taking me in from head to toe; she knows she might not see me in person for quite some time.

My surrogate mother fusses over my hair a little, brushing it back off my shoulders and smoothing it down. I can't help comparing her to a mother bird grooming her little baby before their maiden flight.

"You are precious to me, *ma chérie*. You know I would not send you away if I did not think it best for you, yes?" she asks. She looks into my eyes, making sure I see her sincerity.

"I know. I'll do my best, Eléa; I promise I won't let you down."

I understand the magnitude of the responsibility she's entrusting to me. Decades of blood, sweat and tears have gone into building up this business for her family, and it's hers and Max's legacy she's leaving in my hands.

After all they've done for me, I'll gladly help Chris keep the London hotel thriving for as long as they need. All I need in return is a safe, comfortable space of my own to call home, and a little free time to escape the pressures of hotel management and find fulfilment through a camera lens. For the first time, I wonder what new shapes and skylines I'll be able to capture in my new home.

"*L'été*, you could never let me down. I have sons, you know that, but you have given me the gift of knowing what it is like to have a daughter." My eyes well with saltwater. "And now, I'm blessed to have two—you *and* Brooklyn. You gave me something I always longed for, and now I am *complète*." The lump in my throat thickens, and Eléa gives me a watery smile that almost tips me over the edge.

She gently takes my hand, escorting me out of my apartment—no longer my little sanctuary—for the last time. A porter waits outside to take my bags to the ground floor, leaving Eléa and I to enter the elevator together. As we descend, I mentally prepare for my impending departure. There's not much to do beyond getting into the car that the Houston's organized for me, and then I'll be heading to the airport with New York in the rear-view mirror.

I already said my goodbyes to Max, Jarrod, Bee, and the hotel staff, because otherwise I'd crack. I don't want their last memory of me to be streaks of mascara running down my face and snot dripping from my nose. A girl needs her dignity, and I *definitely* do not want the staff to see me like that.

I'm like the terminator—emotions just get in the way when I'm working. I get the job done with poise and composure, and I'd rather not humiliate myself in front of everyone.

I exit the elevator one last time and walk through the grand foyer, exiting the hotel via the famous golden revolving doors that open onto a magnificent view of Central Park. The fresh winter air triggers my nostalgia, and I begin to remember all my favorite places in the city.

Right now, I'm a nine-minute walk from the Museum of Modern Art, just across the road from Central Park, and a short walk to Rockefeller Center—I love seeing it come alive at Christmas time.

I take a deep breath, grateful for the frigid wind as it shocks away my tears.

"We don't say goodbye, *L'été*, we say *'à bientôt'*. See you soon, my Summer."

And with that, she kisses me three times and hurries me into the town car waiting for me at the curb. I slide onto the heated, soft leather seats, and the last thing I see is Eléa's face before she closes the door after me.

I hear the click of the trunk, and a moment later the driver takes his seat and puts the car in drive, ready to merge into the frenetic chaos of Manhattan traffic.

I don't cry as I look back at hotel, even though I can feel the sting in my eyes. I touch my hand to the window, and Eléa raises her hand in the air in a stationary wave. I continue to look back at her until we turn a corner and my view is blocked by a tall building.

I pull my sleeves out of my thick winter coat, warming up my hands in the stream of warm air flowing out of a vent in front of me. I dressed comfortably for the flight—athletic leggings, a sports bra, and a loose tank. I'm still wearing black for now, but I promised Bee to try out some of the colorful clothing we bought together when I'm in London.

Absent any delays, my plane should touch down at Heathrow in about eight or nine hours, just after midnight. It's fitting for me to arrive under cover of darkness, just like Alice falling into that deep, dark chasm. What will I find when I arrive in London? Will everyone be upside down? Will I be surrounded by talking animals?

I chuckle to myself. *Stop being ridiculous, Summer.*

I decide, right then and there, that no matter what happens I will not lose myself and the resilience I've built over the past two years. I will reestablish order, I will maintain my professional standards, and I will make damn sure The Houston Hotel in London is the best hotel in the United Kingdom!

"We're here, Ms. Hart." I look at my driver as he pulls over in the airport drop-off zone. "I'll get a trolley for your bags, Miss. Give me a moment," he says, exiting the car.

"Thank you," I reply to no one. He's already gone, and in his place is a gust of icy wind that enters the car through his open door.

This is it. I'm about to board a plane to my new home, my new life, my new Wonderland. I really am like a baby bird, flying away.

It's almost as if everything I've worked for, all the years of study, long hours and hard work has been a prelude to something bigger. Something life changing. The unknown is killing me.

I just hope, when I arrive in London, I don't land too hard.

CHAPTER FOUR

JET LAG

The flight was comfortable, thanks to Eléa booking me into business class with as many extra perks as money can buy. I've only ever flown internationally once, and that was as a ten-year-old child when my mom and I left Australia for the U.S. That trip is mostly a blur now, but I still remember it was long and cramped and terrifying.

My mom's relationship with my father was up and down; they didn't even know each other when they conceived me, but they tried their best to co-parent for my benefit. My father, from my memories, was a typical Australian man: outdoorsy, with a great love of the beach. I remember watching him surf the huge waves at the beach where I was too small and weak to swim. I remember him taking me out on the water in his little dinghy boat. Together, we caught bream, flathead, trout, and even a gummy shark on the odd occasion.

I remember those days fondly. He was a noble father. He wasn't wealthy, but he didn't worry about the big luxuries. He worked to pay the bills and enjoy the weekends with his childhood mates and a couple slabs of beer. Peter Hart was a lovable larrikin. He was a hard worker, would help any mate who needed a hand, and loved me with everything he had.

But a boating accident took him from me when I was just six.

My mother, Amelia, struggled to support both of us after that. She didn't have access to the same benefits as Australian citizens. Because she retained her U.S. citizenship, finding a job that paid enough to cover our expenses became much harder after my father's death.

Mom had a couple of relationships, but none of them seemed to work out—until she met Steven. Steven seemed to be the knight in shining armor she was looking for.

My mother was a twenty-seven-year-old single parent living in a foreign country with no family and no connections. My father's family wasn't really in the picture. They lived hours away and only visited for special occasions. His parents were older because they had children late in life. My dad has a sister, but she's almost closer to my age than my dad's, and she couldn't give Mom the support she needed back then.

Steven was some kind of real estate mogul with a fancy car, suits in every color and shiny shoes. He swept Mom off her feet with ease. She needed security and someone to take care of us, and he was able to provide that.

I knew it wasn't genuine love, because she didn't look at him with those eyes—the eyes I saw in Disney movies when the Princess falls in love. Mom looked like a princess with her long, wavy hair, beautiful dark blue eyes, and a distant Spanish heritage giving her an exotic allure.

Steven was nice to me at first, and it seemed like Mom was finally happy even after everything we went through. Then, one day, the world tipped upside-down, and I saw my mom's knight in shining armor turn into a horrible, abusive ogre. I wanted to stop him whenever he screamed or hit her, but I was only a kid. What could I do?

I bit his leg once, when he hurt my mother so badly that he broke her arm and fractured her ribs. The result was me ending up with a split lip and his handprint across my face.

Steven's reign of terror continued for two years. Mom didn't tell me at the time about the control he had over her. He was our sole source of income, and he barely gave her enough money for food and bills. He even took her passport so she couldn't run from him. She was abused, not just physically, but emotionally and financially too.

A local women's shelter allowed us to escape his clutches. We waited until he went to work one day, and then we packed a small duffel bag with our most precious belongings and caught a bus to the shelter. My mother said she met the staff one afternoon while they were collecting money for the shelter at our local supermarket.

About five weeks of living in the shelter later, our new passports arrived. Someone gave us the money—donations collected from the community, I presume—and we booked two economy tickets back to the U.S.

My mom was a nervous wreck the whole time. She looked back at every checkpoint in the airport. She didn't take a deep breath until we landed in LAX. We left everything behind but the clothes on our backs and a small carry-bag filled with the most bare of necessities. We left everything else behind, including all my photos of my father. I have no evidence of the youthful days I spent with my dad in Australia, basking on sunny beaches and strolling under the moonlit sky with sand between my toes.

Mom never pursued another relationship after that, and I understand why.

When I see how Mr. Houston looks at his wife, or how Jarrod looks at Bee, I feel a pang of heartache because my beautiful, kind and strong mother never got to experience love like that in her brief life. Breast cancer took her at barely forty years old, even after she fought for so long. We thought she was in remission, but one day it reappeared, and the doctors said it'd spread to the rest of her body.

She had metastatic breast cancer—that's what they call it when cancer cells spread from the original cancer site to other areas of the body. It would be an understatement to say her youthful body was riddled with it.

I'd just started college. She begged me not to take time off, told me everything would work out, but I think she knew it wouldn't. She knew getting an education was the only way I would survive in this world. I focused all my attention on finding a decent job and earning enough not to worry about every dollar of every paycheck like she did. *And I did.*

Everything I've achieved so far has been for her. I forwent the 'college experience'—no parties, no clubs, no social interaction beyond my teachers and professors—and worked odd jobs in various hotels to make ends meet. I always knew I would go into business management. I wanted something sturdy, a career I could stick with long term. I briefly considered accounting, but sitting in an office crunching numbers was a little too mind-numbing for me. The hotel industry is busy, it's challenging, and it has longevity.

That's what I love about the hotel establishment itself: all the inner workings of a strongly built structure that never stops.

"Ms. Hart, would you like another refreshment before we pack away for landing?" the air-hostess asks me in a quiet voice.

I'm one of few passengers still awake in business. I'm so tired. I haven't slept a wink in two days, but my nervous energy just won't let my brain switch off. I'm going to crash hard soon; I can feel it.

"No, thank you," I reply, and she moves to the next passenger.

Finally, we land safely and without incident. The flight, though long, was very comfortable in business class.

Despite the late hour, Heathrow Airport bustles with activity as staff rush around and passengers come and go. The fluorescent lights hurt my eyes after the dim cabin lights on the plane.

It takes almost an hour to locate my suitcases at baggage claim, clear all the border security checks and pass through customs—'no, I haven't brought any illegal items over', 'yes, I have a work visa', 'yes, I have permanent accommodation'. All my answers feel robotic in the early morning hours, especially while I'm exhausted from my long flight and the whirlwind few days I've had. The physical and emotional jet lag make me want to go to bed for a week.

Finally, as I exit the international arrivals area, I'm met with the chaotic vibrancy of an overcrowded, overstimulating airport. Apparently, Heathrow processes over seventy-five million passengers a year. It's almost like its own country. I'm well-versed in managing large, complex organizations, but this is completely overwhelming. It would take an army of people just to keep the place running every day.

"Ms. Hart." I hear my name from somewhere amidst the sea of people waiting to welcome their loved ones home, and it takes me a while before I spot a young man in a tailored black suit holding up a Houston Hotel branded sign with my name printed neatly on it. I wave to let him know I see him, and drag my suitcases behind me.

"Let me take those for you," he says, freeing my hands one at a time as he stacks my bags onto a trolley. "Welcome to London, Miss." His accent hits home as I'm reminded where I am. I'm here, in this foreign land, nothing more than an outsider. "My name is Geoffrey, and I'll take you to your new lodgings at the Houston. Daniel—Mr. Thompson—has arranged everything for you. No need to worry."

"Thank you, Geoffrey. I appreciate you collecting me at this late hour," I say, as I follow him to a town car waiting just outside.

The wind hits me from the moment I step outside, and I tighten my coat around me, wishing I hadn't packed my scarf in my suitcase. I knew it would be cold, but I can really feel the chill tonight. I just want to have a hot shower and collapse into my new bed, which—knowing Eléa's high standards—would have Egyptian cotton sheets. Thinking about her reminds me how much it hurts to leave everyone behind.

"Here, get yourself warm while I load the luggage, Miss." Geoffrey opens the rear passenger door for me so I can escape the chilly night air. I lean back and try to relax while Geoffrey packs my suitcases in the trunk.

I take a deep breath of British air.

Does it feel different? Will this new air I breathe change me in any way?

What about the water? Will that taste different? Can I even *drink* the water here? All these thoughts are racing through my head, but I try to suppress them, because this isn't a holiday; it's my life.

This is *my* air. This is *my* water.

I just pray that it doesn't pollute me—or, perhaps I should say *dilute* me. I want to remain the same girl my mother left behind. The same girl who gained Eléa's trust enough for her to send me halfway across the world.

I don't want to change myself for anyone.

"We're here, Miss. The Houston Hotel London—your new home." Geoffrey points at a stunning art deco building visible through the car windshield. The hotel is on the corner of a busy intersection, and even though it's almost two a.m., the city is thriving. From my research, I know The Houston is a five-star boutique hotel with elegantly furnished suites overlooking Hyde Park. The unique Grade II listed property offers a Mayfair residential feel, modern amenities, and bespoke luxury services.

I've had brief communication with this property. Mr. and Mrs. Houston run their hotels independently, not like a franchise, but I gather the amenities will be of a similar quality to the New York Houston.

"Thank you, Geoffrey," I answer absently, because I really am taken with the architecture and style of the building—or, at least, what I can see from inside the car.

I know it's completely different to the structures in and around the N.Y. Houston, but this *otherworldly* feel, of history and antiquity, is really something to experience firsthand. It's kind of breath-taking.

Geoffrey opens my door, and again I brace against the frigid night air. "I'll show you to your new accommodations, Ms. Hart. Come in before you catch cold," he says, holding the car door open against the strong gusts of wind.

The automatic front doors of the hotel slide open noiselessly, welcoming me into a stunning atrium. It's quiet at this time of night. No guests are present, but there are a few staff members quietly working; polishing the marble floors, dusting off the sparkling chandeliers, or fluffing cushions on the velvety suede armchairs in the waiting area.

"This way, Ms. Hart." Geoffrey leads me through a door labelled 'Authorised Personnel Only' to a corridor with a private set of elevators. "This is the staff lift and family access. Here is a list of instructions for you from Mr. Thompson—codes for your room and such." He hands me an envelope with my name on it. "Mr. Thompson sends his sincerest apologies for not meeting you himself. Aside from the late hour, he has been run off his feet helping Mr. Houston manage the hotel."

The lift dings softly and opens, allowing me to step inside, followed closely by Geoffrey pushing a trolley with my bags stacked on top.

"Of course. It's totally fine. I wouldn't expect him to attend me at two a.m. I take it you work the night shift, Geoffrey?" He nods. "What is your position here?" I have a lot of staff to get to know; I might as well start familiarizing myself with everyone's name and position right away.

"I work as a concierge, mostly, and V.I.P. guest services, Miss. I work evenings and fill in on day shifts when necessary." He leans in a little closer. "It's good to have you here. We really need the help."

Damn, they must be short-staffed if he's having to fill in day shifts. This is slightly concerning, but I'm sure I'll have this place running more efficiently soon enough.

The lift dings again, and the doors slide open with a gentle *swish*.

"This is your floor, Ms. Hart. That envelope contains your swipe card to access this private lift, and the six-digit access code for your room. Mr. Thompson left you instructions to change the code, for your safety. No one can access this floor other than security, cleaners, and members of the Houston family."

We exit the elevator—or *lift*, as he calls it—and he points to the far right end of the vast hallway. "That big door at the end of the hallway leads to the Houston family suite. Christopher lives there."

We head left, walking down a beautiful, carpeted hallway with dim wall lights that lend a moody atmosphere to the area. On either side is a collection of stunning modern artwork at regular intervals, broken up every so often by walnut timber doors that must lead to various family accommodations. It's different to the hotel in New York, but I can see Eléa's style stamped all over it— and I've only visited one floor so far.

We reach the end of the hallway and stop outside a set of tall, walnut double doors. "This is your Suite," Geoffrey tells me, gesturing to the doors. "I'll bring your bags in, then I'll leave you to rest. I'm sure you must be exhausted by now."

He's right, I'm spent. I'm going to sleep like the dead any moment now. The adrenalin has worn off and I'm crashing hard, like an addict coming down from a massive high.

"Thank you, Geoffrey, for everything," I say sincerely, and I offer to give him a tip for his kind, attentive service. "No need, Miss. We don't really do that here."

I thank him for his honesty and open the envelope from Daniel with the door entry code inside. Inputting the code, I tuck the paper back inside the envelope and slide it into my pocket. I'll reprogram it later. I can't be bothered doing it now, and I doubt I'm going to remember much of this in the morning anyway.

As the door clicks open, a strong whiff of something botanical hits me instantly. I breathe in deeply.

Geoffrey pushes the trolley inside and starts unloading my bags. "Whatever you need," he says, grunting as he lifts the heavier of the two suitcases, "just call the front desk. We'll send it up immediately." With my luggage unloaded, Geoffrey says a quick, "Goodnight, Ms. Hart," and heads out, wheeling the trolley in front of him.

I hear the door click shut, and I begin to examine the apartment with bleary eyes. The living space is gorgeous. Amber light emanates from the wall lights, identical to the ones in the hallway. Plush, dark-gray carpet covers the floor. The walls are freshly-painted in charcoal, my favorite color, and I know Mrs. Houston must have something to do with it. An enormous bunch of flowers rests on the console table in the entryway, with a card poking out the top. I pull the little piece of cardboard out and turn it over, revealing a handwritten note from Eléa.

My dear L'été,

Welcome to your new home. Take some time to settle in. My son, Christopher, and The Wave manager, Daniel, do not expect anything from you for a few days.

Rest, sleep, enjoy. I will speak with you soon, ma chérie.

-E

I put the card down carefully, suddenly feeling like it's the most precious item in the apartment.

Floor-to-ceiling drapes conceal what I imagine are breathtaking views, and though I can't wait to open them, I'm quickly running out of energy. I weave around the expensive walnut dining table and chairs and the gray sofa, heading for a modern kitchenette at the far end of the main living space. The dark ambience has a calming effect, and I can already see myself relaxing in this room after a hard day of work. I run my hand over the handsome gray veins of the white Italian marble countertop on the little kitchen island that just fits two barstools behind it, and I approach a tall fridge with a brushed-steel door.

I pull on the black handle to discover the fridge is fully stocked with my favorite brand of sparkling water, a fresh loaf of sourdough, a carton of milk, a stick of yellow butter, a colorful variety of local produce, and even two blocks of Lindt dark chocolate—which Eléa knows is my one true weakness. She certainly has made sure I feel welcome.

Leaving the kitchenette, I approach a set of double doors leading to the bedroom, and when I push them open I gasp.

"Fuck…" I swear, because what else can I say to explain the beauty before me?

Custom wallpaper lines the walls, almost identical to the one in my old apartment. Empty picture frames hang from the walls, ready to display any new photographs I take. This must be Eléa's way of making sure I continue my hobby here in London.

I enter the large walk-in wardrobe with floor-to-ceiling hanging space, built in shelves, and a large dresser. I don't think I'll be able to fill this much space even with all the clothes Bee and I bought. A full-length mirror with built-in lights and an art deco chandelier make the room feel even more distinguished.

I pass through the walk-in robe into the most luxurious full bathroom I have ever seen. A large oval tub, almost the size of a jacuzzi, sits by the window, low enough to provide a stunning view of the city. A massive double basin extends along the center of the far wall, topped with the same Italian marble as the kitchen island. A huge shower, seriously big enough for three or four people, with a sitting bench and body jets, takes up most of the other wall. A large T.V. is mounted to the wall beside the shower, visible from everywhere in the room.

This is too much. I mean, *damn*. The New York hotel is stunning—even after living there, I still admire the five-star luxury—but this is next level.

A basket filled with The Houston Hotel's own range of spa and pamper products rests on a square leather ottoman in the center of the room. As I rifle through the collection, I'm even more astonished. Eléa—I know it's her doing—has given me a stock of luxury soap, shower gel, moisturizer, face cream, bath salts, and even more. I open the lid on one of the bottles and take a sniff.

Mm, delicious—grapefruit and mint. A signature scent.

I decide to wait until tomorrow to take a proper look around, because right now I *really* want to shower and climb into the huge, cushion-covered bed I glimpsed in the bedroom.

After a much-needed, glorious shower that leaves me smelling like a fruity, minty cocktail, I decide to hit the sack.

Sure enough, the bed has the softest black Egyptian cotton sheets, a thick down comforter and pillows soft as clouds. The duvet cover is charcoal grey linen, my preferred feel and color. The dark hues encourage complete relaxation, soothe my nervous system, and induce sleep. Black is my go-to color; what can I say?

Maybe that's why I print most of my photographs in black and white. I find it more emotive when you strip away the color. It gives every photograph a feeling of timelessness.

I collapse into bed, completely spent. This past week has worn me out like I ran the New York City Marathon ten times.

I don't even dream after I drift off to sleep.

I awake to a pounding in my head and a feeling of disorientation. I don't know what the time is, but I'm pretty sure I haven't slept long enough to wake up naturally. A loud bang coming from outside my apartment makes me jump. What the heck? I strain my ears, but I don't hear anything else for almost a minute.

I roll over to get comfortable again, but the pounding in my head continues. *Fucking jet lag.*

I need a drink of water. Sitting up, I look over at the dimly illuminated digital clock on my nightstand. Four thirty a.m. No wonder I feel like shit.

I hear another loud bang, closer this time, followed by someone cursing loudly outside my apartment door.

Panicking, I step out of bed and reach for my oversized t-shirt to cover my black lacy bra and underwear. Afraid of what might be the cause of the noise, I tiptoe over to the apartment door as quietly as I can. Geoffrey said no one could access this floor, so who's outside?

Five seconds is all I'm giving the person outside my door to explain themselves before they're murdered—in self-defense, of course. I crack open the door, peering through the gap while trying to keep my half-naked body semi-hidden.

What I find outside leaves me momentarily speechless. The most sublime creature I've ever seen lies, splayed, across the carpet just beyond the threshold.

I blink a few times, making sure I'm awake and not hallucinating. Did I actually fall down a rabbit hole? Because *damn*, the person passed out on the floor in front of me is too beautiful to be real. He really belongs in some kind of fairy tale.

He has brown hair, like my favorite dark Lindt chocolate, not too long but long enough to run my fingers through it.

Stop it, Summer, I tell myself, but he really is a specimen.

His face is perfectly symmetrical, with lashes so long they almost touch his cheeks while his eyes are closed. I can't see the color of those eyes, but I imagine they're just as stunning as the rest of him. A pink blush flushes his cheeks as though he's had too much wine, and, my god, he has the softest, most luscious lips I've ever seen on a man. I have to catch myself before I start thinking a little too deeply about those lips.

Why is he on this floor, and what the heck do I do about it? My jetlagged brain can't handle this at four thirty a.m.

I nudge him with my toe, just to make sure he's real, and, sure enough, the freakishly hot lump is warm. I take another second to inspect him. His navy-blue shirt is untucked and has risen enough to give me the tiniest glimpse of smooth skin. Lines of well-defined abdominal muscle peek out, tormenting me just a little. His denim jeans are sitting low on his hips, fitted in all the right places, and my depraved, frustrated brain wants to look at the package I know he's packing, but my logical, professional side is shouting at me to ignore the *pretty* and do something.

I walk back inside my apartment and pick up the hotel phone to call the front desk.

"Good morning, Ms. Hart. What can I do for you?" The voice on the other end of the line is unfamiliar, but gentle and kind.

Wow. I'm already in the system here. Mr. and Mrs. Houston must have worked hard to make sure everyone and everything was ready and waiting for my arrival.

"Um, hi. This might sound odd at four thirty a.m., but there's a random guy passed out in front of my suite. I don't know him, or how he got here. Can you… send security?" I ask, trying not to let my panic come through in my voice.

"Oh! Of course, Ms. Hart. I'll send Victor up right away, but I'm sure it's not a breach. That floor is very secure. Perhaps it's just Mr. Christopher. He comes in late some nights."

I relax a little. Surely the concierge on the phone is correct and this isn't just some random guy that ended up on the wrong floor.

"Thank you. I appreciate it."

As I disconnect the call and head back to the front door, I notice sleeping beauty still hasn't moved. I check, and he's still breathing, which is a positive.

The elevator dings its arrival, and out steps a huge hulk of a man in a Houston Hotel security guard's uniform. This must be Victor; it's reassuring how quickly he arrived.

"Ms. Hart, sorry to disturb you at this time of the morning."

I just now remember I'm standing there with no pants on, and I yank down the hem of my black t-shirt to cover my upper thighs. Victor deserves a medal for the professional way he averts his eyes from the half-naked, jetlagged girl standing in the doorway.

"It's alright. You weren't the one who disturbed me," I reassure him, gesturing towards the man passed out on the floor. "Do you know who this is?"

Victor bends down to check sleeping beauty's pulse, and looks up at me with an apologetic expression. "It's Mr. Christopher. He went out tonight and must have had too much to drink." I can see it now—the resemblance to Jarrod. Christopher's hair isn't so dark, but I can definitely see the Houston DNA in that tall, well-built, sickeningly handsome lump asleep across my entryway.

"His suite is down the other end of the hall, so perhaps he was too intoxicated to find his way there. I'll try to wake him," Victor offers.

Thus, Victor, along with some hesitant shakes from me, tries to wake sleeping beauty for the next two minutes and twenty-nine seconds, to no avail. We manage a couple of grunts and moans, but Christopher doesn't stir. He's so wasted he doesn't even open his eyes when Victor taps his cheek.

"Can you just carry him to bed?" I ask.

"I'm sorry, Miss, but no one has the code to access his suite. That's the Houston family suite. It's private. There's no card reader to enter, just the keypad. No hotel staff can access the apartment without a Houston to unlock it, I'm afraid." He looks at me and shrugs.

"Well, what am I supposed to do? Leave him here at my door? What if he gets sick or something?" That panicky feeling is quickly rising, and I'm not calm or collected any more.

Eléa would have a meltdown if she knew this was how I would meet her beloved son for the first time. Damn it! I can't just leave him here—I have to look after him; I promised Eléa.

This isn't the first impression I expected, but what can I do?

"You know what?" I ask, looking at Victor with a sinking feeling in my stomach. "Can you lift him onto my sofa?" By the looks of it, Victor is the *only* person sizeable enough to lift the dead weight of Christopher Houston into my apartment.

"Are you sure, Miss? I could see if we can find a vacant room on another floor." While I appreciate Victor's offer, I'm terrified that something terrible might happen if Christopher is left alone.

How would that look for me, murdering the owner's son on my first night? Well, maybe not murder, but I would be an accomplice or something, wouldn't I? I'm aware my brain is slightly wonky because of my jetlag and all, but the thought still makes sense to me.

For now, I'll keep him alive and well. I can murder him for doing this to me when he wakes up.

"Yes, it's OK. I don't want him to get sick, so just bring him in. I'll sort it out tomorrow."

Victor gives me another apologetic look, then he hefts Christopher over his shoulder in one move, like a professional wrestler would, and carries him into my private space, my new sanctuary, and lays him down gently on the sofa. The big lump doesn't even wake up. Gosh, he must be completely out of it.

"Call if you need anything, Miss. I'm on until ten a.m."

Victor takes his leave, leaving me in my t-shirt and underwear, alone with the most perfect human ever to walk on planet earth.

Sharp angles and soft lips… It really feels like he's waiting for a princess to kiss him and wake him from his slumber.

Well, I'm not a princess, and I will *not* think about kissing anyone. I'm certainly not going to look at him in any way other than professionally. I have to work with him.

In fact, I won't look at him at all. I'll just close my eyes and pretend he's hideous and has a teeny, tiny penis. That'll help turn me off him.

Small penis, small brain, ugly—that's what I have to tell myself for the foreseeable future, otherwise how the fuck am I going to work with him every day? This is the worst thing that's happened to me in years. Why couldn't he be average-looking, with bad skin and a balding head?

I sigh out loud and throw a blanket over him, then I head back to bed, chanting my new mantra: "Small penis, small brain, ugly face, small penis, small brain, ugly face." I think I fall asleep after about the twentieth repetition, because I don't remember anything else. It's a good thing, really, because I need my rest.

Clearly this strange new world I'm in is going to test me at every turn.

CHAPTER FIVE

WHO'S THE BOSS

I detect a subtle hum, as if someone is breathing out and producing a low, throaty vibration. Not a growl, but more of a laryngeal resonance. I'm so tired and foggy. A mix of jet lag and exhaustion hangs over me like a rain cloud, threatening to dump its load onto my head at any moment.

"You talk in your sleep."

My eyes ping open at the softly spoken but very obviously male voice, so close I can feel his breath on my face.

What the actual fuck?!

I'm almost nose to nose with another person, and an unfamiliar pair of baby blues is right up in my business. His closeness obscures any other details; we must be less than an inch apart.

I take a full minute—*sixty whole seconds*—to unravel this situation I find myself in. The how, why, and finally, who.

Of course! It's all coming back to me now.

He waits patiently for things to click as I stare blankly at him, and when they finally do, I'm fucking mad!

Inhaling a sharp breath, I scoot backwards, giving myself more room on the bed—actually, *my* bed! He's on my bed!

"Can I ask why you are *in my bed*, staring at me like some kind of nut job?"

My polite, professional side has left the building. Honestly, I think it vanished last night when I found him on my doorstep. His expression is simply curious, and his eyes are absorbed in studying my face up close. He sees everything. There's no barrier between us. I feel naked. Exposed.

"I heard you talking; you woke me up. I have no clue how I got into this room, so naturally I had to explore and find out." He still doesn't make a move. He seems so comfortable, as if he's done this a hundred times. As if he owns the place.

Yes, of course he owns the place, but this suite is mine! He definitely shouldn't be this relaxed on *my* bed, with that accent that makes him sound like a nice, proper gentleman.

"And *you're* the 'nut job'. You kept repeating something about an ugly man with a small penis." At this, my face spontaneously combusts, making my cheeks turn fuchsia, and I can't maintain eye contact. I shut my eyes briefly, fighting back anger and frustration at his offhand use of 'penis', like he's discussing the weather.

"I am not. I did not!" I splutter, barely able to control my words.

"Did too." Again, so casual—and then I see his smile. His lips have quirked up at either end. He's *enjoying* tormenting me.

As angry as I am, I can't help wondering if he has perfect teeth too. I'm yet to observe an ugly feature on him, which just makes me even madder.

Please, universe, I beg. Show me something hideous, something that will turn me off this far-too-attractive man in front of me.

"Well, if you weren't passed out and on the brink of death, I would have had Victor carry your drunken ass to another room," I snap. "It's nice to meet you too, *Christopher*," I say snarkily. This is obviously *not* the introduction I expected, nor the wake-up I wanted on my first day here in London.

"Pleased to meet you, *Wednesday*. I wondered why my mother insisted on decorating this suite in such festive colors, but now I understand."

'Festive'? Did he just take a jibe at my favorite color scheme? This asshole thinks he's a comedian.

"And I wasn't on the brink of death, Wednesday. I was merely a couple pints over my usual Friday night quota," he tells me with pride, like he won some kind of college drinking game. Does he want a ribbon?

"My name is Summer. Why are you calling me Wednesday? And I don't care what you do for fun around here; next time, crash into *someone else's* door. And preferably not at *four thirty in the morning*!" I swear there's steam coming from my ears.

"Summer doesn't suit you," he remarks, gesturing at the room's dark colors before shaking my black linen comforter in the air, as though I'm not already aware that it's black. "You're more of a Wednesday Addams with the dark walls, dark hair and gray eyes." Again, he fixes those baby blues on my stormy-gray ones. For a moment, we just stare intensely at each other. I roll my eyes, trying to show him he's not anywhere near as funny as he thinks he is.

"Summer is my name. Please use it! And now that I see you haven't died of alcohol poisoning or choking on your own vomit, can you kindly leave my bed—my *suite*," I correct, "and let me recover from my three-thousand-four-hundred-and-seventy-one-mile journey without interrupting my sleep for the *third* time?" I don't even bother trying to be polite anymore.

"As comfortable as your bed is, freckles, I have important things of my own to take care of." He rolls effortlessly off my huge king bed, straightens his shirt like the creases don't even matter, and winks at me.

Wait. He winked at me… like I'm a one-night stand he just slept with. Before I even have time to get offended, he ambles out the door of my bedroom. This sets my anger to a new level. I close my eyes, scrunch them tight so I don't get a view of that ass walking away—I don't need that kind of visual when I'm trying to be mad.

"MY. NAME. IS. *SUMMER!*" I yell, like a petulant child. This guy has brought a foot-stomping tantrum out of me from a single conversation. I kick my legs angrily under the covers, just to cement my behavior as childish.

"See you soon, *Sunshine.*" The sound of his laughter fills the air before my apartment door clicks shut, leaving me in stunned silence.

"Asshole," I mutter, all-too-aware he can't hear me. "Ugh! Hideously ugly, teeny tiny penis, and I'm sure he has a beer gut somewhere under those clothes," I tell myself, even though I know it's a big fat lie.

Unfortunately, I know my words are empty, because holy mother-of-dragons! Christopher Houston embodies the Houston family genes effortlessly. He has his father's blue eyes, lighter than Jarrod's, and his mother's fiery personality. Even worse, Christopher has his own blend of charisma that may well be the end of me. I don't do well with being taunted or teased, and I sure as hell don't do well with being winked at! The *nerve.*

I really need to set some boundaries before it's too late—if it isn't already.

I spend the remainder of the day resting.

I don't emerge from my suite at all, because I'm far too busy reading the hotel's logbooks from the last couple months: clientele details, front desk check-ins, room service, room turnover rates, restaurant and cocktail lounge patron numbers, everything.

It seems to have been operating very well prior to Jarrod's departure, but everything is a bit of a mess since he left. Rosters are inconsistent, with too few staff on some shifts and too many on others, and an overall lack of authority, it seems. Well, I'm here now. I'll get this hotel back to perfection in no time.

I skim over the amenities books while I enjoy a nibble of my favorite dark chocolate. Hopefully I don't eat it all in a week due to homesickness. This place and its blue-eyed owner will give me more than enough to worry about; I don't need to pack on the pounds, too. I need to be physically and mentally healthy to deal with everything coming my way.

Studying a map of the hotel, I can see there's an indoor gym and pool on the third floor, the roof top is a bar and function area, the first floor holds The Wave, where Bee used to sing, next door to Aqua, a casual dining restaurant, and the ground floor houses Sable—'sand' in French—an *à la carte* restaurant.

It's not as large a building as the New York hotel, and it caters to select clientele—international guests and well-to-do locals looking for a classy place to unwind on weekends. This was Mr. and Mrs. Houston's first hotel, established thirty years ago but fully renovated within the last five years. Just like New York, it's all art deco styling, gloriously posh but tasteful.

Old-world charm meets modern amenities in London's historic city center. I haven't yet had a chance to walk the streets with my camera, but doing a Google search shows me a mix of old and new. This city has so much more history than New York, with its remnants of war and the gilt of aristocracy. It's a rich display of art, a network of interconnected structures. It's beautiful.

I can't wait to get into the daily grind here. Work is what I do best, but I'm looking forward to exploring and taking some time off to settle my mind, ground myself, and learn about this new life I have in London. I'm excited to wander around with my camera and see new shapes through the lens. I wonder what new discoveries that little window will compose for me.

I note where the gym is located because tomorrow I'm going to work out all my frustrations on the treadmill. After that, I'll unpack my clothes and take a walk around the hotel, from the ground floor to the fifth floor and rooftop. I'll try to sleep early, too, so I'm ready for Monday; my first official day as the general manager of The Houston Hotel London.

Somehow, I'm less nervous about managing a hotel than I am about working with a tall, *unfortunately* not ugly, blue-eyed hottie that refuses to call me by my name. This, no doubt, will be my biggest complication in London… The fucking gorgeous asshole.

My alarm buzzes, instantly waking me. I don't usually need to set an alarm, because my body clock is perfectly in tune with my daily schedule back in New York. This morning, I was worried that the jetlag and unfamiliar surroundings would throw me off, so I set an alarm just in case. Judging from my grogginess, the alarm was a good idea. I want to get a good workout in before I familiarize myself with the hotel and meet the team.

After a strong cup of coffee, I brush my teeth, tie my long hair up in a messy bun, and apply skin serum to my face so the sweat I'm about to leach doesn't stick for the rest of the day. I rummage around in one of my suitcases for some active wear and find my regular black gym shorts and crop top, avoiding the beautiful but far too bright pink number Bee made me purchase on our shopping spree in New York.

That would attract attention, and I don't need—or want—to be that noticeable, especially in a new place and out of my comfort zone. I guess you could say I like to fly under the radar.

I saw my beautiful mother attract the male gaze, probably more than she realized, and it didn't do her any favors. I don't need to use looks to gain success. I rely purely on education and bloody hard work.

I grab a bottle of chilled water from my fridge and head out the front door. It's great not having to carry a separate keycard with me for the door, and I'll never forget the code I programmed into the keypad—my mother's date of birth.

The one card I have unlocks everything in the hotel, including elevators, guest rooms, the gym, the pool, and the hotel safe where cash and guest valuables are stored. I make sure to zip it into the pocket of my gym shorts to keep it safe.

As I ride the elevator, I surmise it will take me a few months to establish a good rhythm here. During the first month, I'll learn the ropes, see how this hotel operates, implement a plan for continued success, and make sure we hire the right people for management positions. From what I've heard, Daniel is fantastic at managing The Wave. Different musical acts perform there regularly, but their patron numbers have steadily declined over the past few months.

I heard Bee literally drew a full house every time she sang, and the attendance was so high they had a waiting list for weeks.

Though I know Bee is truly one of a kind, I'd like to scout out another musical act that can match her talent as closely as possible. I need to discuss this with Daniel and take some time to venture out and observe potential acts in person. For all I know, we could uncover the next Ed Sheeran or Ellie Goulding.

Keeping a fresh and exciting line-up means we're able to keep the local clientele coming, so letting things get stale is the last thing we want.

Exiting the elevator on the third floor, I see the glass doors at the end of the hallway. The east wing holds several guest rooms, and at the west end of the building is the indoor pool and fitness center.

As I walk through the doors into the quiet recreational space, I see stunning floor-to-ceiling windows, with breathtaking views of Hyde Park and a colossal structure I believe is the Marble Arch. It's a nineteenth century white marble-faced triumphal arch that stands about forty-five feet high. I'm not sure if it holds any royal significance. I'll have time to do research and learn all about local landmarks and historical monuments on my days off.

The gorgeous, mosaic-tiled, clear blue pool is to my right, and I can't help comparing it to a peaceful oasis that guests can enjoy all year round. It's winter now, but the climate-controlled heat and humidity make it the perfect temperature to relax and take a dip.

I'm sure as heck going to partake in all the perks of my job, starting with that pool, just as soon as I work out when the least congested times are. I don't like the staff and guests seeing me in my personal time, so I tend to use the amenities either very early or very late in the day—like now.

I enter the fitness center and realize I'm the only one here. The guests must be staying warm and cozy in their beds, but I'm sure the fitness center will be busy later in the morning.

The room is filled with high-tech cardio equipment, weight training machines, hand weights, skill tools, and Pilates reformer machines—I'm yet to try using one of those. The closest I've come is practicing yoga with Eléa. We used to make time once a week for a girls' yoga session at a great studio just down the road on West Fifty-Fifth Street.

We would sweat it out for a full hour, then hit up a little contemporary French bistro called *Benoit*. It has the cutest façade—a white painted exterior with blue-striped canvas awnings—like it jumped right out of a Parisian magazine. The light color palette and red velvet banquettes bring a bit of France to the heart of midtown Manhattan.

I get that little heart pang again, as I'm reminded that the girls' time I cherished so much is over. I suppose I could attempt to make friends here, but I'm unsure how, given my history of lacking stable social connections.

Relocating to the U.S. at age ten was an emotionally turbulent experience. My mother and I moved multiple times before she found regular work, and by that time I was starting college. College was really the only time I had a permanent home until I moved into the Houston. The past couple years in New York were my only stable refuge.

I start warming up at a slow walk. Music plays from hidden speakers in the ceiling. It's a Miley Cyrus song, not loud enough to be disturbing, just nice background noise for those of us who don't have headphones on. I find that headphones often move around and fall off, so I never wear them while I work out.

The large flat-screen T.V. on the wall is muted, with captions on. This doesn't bother me, because it's just the news on right now. The day's weather is looking average. There's no rain in the forecast, but it'll be cold—not that I'm leaving my sanctuary any time soon.

"If it isn't Little Miss Sunshine."

I hear the familiar voice, but I can't do much more than turn my head without falling off the treadmill. It's him: my archrival. Well, not really a *rival*, as such. More like a nuisance I have to put up with for the indefinite future.

I roll my eyes at Christopher's title for me. He's still not using my name. My stomach dips a little when I notice he steps onto the treadmill next to me. He has an entire room to play around with, and here he is crowding my personal space *again*.

"Well, if it isn't Mr. I-get-so-wasted-I-pass-out," I retort. With a smirk, I turn to face him, but I realize my mistake as soon as I look up into his face.

Fuck, I kind of forgot how damn *hot* he is—or maybe my jet lag and throbbing head the other night prevented me from appreciating the true depths of his attractiveness. The Nuisance is not just *good looking*, but really beautiful. He's taller than I expected; now that we're standing—or walking—beside one another, he looks to be… six-foot-two? Six-foot-three?

His lips curve up into a smirk again, that mischievous glint betraying him. He must be one of those impossibly good-looking men who always gets away with everything.

Those baby-blues take a long wander down my body, soaking up my bare legs and athletic shorts, and then meander on up to my top half where they finally settle on my face. His inspection makes me feel like I'm applying for *America's Next Top Model*.

I'm a little shocked at his blatant examination, but then I think, well, fair game. I can do the same.

I rake my gaze over his mid-length gray running shorts and muscular legs dusted with dark hair. He has a natural tan about him, closer to his mother's warm skin tone than his father's pale British countenance. Christopher is wearing a black muscle tank with The Rolling Stones' logo printed on the front. His arms, though long and corded with muscle, are not as large as Jarrod's. Christopher's are closer to the lean arms of a tennis player or rower.

He really is perfectly formed, like he was carved by a master sculptor, and I have to drag my eyes back to the TV just to get a breather from his genetically-blessed physique. He's an asshole. A good looking, smirking, blue-eyed asshole. And he knows it.

"They're some fit legs you have, Sunshine." I avoid looking at him again, because I don't want to be enchanted by his intoxicating face and body. He's so striking in the morning light, with his perfect skin and neatly cut dark hair with the little wave on the ends.

Fuck, I'm losing my mind, and it's not even breakfast time yet.

I speed up the treadmill, hoping he'll leave me alone to continue my workout.

"It's Summer. And stop looking at my legs, thank you," I say, breathing a little heavier. Unfortunately, I don't think it's the pace causing my lungs to tighten.

I don't feel objectified so much as appreciated. I've put a lot of effort into my fitness, and he's clearly noticed. I don't use baggy clothing to hide my body. I'm aware that men look, and I'm fine with it as long as they're not sleazy or making me uncomfortable.

"It's hard not to, Sunshine. You have an amazing rig," he tells me, in all seriousness. I realize his compliments on my fitness must be because he's into fitness himself. "How do you find your room? I hope it's up to your standards."

I'm glad for the change of subject. The two of us clearly need a different direction—a new beginning, really, if I'm being honest. Meeting Christopher the way I did hasn't exactly kept us in 'professional' territory.

"You mean your *mother's* standards, which are astonishingly exquisite? Who could fault her taste and style? The whole hotel, from what I have seen so far, is magnificent." I'm not playing around now. I want him to know I really do love The Houston Corporation's hotels. "I would do anything for your parents—Eléa especially. I mean, here I am in a different continent, just because she asked me." With my gaze fixed on the treadmill's display, I avoid meeting his eyes.

"She thinks the world of you, Sunshine, but I don't need help. I appreciate the huge life-changing effort you made for my parents, but I can handle things here. I just need some time to work things out," he says, confident and a little condescending.

I pause the treadmill so I can look at him without tripping. Knowing my luck, I'll break my ankle before my first day on the job. He doesn't seem mad, but he's clearly resistant to being helped. It's now I realize he was the one arguing with Eléa on the phone before I left.

"Christopher, I'm not here to undermine you. I'm here because you clearly need help running this hotel. Jarrod isn't coming back right now, and it's too much for one person. Don't think of me as your boss, more like a partner to share the load," I say sincerely.

"Boss? What are you talking about?" he asks quizzically and stops his own treadmill to face me with those blue eyes. Blue I could drown in.

"Didn't your parents tell you I'm here as G.M.?" My stomach sinks as I see the confusion on his face. Shit, they didn't tell him.

"No. *I'm* GM now that Jarrod's gone. I assumed you were going to be my assistant or operative manager." He frowns. A small line forms between his dark brows, and he sucks his lower lip into his mouth. I know it's not meant to be flirty or sexual, but that lip has me feeling all kinds of warmth. God, I can't even concentrate on the current situation.

"I think you need to speak to your parents, Christopher. I came here to take over as the general manager. I assumed they would've informed you of that."

I take a breath, because this situation is growing more hostile by the second. Christopher's face has lost its carefree visage and now showcases indignation and frustration.

"Well, fuck, Sunshine. My own parents have duped me." He takes a minute to process, looking up towards the ceiling. Taylor Swift singing about a 'lavender haze' fills the awkward silence.

I watch him run his hand through his hair and over his face, like he can wipe away his feelings, then his gaze returns to me. We lock eyes, blue and gray, and I see his own change. The blue gets just a little deeper, and his pupils dilate like a lion sensing his prey, ready to begin the chase.

The smile that comes next is a shock. He shows me the set of perfect white teeth he's been hiding behind those juicy lips, and I really feel like I've fallen down some deep, dark hole.

Why is he looking like he wants to devour me?

"Well, Sunshine, this is going to be interesting." He puts his face so close to mine that I feel his breath on my lips. Christopher clearly has an issue with personal space.

"What is?" I ask cautiously.

"You and me. This…" He waves his hand between us. "It's going to be fun working out who the *real* boss is here. I look forward to the challenge."

Without another word, he walks right out of the gym, leaving me open-mouthed with a hundred unanswered questions and a heart beating way too fast considering I've been standing still for several minutes now.

"Asshole," I mutter.

It makes me feel marginally better to call him names. It would be a lot more satisfying if I could say it right to that obnoxious, stupidly fucking pretty face. I don't like him. He's going to be a giant headache for me, I know it. What I *don't* know is what to do about it.

I guess I'll have to outsmart him and work even harder than usual. I'll show him I can thrive in a competitive work environment.

Yes, I'll play his game. I'm going to enjoy making Christopher Houston surrender.

I may just have to engage in some questionable tactics, because if there's one thing I can be certain of, it's that Mr. Blue-Eyes plays dirty.

CHAPTER SIX

LET THE GAMES BEGIN

Monday morning is finally here. I've spent the last couple days adjusting to the new time zone and trying to reset my inner clock, all while reading as much about this establishment as my jetlagged brain can digest.

Now, after a strong coffee, a focused gym session, and an almond croissant for breakfast, I'm ready to begin my mission.

Today I chose to wear a sleeveless black bodycon dress that stops just above the knee. I avoid wearing a jacket because I'll no doubt be hot and bothered with Christopher around for eight to ten hours. What kind of punishment did I unknowingly self-inflict by coming here?

I tie my hair into a knot at the nape of my neck and touch up my neutral lipstick. I strike a pose in the mirror and laugh at my expression.

My phone starts to ring, and Eléa's name lights up the screen.

"Good morning," I greet her. "It's almost eight a.m. here, so it must be… three a.m. in New York?"

"*L'été*, my dear! It's so good to hear your voice. And don't fuss over the time—I am taking a spa day tomorrow. Jarrod will manage." I love how her accent makes Jarrod's name sound like '*zha-rod*'. "Are you excited to begin, *ma chérie*?" she asks, with all the warmth I've come to love.

"Yes, I'm ready. But Eléa, didn't you tell Christopher about my position? He seemed a little surprised. I mean, I don't want to get in the middle of family business."

"Shush you, don't mind my son. He can be headstrong, like his mother." She laughs, and I sigh in frustration as she dodges my question. "You're family too, L'été, and my son's too stubborn to ask for help. I send you to fix him. Fix everything. Yes?"

While I appreciate being welcomed into the Houston family, I can't help but think there's another reason I'm here. Maybe with more time Christopher could have handled this hotel on his own.

"Alright. As long as he accepts me, and my position, we can work through this together. I think."

I spray on some of my favorite perfume, my mother's old favorite, by Lebanese fashion designer Elie Saab. I close my eyes and breathe in the floral orange blossom and jasmine fragrance that reminds me of Mom. It's my go-to perfume. It's classy and feminine, but within my budget.

"Of course, *ma chérie*, of course. You take all the time you need. I will call once a week to check in, but *L'été…*" She pauses for a moment.

"Yes?" I ask, waiting for her to finish before I leave my new little sanctuary where I've cocooned myself for the last few days.

"You can always call, no matter what. Your home is with us now. If you need anything, *chérie*, we are a phone call away." Her words bring a little pool of salt water to my lashes. Damn, I just did my makeup.

"I know, Eléa. Thank you."

After I end the call, I pause and take a few deep breaths, staring at my apartment door. My future awaits beyond that door. I don't know why, but I feel some kind of pull, like an invisible rope tugging at my insides. It feels less like a job and more like destiny.

I glance at my watch. Seven fifty-two. Time to go! I pick up my bag and head out, finally taking those first steps towards whatever inevitable situation awaits.

"Morning, Ms. Hart," a young housekeeper greets as she takes an armful of fresh linen to another floor. So far, the staff I've met know exactly who I am, and they've been nothing but lovely. Someone must have briefed them before my arrival.

"Good morning, Anita," I respond, quickly scanning her name badge. Thank goodness the London hotel has the same protocol, otherwise learning so many new names would be mind-bending.

Of course, as upper management, we don't wear a uniform or name badges. We dress like corporate executives in suits and tailored garments. I usually stick to my conservative and familiar black, but I have a few pops of color Bee packed for me that I'll try out as I go.

After several more 'good morning's, I finally make it to the main office suite on the ground floor, behind the back-of-house facilities. It's quiet, as expected on a Monday morning. A few of the night staff flutter around, finishing up the last of their work before heading home. The day staff are mostly huddled around the sole espresso machine, exchanging yawns and low-energy greetings with one another.

The office space features a beautiful entryway, with marble floors and comfortable seating for visitors. On the right is a conference room for managerial meetings, a lunchroom with a long table featuring several stacked-up fruit bowls, and the busy kitchen, with its state-of-the-art coffee machine—now boasting a queue of half-a-dozen staff—and tea bar. There must be fifty kinds of tea here from around the world. The English really do love their tea.

My office, which I visited yesterday, is located down a long hallway with several adjoining rooms. It's a gorgeous space, with plush gray carpets and a stunning 'Flowers and Birds' mural by William Morris. After admiring his artwork, I looked him up online and discovered he was a celebrated local artist in the nineteenth century.

This is Eléa's office when she's in town, and I guess Christopher has the room next door now that Jarrod has moved on. From my window, I observe the bustling morning traffic of central London. Though the city is quite congested, it's calm compared to the frenzy of Manhattan that I've grown used to.

The only sound I can hear is the soft hum of the climate control and the gentle buzzing of the lights, reminiscent of a beehive. All outside noise is completely blocked out by the soundproofed walls, and I'm grateful to have a quiet place to work.

I'll have to walk around the hotel later this afternoon to get acquainted with the staff and their zones, but for now, it's time to hit the books. Paperwork will have me busy 'til lunchtime, no doubt.

I'm about twenty minutes into roster modification, my fingers flying over the keyboard at the speed of light, when I sense someone watching me. I pause my fluttering fingers and look up to find a stunning creature staring at me, like I'm one of those animals at the zoo that people pay to see performing mundane human tasks.

Christopher wears a tailored midnight-blue suit, darker than his eyes but no less captivating. A white shirt and gray tie complete the ensemble and offer a striking contrast to the dark suit.

My mouth suddenly goes dry, and I regret not getting a coffee on my way in. Damn, if I thought he looked good in jeans and gym clothes, this is something else. This is GQ magazine.

I'm not prepared for this kind of perfection at eight a.m. on a Monday. Bloody Houston family. Why do they have to be so goddamn beautiful? I blink slowly, hoping he's just a mirage that will disappear, but nope… still there.

He leans on the doorframe, as imposing as an ancient Greek god, and I have no words. My brain is a mess of frustration at how casual he looks, anger at how easily he's able to affect me, and lust. I force my eyes back to my computer screen and pretend I've barely noticed his arrival. I can pull off a detached, aloof co-worker vibe easily; I've been doing it for years.

"Morning, Christopher. May I help you with something?" I don't look up as I speak, hoping he'll take the hint.

"While there are *many* answers to your question, Sunshine, my response this morning is yes." I stop typing and look up, curiosity piqued against my will.

That lazy smirk of his is back. He's holding a cup of coffee, and as he sips, I watch his tongue snake out and wet those luscious lips. Lips that look way too soft… and warm… and I'm losing my train of thought.

Snap out of it, Summer.

I can't allow him to do this to me. I bet that's his *modus operandi*—derail me so I'll go back to New York and let him run this hotel on his own. Not happening.

"And what would that be?" I ask, finally responding.

He saunters into the room, ambling like he has all day, and walks right up behind me to see what I'm working on. Leaning over the back of my chair, his chin nearly touches the top of my head, and I get a whiff of his cologne. I breathe through my mouth, so I don't inhale more of the provocative, woody scent.

Why is he wearing it this morning? Surely it's a night-time, 'hitting the town' kind of aftershave. It's inebriating.

"What are you working on, Sunshine?"

My chair angles back slightly with a creak as he leans his arm on the backrest. Didn't anyone teach him about personal space growing up?

"The rosters are a mess. I'm trying to sort them out." I turn my head to look at him and get a read on what he's up to. "So, what is it, Christopher? What can I help you with?"

He shifts his attention away from my screen, and the sudden force of his intense gaze lights my face on fire like a solar flare. His eyes roam, meandering across the planes and angles of my face. I can feel him looking at each individual freckle across my nose and cheeks.

Now I *really* feel like a caged animal at a zoo.

"Where did you get the freckles, Sunshine? Certainly not in New York," he adds, as a statement and not a question. I debate whether I should answer him, and I decide that he might leave me alone if I give him what he wants.

"I grew up in Australia, on the coast." And that's all the personal information he'll get from me today.

"Ah, that explains the accent." He leans back, walking around to stand on the opposite side of my desk, like a *normal* co-worker. I draw in a breath of relief, glad to have my personal space back again.

"I don't have an accent. Anyway, what do you want ?" I repeat my question from earlier. He side-stepped it before, but I'm not letting him get off track again.

"What I *want* and *need* are worlds apart, Sunshine, but let's start with the latter. We should sit down at some stage today and divide the workload. We don't want to inadvertently cross territories, so to speak."

I nod in agreement. We need to cohabit in a mutually respectful way. "Sure." I bring up my day planner. "How's five p.m.? That gives me time to get through everything I need to do today, then you and I can discuss the long-term plan." I await his answer, pretending to type on my computer so I don't have to look at his face for a second longer than is necessary.

"Done. Oh, and Sunshine, I'll order dinner in. Be outside my apartment at five." Mr. GQ walks out of my office without even waiting for my reply.

"Asshole," I mutter. It's my new favorite word. Inwardly, I mutter about ten varieties of vile insults at him, which is a surprisingly effective way of alleviating my anxiety about starting this new job.

The rest of my day passes surprisingly quickly as I get to know the system here. It's familiar in some ways to how I run New York, but there are some things I'll need time to pick up.

On the plus side, I think I fixed the roster issue, and I sent a new schedule out to all the employees via the Houston Hotel's in-house application. Technology is fantastic when it works. The employees' app allows for everything from rosters to pay slips, shift swaps and emergency plans to be sent between staff and management immediately and confidentially.

The staff can see every update as soon as they open the app, which they're required to do at the start of each shift if they want to get paid. It's an employer's dream, allowing for less time talking to people face-to-face and more time for, well, managing.

I was able to tour the entire lower level and meet several new faces, both staff and guests. I spoke with a few guests who have stopped over for a few days on their way home to Germany from Spain. I love how easy it is to plane-hop, or train-hop, to so many countries in the same day. It's mind-boggling. Maybe I'll catch the Eurostar and treat myself to a weekend in Paris soon.

I put my Parisian dream-weekend out of my mind for the moment as I exit the elevator. My next stop is The Wave, where I'll be meeting the manager, Daniel Thompson.

I check my watch. Four thirty. I have thirty minutes to finish with work before presenting myself for my meeting with Mr. 'Be-there-at-five'. I really want to turn up late out of spite, but my time-management OCD won't let me. I'd be a flustered, anxious mess if I did that, and I can't let him see me as anything less than calm and professional.

As I walk through the huge double doors of The Wave, I feel like I'm instantly transported into a Leonardo DiCaprio movie. I had a quick peek a few days ago, but I couldn't appreciate its beauty until now. Art deco styling in shades of pale blue and touches of gold shimmer in the afternoon light.

Hardwood floors in a herringbone style lead the eye towards an otherworldly turquoise-and-green marble bar with black veins. That slab of stone alone would have cost a few hundred thousand, which makes the room that much more impressive. Pale blue paint coats the walls, accented by architectural molding and antique gold mood lamps in a classic style. Eléa's signature touch is all over this place, but I don't doubt that she consulted an expert interior decorator just like in New York.

A glossy black piano and small stage take a regal position to the left. The room is large enough to host a variety of functions, from high tea in the afternoon to cocktail parties and formal functions. I must remind myself to look around for another musical act. Bee will be hard to top, but I'm sure London has some undiscovered talent hiding somewhere.

"Summer." Recognizing my name, I turn towards the sound, spotting the person I came to see standing behind the bar. Daniel is filling out some kind of paperwork with another employee who's wearing a neatly ironed bartender's uniform. I start walking over, giving him a polite smile and wave as I approach.

Because I'm younger than many of my colleagues, I favor a first-name approach when dealing with management, but I prefer the junior employees call me Ms. Hart. I am, after all, not here to be their friend.

"It's good to finally meet you in person, Summer," Daniel greets me, extending his hand. I grip it tightly, and after a quick shake he releases it. "Eléa and Max spoke highly of you, so I know we're lucky to have you here." His accent is slightly different from most of the other staff here. He speaks with a Scottish burr when he pronounces his 'R's.

"Thank you. And thank you for organizing my transportation on arrival, Daniel. It was great not having to work out how to get here after a long flight."

Daniel is in his late thirties and quite handsome. He doesn't wear a wedding ring, which doesn't surprise me. The hours he works aren't exactly conducive to a healthy relationship. The Wave is busiest on weekends and late at night, so he'd have to have a very understanding partner.

Daniel wears an expensive, black tailored suit that contrasts with his light hair. He's quite muscular, which I can tell by the way his clothes hug his chest and arms, like a well-dressed rugby player.

"Come, take a seat." He gestures to a plush, blue velvet couch off to the side, and we sit beside one another. A server approaches us to offer refreshments, but I've been on a caffeine high since lunch, and I think alcohol is the last thing I need before I meet Christopher later. I want to be clear-headed and ready for anything he throws at me.

"Just water, thank you, Sarah," I answer, and she smiles. It's polite to use employees' names, and makes the interaction more personal. We pride ourselves on our low employee turnover rate, and it's the little things like using their names that show them we care.

Daniel and I spend the next twenty minutes going over the inner-workings of The Wave, but honestly, he's magic. He runs this part of the hotel like a dream, and I can see why either Mr. and Mrs. Houston or Jarrod hired him. He's a true asset to the company.

"So, other than finding a new musical act, everything looks perfect, Daniel," I tell him, and he bestows a very handsome smile on me, hazel eyes sparkling.

"Summer, you don't know how happy I am to have you here. Not that Chris was doing a poor job—he's great—but it's not a one-man job, if you know what I mean, and I can only offer so much before I burn out. I have a daughter to spend time with, and this hotel needs someone who can give a lot more than I can right now." He continues thoughtfully, "I love this place. I'm happy here, but I have no ambition to take on any more currently." I nod, because I understand better than anyone how big of a commitment this job is. You invest your whole life into it.

"I understand, Daniel. Everyone truly appreciates your help so far, but I'm here now. I can take that burden off you, and I have the time to do it. How old is your daughter?" I ask, not wanting to make things too personal but wanting to get to know him a little more.

"Thank you, Summer. I'm confident that you and Chris can work everything out. I was happy to step in, temporarily, when Jarrod left. I look forward to working alongside you.

"And yes, my little girl is eight this month. I promised I would take a couple days off and take her to Warner Bros. studios where they filmed the Harry Potter movies. She's just getting into all that now. We watch the movies together." Pride shines in his eyes.

"That sounds awesome. I'll add that to my list of places to visit. Thank you, Daniel. It's been a pleasure finally meeting you in person." I stand, ready to head to my last appointment of the day.

"The pleasure is mine, Summer. You should take a well-earned break; you must be overwhelmed by everything. I'm going to have a nice, smooth scotch and head home. Let me know if you can spare some time on Wednesday night to check out two or three singers with me that I have in mind for The Wave."

"Of course! Just email me the details. I'd love to explore the local talent here."

"Will do. Have a great evening, Summer." He heads back towards the bar.

I check my watch again as I take my leave. I'm two minutes over my mental time allocation for Daniel, but still within my schedule to arrive at Christopher's by five p.m.

As I ride the elevator up, I smooth over my hair, suddenly feeling a little nervous. My lips feel dry, so I apply some lip balm. I rub on some mint and grapefruit hand lotion, the one from my welcome basket from Eléa, and take a few deep breaths.

The elevator dings to announce my arrival at the private Houston floor. Instead of turning left towards my little sanctuary, I take a right and head straight to the large timber door at the opposite end. Just like with my apartment, there's a keypad and buzzer on the wall, so I press the button and stand back to wait.

I look at my watch again. It's three minutes to five and I think maybe he's forgotten. Wouldn't that be awesome? I'd get to go home, take a hot shower, open a bottle of wine and celebrate my first official day in London on my own. Maybe I could video chat with Bee and tell her all about it.

Two minutes have passed, and I feel my patience wearing thin. This is incredibly rude on his part. Seriously, I'll give him one more chance, then I'm leaving. I lean over and press the buzzer again, this time holding it down for three full seconds, and wait. Another full minute goes by, and by now I'm fuming.

Christopher has left me standing outside his apartment looking like a fool. He probably left to have drinks with someone and forgot about our meeting. "Asshole," I mutter, and turn around to leave. My heels would normally make a loud clicking noise, but seeing as I'm on soft carpet, I don't get the dramatic stomping effect I deserve.

He's playing a game with me, like I'm a fish caught on a hook, which means I'll just have to come up with something equally humiliating. As I ponder my revenge, I hear the door open behind me. I spin around, ready to give him an earful, but instead what I see leaves me shocked.

My mouth hangs open wider than a laughing clown at a carnival, because standing in the doorway is Mr. Asshole, clad in nothing more than a towel. Water cascades down his stunningly-tanned skin—far too bronzed for a British winter—tracing a path over his chest and disappearing into the white Houston Hotel-branded towel wrapped around his hips. My eyes follow the path of the water over the muscular surface of his body, completely entranced. The 'V' shape of his hip bones points downwards, interrupted abruptly by the towel, and for some strange reason I feel disappointed. It's like going to see the Mona Lisa and having half her face covered up.

I can't speak. My throat feels tight and dry.

He'd be more suitable as a Ralph Lauren model than a hotel manager, surely.

"You're early, Sunshine, and I'm not decent yet." Those baby-blues sparkle at me, and suddenly I'm very aware that he knows *exactly* what is going on inside my head. He doesn't seem even a little ashamed about being half-naked and dripping wet in front of his colleague.

I swallow a few times to lubricate my dry throat, and finally I find my voice.

"I'm not early, I'm on time. You're running *indecently* late," I say, emphasizing his indecency so he understands how *not okay* I am with the state of him. I doubt he cares, though.

He just gives me a smile, then readjusts his towel to make sure it's tucked in properly, and my traitorous eyes follow the movements of his hands. I can't look away, no matter how much I mentally pep-talk myself about propriety and professionalism.

"You seem to be obsessively punctual. I gather you *come* on time to everything, right, Sunshine?" he asks with an amused smirk.

I pick up on his double entendre, but I ignore it and continue trying to keep this situation… legitimate. I refuse to play his games.

"How about we reschedule for another night, when you can actually keep to your own time commitment?" I smirk back at him.

He knows I just not-so-subtly insulted his time-management skills.

"How about we don't?" He steps aside and opens the door wider, inviting me to walk past him. My thoughts are conflicted, wondering if I should accept or decline his challenge—because it *is* a challenge, that I know for sure.

I decide to take him on. We have work to discuss, but I'm also not a quitter. I don't back down, not for anyone, and *especially* not for him.

"Fine. I'll have some wine while you make yourself presentable." I enter, unsuccessfully attempting to ignore his intoxicating, just-showered scent as I duck past him.

"I'm more than presentable, Sunshine, but I'll get you the wine. Relax while I throw something on." He leads the way into a stunning apartment that I can't appreciate in the slightest. Not when the asshole in front of me is wet, naked, and so much more attractive than the modern furniture. I could be walking into an empty warehouse, for all I care.

What have I gotten myself into? I'm in a metaphorical bull-fighting ring. Red flags are flying all around me, and he is the Matador, flaunting his best assets right in my face.

In the end, only one wins, and right now I don't know how this game will end. All I know is I desperately need wine. I'll probably need an entire bottle to erase the image of an almost-naked Christopher from my mind.

CHAPTER SEVEN

DINNER FOR TWO

I'm in the lion's den. It looks like an elegant apartment, but I know these walls house a deadly predator in his natural habitat.

While Christopher's demeanor is usually polite and cheerful, I know he's also bold and unapologetic. It's not like I don't encounter men like him on the daily, but it's difficult to go up against one as attractive as him.

Him, with his pale-blue eyes staring into my soul, a chiseled jawline that's undoubtedly hereditary, meticulous attention to his neat appearance, and an amazing scent that surrounds him. And those lips... he certainly doesn't need any cosmetic filler, not when they're already so plump.

His smile reveals a set of too-white teeth, and I can't help comparing him to a ferocious animal ready to tear into his prey. I'm not his meal, though, and it's high time I make that clear. Whatever Christopher's thinking right now about our *situation* needs to be curbed as soon as possible. I came here to do a job, and I won't let him distract me.

The Houston family wing is just stunning. Marble floors line a long hallway that opens into several rooms. The home features a modern kitchen with stainless steel appliances and dark wood cabinetry, and a sunken living room with expansive windows overlooking the city. I gaze at the horizon, admiring the sun as it sends dazzling hues of orange and pink across the evening sky.

I haven't been out to explore yet, but I'll find time once things are settled here.

The hotel isn't a skyscraper like in New York. This heritage building is much lower to the ground, offering a view of Londoners heading home during rush hour. The traffic reminds me of New York, and I smile at the memory of home.

"Are you enjoying the wine?" His voice comes from right behind me. I must have been so engrossed in the view outside that I didn't hear him come back in. I take one last peek at the park across the busy road and the marble arch in the distance, then turn around.

I'm puzzled by my strong reactions whenever I see him. What is it about him that always leaves me breathless? Christopher is wearing worn-in jeans and a dark grey T-shirt. It's not fancy—he's not even wearing shoes—he reminds me of the leading male in a romance movie. It's frustrating that with such little effort he's suddenly photoshoot ready.

I take a sip of my wine, realizing I must have been too engrossed in the view to notice him pouring me a glass. I savor the taste, intentionally making him wait for my response.

"It's lovely. Is it French?" The palate is new to me, and I'm certain it's not American or British.

Those blue eyes latch onto my face, inspecting me again like I'm 'Exhibit A', leaving no detail unseen. He makes me nervous when he does that.

"Italian. Colli Orientali del Friuli." He takes my glass and swirls it around before taking a sip. Okay, then. Don't bother pouring your *own* glass, just contaminate *my* glass with your mouth.

My indignant expression seems to amuse him, judging by his smirk. "Relax, Sunshine, I don't have cooties."

I snatch my wine back from him, our hands touching for just a fraction of a second. "I wasn't worried about *cooties*. I'm more worried you have something contagious, if you must know."

He laughs as he heads over to the kitchen to pour himself a glass. "I don't have any infectious diseases, let me just make that clear right now. Do you?" he asks, point blank.

Part of me thinks he's serious, but his playful smile is still there. I don't owe him a response, but the last thing I want is for him to think I have a disease.

"Not that it's any of your business, but I'm in perfect health." I raise my chin defiantly. This is way too personal a conversation for coworkers. "Now, can we get down to business?"

"Sunshine, I agree it's none of my business, but I'm glad to know you're healthy. I'll put you to the test soon enough."

Settling onto the inviting sofa, he sets his wineglass down on the coffee table. I sit opposite him, just to put a little distance between us, aware of his tendency to crowd my personal space.

"I'm more than up for the challenge, Christopher. Just in case you forgot, I was running New York City—*alone*—which dwarfs this hotel in size."

I open the bag I brought with me and take my laptop out, ready to fire it up and get this meeting over with as soon as possible.

"So, you think bigger is better, Sunshine?" His innuendo hits me right in the gut when I realize he wasn't talking about work at all. "I do agree, greater size has its advantages, but what good is having the proportions without performance?" He speaks so calmly, so seriously, it feels like he's not being lascivious at all, but I just know he's talking about sex.

Christopher really does challenge my ability to stay focused on work. How does he always manage to turn these chats into something inappropriate?

I opt to give him a little salacity in return, hoping he'll see I'm not so easily beaten. I smile at him, the same way he smiled at me just moments ago.

"Oh, size is everything, Christopher. Once you've had the pleasure of working with as substantial an asset as I have, it can be a bit of an adjustment to downsize, you know. I mean no offense, of course. Your *asset* is quite charming, just... petite. Diminutive." Sipping my wine, I meet his eyes haughtily. "Definitely smaller than I'm used to, but I'm sure I can make it work."

His face glows in the last rays of the sun before twilight hits, and he reminds me of a Renaissance painting come to life. Like an Italian work of art; the perfect example of chiaroscuro, dark and light.

"You'll be pleasantly surprised, I'm sure, when you experience it in its entirety. You haven't yet had the satisfaction of judging its performance. When you do, I'm certain you'll see that what you see now is just the tip of the iceberg, with much more hidden below the surface." Blue eyes sparkle at me humorously over the coffee table.

Fuck me, he doesn't give up either. We could get stuck debating this all night unless we stop discussing the size of Christopher's *asset*. How the hell do I get out of this now?

I take another sip of the delicious Italian wine to stall for a moment as I plot my escape.

"Can we just move on to co-parenting this hotel? How about you be the Daddy and I'll be the Mommy? I'll give you a list of chores, because we both know who the real boss in this marriage is, am I right?" My smart-ass mouth knows no bounds when I'm annoyed. I know my attitude is unprofessional, but Christopher started it. Besides, technically I'm off the clock for the day.

Christopher looks flustered for the first time since I met him. He lifts his gaze to the high ceiling, hands combing through his chocolate-colored hair, and I wonder if I won. I'm proud of myself. Yay, me.

He clears his throat, then looks at me. That sparkle from earlier is suddenly a fire, and the room feels like it's rapidly heating up. Now *I'm* the one getting flustered. He isn't saying anything, but he doesn't have to. His stare is so intense it's burning me up. That cheeky smirk is gone, replaced with an unsettling intensity in his eyes, and I don't know where to focus my own.

Perhaps I may be his dinner after all.

"What did I say?" I say into the silence. My mouth and throat are so dry now, my voice comes out as barely a whisper. His gaze drops to my mouth, those pale eyes fixating on my lips, and I grow self-conscious. I look away, unable to maintain eye contact anymore.

A buzz sounds from the front door of the apartment, and I take a much-needed breath of relief. Saved by the bell, literally. I look back at Christopher, who takes in a deep breath before gulping down the rest of his wine.

"Dinner is here," he says, and stands up. Without another word, he walks out into the hallway towards the front door.

I stand and shake off the unnerving feeling that settled over me during our silent interaction. Holy heck, what was that crazy chemistry? I don't know what I said to set him off, but I've never felt like that before.

My eyes wander back towards the window. Dusk is well on its way, and with it some strange emotions.

I lean down and grab the wine bottle off the coffee table, refilling both my glass and Christopher's, just as he returns holding two paper bags. Something smells amazing, and my stomach rumbles at the thought of whatever is in those bags. I need some food to go with this wine, or I might end up making a fool of myself in front of Christopher—and that would be devastating.

"I hope you like Mexican. It's from Kol, a block over, on Seymour Street." He sets the bags down on the kitchen island and takes out the food. I bring over our glasses and the half-empty bottle of wine and take a seat at the island. Christopher opens cupboards and drawers, pulling out crockery, cutlery and napkins, which he places on the marble bench top.

"I didn't expect to find Mexican food here. Is it good?" I ask, opening the take-out containers and taking a peek.

"It's more like a Mexican-British fusion. I'll take you to the restaurant, if you like. They have an amazing nine-course tasting menu that's out of this world. My favorite dishes are the smoked chili scampi taco and the crab chilpachole." He takes a seat on a barstool opposite me, seeming more relaxed now.

"It looks and smells amazing. Thank you." I also feel more at ease now that we have food between us. This is more my climate than the scorching heat earlier.

As we begin to eat and sip the wine, we settle into the comfortable silence of neutral territory. I know the flame behind those baby-blues must still be lit, but right now he's keeping it in check.

"Let's see if we can come up with a plan to run this hotel that maximizes our individual qualities," I say, around a mouthful of incredible food.

"Sure, Sunshine, but can we enjoy dinner first before we suit up for battle? I need nourishment before we clash heads again." He eats like it's his last meal, which makes me wonder where he puts it all. If I ate like him, my weight would double in a few days. The man is basically a bottomless garbage disposal.

He looks up at me while I gawk at him. "What?"

"You eat like a hyena," I answer, amused. "Seriously, you ordered so much, and I promise I won't steal it off your plate or anything. Is this… normal for you?" Only half-jokingly, I wonder if I should get him a shovel.

"Yep," he responds, barely stopping for long enough to avoid choking on his food, then goes back to shoveling it into his mouth. I haven't even taken my third bite yet.

"Okay, then. You do you, and I'll be here eating like a normal person." I continue eating despite the hungry caveman across from me devouring everything in his path. I wonder if it's a guy thing, but I've been on dates before and I've never seen this kind of ravenous consumption.

I look away, because even though the animalistic way he's eating is humorous, there's something carnal about it that makes me wonder if he consumes *every* kind of meal with that same desperation. My face heats up at the thought.

"You all right, Sunshine?" he asks, licking his index finger, which does anything but help.

I reach for my wineglass. "The chili got me." I take a large gulp.

"You don't like it spicy?" His innocent expression fails to mask the taunt behind his ever-present ambiguity.

"I like some spice, yes. It just took me by surprise." I cough out my reply to drive home the charade.

"Variety is the spice of life, they say. You'll never know if you're going to like something until you try it." His easygoing smile is back. Flirty, teasing Christopher is back in business.

"I guess that's true, within reason. I mean, I won't swim with sharks just to find out if I like it or not." I muse over my wine. Our eyes lock, blue to gray once more.

"I acknowledge your reasoning. Where sharks are concerned, I agree; however—" He leans in, invading my space again. "—there are other ways to get that same adrenalin rush." Why do I feel like he's not talking about bungee jumping?

"I think I'll leave that adrenalin junkie stuff to Tom Cruise."

He shakes his head, mock disappointment on his face.

The rest of the night goes well. We banter, sure, but we also manage to get some work done. Christopher is quite fascinating when he's in work mode. It's like a switch is flipped and he's suddenly serious and professional. I haven't seen that side of him before tonight, and I must admit I'm a little impressed.

His knowledge of the hotel is extensive, and I'm certain the only issue is that it's too much to handle for one person alone. We brainstorm ways to share the load in some areas and individually split the manager portfolio in others, and finally it seems like we really *can* co-parent the hotel like adults.

Hours later, I start to feel tired. I can't wait to take a hot shower and watch some mindless TV in bed. It's been a long day.

I unleash an enormous yawn and close my laptop.

"Tired already, Sunshine?" Christopher muses at me over his own laptop.

He's been sitting on the sofa, left ankle resting on his right leg, tapping away at emails. I'm about to respond when his phone rings at full volume, disturbing the peace and quiet.

"I have to take this. Give me a minute."

"Sure." I tuck my own legs under me as I lean into the soft fabric of the couch.

"*Bonsoir maman.*" I look up sharply, eyes fixed on Christopher's face as he starts speaking French.

God, did I think he was attractive before? He just hit level ten, like this interview I saw where Bradley Cooper was speaking in French. Like, hello! Gorgeous, bilingual, and stunning blue eyes...

Oh, shit. It's just a coincidence that my celebrity crush has just manifested into a younger, taller, but just as beautiful human, right?

Christopher sits there, speaking words I cannot understand, but my stomach suddenly flutters like a dozen hummingbird wings.

"*Oui, L'été est merveilleux... un trésor.*"

I hear him use Eléa's name for me, and I realize he's speaking with her—about me. I wish I knew what he's saying. This is so annoying. I narrow my eyes at him, showing him I'm aware of the subject of their conversation.

"Of course I will, don't worry," he tells Eléa reassuringly, looking over at me. I wonder why he switched to English. Does he want me to understand what he's saying? "It's fine, we have an understanding… *je promets… ça va être bien.*"

His eyes remain locked on me. Is he waiting for me to disagree? For me to grab the phone and beg his mother to bring me home? As much as I'd love to get on the first flight back to New York, I'm not going to let him win that easily.

I'm unshakable… even if the view is stunningly pretty and smells like expensive aftershave. His sparkling eyes and far-too-kissable lips won't break me.

Christopher Houston is nothing but a business colleague. I mentally start listing the reasons why he'll never be anything more than that.

We work together. He gets on my nerves. He's probably a total man-whore in his private time. He drinks like an Aussie on a Friday night at the pub—not that I'm against drinking, but I don't need a man that drinks to excess either. Or a man, period.

Who knows what Christopher gets up to on his nights off? Not that it's my business anyway. I don't care what—or who—he does. I'll just manage this hotel with style, intelligence, and efficiency, like I always do.

Eyes closed, I listen to the rest of his conversation with Eléa.

"Yes, I will. Say hello to dad. I'll call him tomorrow." After a beat, Christopher closes out the conversation with, "I love you, too."

Those words sound so beautiful coming out of his mouth. How many men can express such love openly to their mothers? He could have answered in French, but he didn't. Those sparkling blues fix on me as he puts the phone down.

"*Tu es une belle femme*," he murmurs.

"Pardon? Christopher, you know I don't speak French." He pauses for a second whilst continuing to watch me. "What did you say?"

I'm sure he used the word '*belle*' which, thanks to Disney, I know means 'beautiful', but my tired brain probably misheard him.

"You're tired, Sunshine. I think it's time for bed." He stands up, stretching his arms above his head and giving me a peek at those hard abs beneath his top. I avert my gaze. I don't want him catching me checking him out. That would give him too much ammunition for our future interactions.

I sit up and rub a kink out of my neck. I slide my laptop back into my bag, then I stand, ready to leave.

Christopher walks with me to the door, but before he opens it, he leans back against the massive walnut slab and observes me. His arms rest casually in the pockets of his denim jeans. I wish I had my camera to snap a picture that would, no doubt, appear on Times Square billboards.

"What?" I ask, getting frustrated now. I really need to limit the time we spend alone together. Christopher is way too potent to be around in a private setting, especially with how close he likes to stand.

"You amuse me, Sunshine. I admit, your arrival disrupted my momentum a little…" He leaves the sentence unfinished.

"But?" I ask, looking up at him with curiosity.

"But," he repeats, pushing off from the door and taking a step towards me. He is so close, his t-shirt is practically touching my chest. He leans in, his mouth right next to my ear. I can feel the warmth of his body and smell that dizzying scent of his cologne.

"I'm thinking that my parents knew exactly what they were doing sending you here."

I inhale his scent for another half a second before I step back. Maintaining a professional distance is difficult, but I force myself.

"Christopher, whatever you think, it's not the case. Your family was worried about you here alone, and honestly, I can see this hotel needs two people. You managed with Jarrod; we can achieve that, and more, together," I state, honestly. "But I'm here for work only. I have no intention of getting personal with anyone, especially at work. So, if you could give me a little space, I'd appreciate it."

I make sure to show sincerity in my expression. Even though I have a *miniscule* twinge of attraction I'm trying to bury; my poker face is competition-level. What he sees on the outside is what I want him to see. He doesn't need to know the inner battle I'm facing every time he's in the room, even though I've only known him for a few days. Hopefully, whatever's between us dies soon, so I can focus all my efforts on work.

"All right, Sunshine. I'll play nice… for now." He steps back to open the door for me.

"Great." I extend my hand to shake his, and his amusement returns, the hint of a smile under the surface. "So, we have a deal. We'll work together to make this place even more amazing than it already is. Purely business."

"As you say." He takes my hand, giving it a firm shake, but he doesn't let go. He maintains his focus on my poker face while he keeps a firm grip on my hand.

I wiggle my fingers to get him to release me, and he does. "See you tomorrow, Christopher."

I walk down the hallway to my apartment. He's silent, but I don't hear his door closing, and I can feel his eyes on my back the whole time. I reach my suite and punch in the code to open my front door.

As I step inside, I turn, and there he is: the beautiful headache I'll be dealing with on the daily, leaning up against his door frame, watching me. He doesn't move an inch, and I can feel his intense aura all the way over here.

I close the door, wondering how long he'll stand there after I'm gone.

CHAPTER EIGHT

AMBIVALENCE

The next forty-eight hours are a flurry of employee introductions, paperwork and collaborative project work with Christopher. Somehow, even though I've avoided him as much as humanly possible, we're making it work.

Though we live so close to one another, there's more than enough work to keep both of us busy. Our paths have crossed a few times, and can I still feel him intensely studying me every time, but I ignore it as best I can. It's the only way I can do my job effectively. I don't want or need his distracting presence.

I'm currently on a video chat with Bee in New York, while I get ready to meet Daniel for our Wednesday night scouting trip. I'm excited to get out and see a little of the London nightlife while we search for a new musical act to perform at The Wave.

"How about this?" I ask Bee, modeling the current outfit of choice: fitted black slacks with a black bralette under a sheer lace shirt.

"Uh… no," she replies with a roll of her eyes, while drinking a grande-sized americano. "Summer, we talked about this, remember? Trust me, you'll look smashing in the red dress." Jarrod pops his head in from the side of the screen, looking like a Hugo Boss model in his statement black denim and fitted black t-shirt.

"Summer, you look lovely in everything, but my angel has an eye for style. Take the risk, wear the red dress." He winks at me and disappears once again. Bee's admiring gaze follows him out of the room before she looks back towards me with a knowing smile. "See? Just try it on. I promise it'll be the perfect choice for tonight," she assures me.

"OK, give me a few minutes. I'll be back." I run off to my walk-in robe on the other side of the room.

While I change, I hear Bee's angelic singing voice coming through my laptop speakers. She must be working on new music, because it's not a song I recognize.

Then I hear Jarrod's voice join hers, and I'm transported back to Le Soleil in New York. Suddenly, silence falls, and I bet they're engrossed in some PDA. Well, not public, per se, but they aren't exactly alone.

"You two'd better be keeping it P.G. over there. I'm almost ready," I call out. I hear Jarrod laugh, that masculine chuckle, and Bee goes back to singing.

I step in front of the camera again, wearing a red bodycon dress we purchased from a small boutique in Manhattan. It's made of a ribbed, stretchy fabric and falls just below the knee. The neckline is a low 'V', and the long sleeves hug my slender arms. I pair it with a pair of black ankle boots with a killer stiletto heel. As I walk into camera view, I hear a whistle.

Jarrod gives me the thumbs up, and Bee claps her hands together in excitement.

"I knew it!" she yells. "Summer, you look fabulous, you sexy bitch." She spins her index finger around in the air. "Give me a three-sixty-degree view, girlfriend."

I laugh at her excitement but do as she says, feeling just a little embarrassed to be modeling while Jarrod is in the room.

"I was thinking of wearing my black leather jacket. Do you think it will work?"

"Fuck yes, you're like a hot businesswoman with a rock 'n' roll edge, the perfect blend for tonight. Damn, I'm good. I knew that dress was perfect for you the moment I saw it on the rack." She gives herself a pat on the shoulder, causing me to chuckle again.

"You definitely forced me out of my comfort zone, Bee. I'm still debating if I'm thankful for that yet," I say, taking a sip of my wine. "No way anyone'll call me Wednesday Addams in *this* dress," I remark, admiring the bold fire-engine-red.

"Who called you Wednesday Addams?" Jarrod pipes in from somewhere off-screen.

"Have a guess, Jarrod. He's about six-foot-three and annoys me daily. I swear that brother of yours is a handful." I shake my head and take another sip of wine. "I'm not sure if he enjoys messing with me for the fun of it, or if he really is a jerk-face asshole just out to traumatize me so I'll run back to New York."

Bee laughs, shaking her head at the camera, "Summer, give him hell. Don't let him play you," she instructs me from the other side of the world. "He needs to learn to share, and maybe you're the perfect person to help him learn that lesson." She gives a sly wink to Jarrod, who I still can't see.

Jarrod walks back into frame, looking at me through the camera. "Summer, Chris is stubborn, like my mother. He works hard to get what he wants, but don't let him tell you what to do. And if he fucks around, just let me know and I'll fly back and pin the idiot to the floor for you." He grins broadly, as if the thought is the most hilarious thing imaginable.

"Thanks for the support, guys. I'll try to handle things here—*without* violence—but if I need someone to throw a few punches into his smug face, I'll definitely call you, Jarrod."

I place down my wine glass, ready to head out for the night.

"I'll let you lovebirds go. Thank you both for the wardrobe advice. I need to finish my hair and makeup. Fingers crossed tonight's a success and Daniel and I find someone half as good as you, Bee."

"I'm sure you will," Jarrod responds confidently. "Daniel's an expert on what The Wave clientele want."

Bee blows me kisses. "You look fabulous. Have fun. And send me a pic of the whole outfit! Kisses to you, babe."

"Have a fantastic night, Summer," Jarrod adds. "I know it's technically work-related, but let your hair down a little. Have some drinks and enjoy yourself. You've earned it." Jarrod gives me a salute, and the video call ends. Time to have some fun.

There's less than half an hour before I'm meeting Daniel downstairs, so I quickly finish my wine, a beautiful dry red from the Rhône Valley, and head into my bathroom to work hair and makeup magic.

My mom taught me the importance of taking pride in my appearance and looking my best. I think she just wanted me to prioritize self-care, because when you feel good, you look good, and vice-versa.

My mom was a beautiful woman. She was active, but didn't obsess over her body. I guess her adolescent backpacker days stayed with her, because she walked every day, and I remember walking along the beach with her for miles when I was young.

Although our move to the U.S. meant no more beachfront walks, she compensated by finding and using forest paths and hiking trails wherever we lived. She always found solace in nature.

As I enter The Wave, I'm unsure if it's my attire or my position as a manager that makes me feel out of place, but I'm acutely aware of all the eyes on me. My hair is pinned off my face to one side, the rest of it flowing down with the ends slightly curled. I opted for a smokey eye tonight, dark gray to match my eyes, and I've kept my lips neutral with a pale nude gloss.

I pause to take in the venue's occupants. It's not at capacity, but still busy for mid-week, which is a good sign. There's a mix of junior executives standing around the bar, laughing heartily as they have a drink after work; and some older patrons wearing expensive suits and dresses—doctors and lawyers, I'd guess, judging by the designer brands.

A silver fox at the bar decides he likes what he sees and performs a very conspicuous head-to-toe inspection. He shamelessly holds up his glass of scotch to toast me, nodding in my direction. I smile at his contagious confidence and strut over to where Daniel is waiting by the plush blue velvet sofas.

"Summer! Wow!" He takes my hand. "You look beautiful." His eyes alight with admiration. So, Bee was right. This dress is a bit of a showstopper.

"I appreciate it, Daniel. Are you ready to head out and find some raw talent tonight?" I can barely contain my excitement.

"Here's hoping. I have three places on my list for tonight. Would you like a drink while we wait?" He gestures towards the bar.

"Wait? I thought we were heading out now?" I ask, tilting my head to the side quizzically.

"For Chris. He's running a tad late, but I'm sure he won't be much longer." Daniel nods amicably to a passing gentleman.

Knowing that Christopher is going to be close by all night, most likely getting on my nerves, irritates me. No doubt, his fragrance will make ignoring him nearly impossible. The man smells amazing.

I wish I could ignore him, but I need to act with at least a modicum of professionalism, especially with Daniel around. I'll act friendly, but internally I'll wage war against my attraction to his incredible beauty. Dammit, this is not what I wanted.

"I need to make a quick bathroom visit. Back in five," I tell Daniel. I need to psych myself up to ignore those sparkling blue eyes… and soft lips…and tanned skin.

As I turn, I collide with a wall of muscle.

Strong hands clasp my arms in a firm hold, steadying me. The intoxicating fragrance of sweet tobacco and sandalwood surrounds me, causing an audible gasp to escape my lips. A thin, shining gold chain snakes around his neck, resting against the smooth skin of his throat.

I venture a look at his face, and I know even before I meet his eyes that tonight is going to be a testament to my strength of will, because Christopher Houston is a fucking Adonis. My professional suit of armor will face its ultimate test. I'm so mad it hurts.

"Careful, Sunshine. Mind where you're going." There's that familiar deep voice, gravelly despite his polished British accent.

I lift my eyes and see his sky-blue eyes locked onto me. He holds me close, like I might fall at any moment, and then he starts taking me in. His gaze slides down my body, agonizingly slow.

Hair, lips, neckline… It's unnerving. Why does he have to stare so profoundly at such close range?

I extricate myself from his grip and step backward to get some air back in my lungs. "Christopher," I murmur, tucking my hair behind my ear. "Sorry for crashing into you. I'll just be a few minutes." I step around him and head towards the ladies' room with as much grace and poise as I can, knowing he is watching me walk away. I can feel it. Goose bumps have erupted over my body.

In the bathroom, I take a few minutes to breathe and ground myself. *Why does he do this to me?* I'm not that kind of person. I'm usually impervious to distractions at work, but he agitates me with such little effort.

I head back to the bar a few minutes later, with renewed confidence and my mask back in place. I see Christopher and Daniel waiting for me by the entryway. A beautiful blond woman is with them, possessively petting Christopher's arm as one might a domesticated animal like a puppy. Her long pink nails scrape over the cuff of his crisp shirt.

I look up at his face. He seems unaffected by her yet he doesn't move her hand. Maybe they're sleeping together. Maybe she's his girlfriend…

Or maybe I should stop caring and mind my own business!

I glance away as he looks up at my face. I shouldn't have any opinion whatsoever on what he does in his private life. Daniel spots me and waves me over, and as I take the last few paces Christopher whispers something to the blond that prompts her to pout and walk away, chest pushed out in front of her like an affronted penguin.

"Summer, are you ready?" Daniel asks, and I nod.

"Yes, I'm ready now." He gestures for me to lead the way out.

When we make it to the elevator, I press the down button and wait, refusing to turn around. I can sense Christopher standing behind me, and the scent of his cologne wafts over me. The elevator dings its arrival, and we all step into the enclosed space together.

I move to the right, and the men take the opposite side. Daniel pauses a moment to fix his shirt and cufflinks as Christopher leans back against the polished and reflective steel wall, hands in his pockets. Staring at me.

Elevators are always so awkward, or is it just me that thinks that? I feel his eyes wandering, yet again, over my face, my hair, my clothing, as though he's appraising a painting or sculpture he might buy.

Clearing my throat, I break the silence. "Daniel, who's the first performer we're seeing tonight?" I adopt a polite tone, attempting to keep the conversation professional and discourage any funny business from Christopher.

"Geoffrey's waiting out front to take us to an up-and-coming venue on the east side. It looks like an old-style tavern, but it's actually a cocktail bar with live music on Wednesday and Saturday nights. Tonight's lineup includes an all-female trio called Triptych. They're a unique blend of indie, soul, and jazz."

The elevator doors open, granting us access to the ground floor. We head through the atrium towards the main hotel exit.

"Good evening, Mr. Christopher, Ms. Hart, Mr. Thompson," Geoffrey greets us, looking dapper in a black suit. His hair is neatly combed and his gold name badge is polished and pinned, perfectly straight, onto his lapel.

"Nice to see you again, Geoffrey. I hope you've been well?" I inquire, genuine in my interest. I liked Geoffrey from the moment I met him at the airport.

"Very well, Miss, thank you for asking," he responds as he opens the door for us. I move in and over towards the window as Christopher joins me in the back. Daniel, I notice, takes the front seat next to Geoffrey, and as we take off they start up a conversation about football. I hear something about Liverpool and Manchester United.

"You look beautiful, Sunshine," Christopher states in the quiet of the back seat. I had that compliment earlier from Daniel, but somehow it didn't feel the same as it does in this intimate setting with *this* man sitting next to me. Engrossed in conversation, the men in front are unaware of the tension between Christopher and me. I face him, ready to thank him for the compliment, but I freeze when our eyes meet.

That silent, intense telepathy thing of his is happening again. As if he can whisper in my brain without saying anything out loud. The energy is palpable. I feel his desire. It's a lot to take in, and in this moment I know if something were to happen between us, it would be explosive. Sometimes you meet people who speak to you, body and soul. And, unfortunately, Christopher Houston is my new kryptonite.

"Please," is all I can say. He understands. He knows exactly what I'm asking. I'm asking him to stop whatever *this* is, because it's too much.

"Sunshine," he begins, and I cut him off.

"It's Summer," I reiterate for the millionth time. His pet-name for me is feeling a little too intimate tonight, especially with his proximity.

Christopher expels a non-committal grunt and remains quiet for the rest of the ride.

We arrive at the first stop: an eighteen-fifties corner house converted into an all-day craft beer and cocktail den. As we enter the old building, I run my gaze over exposed brick walls, industrial lighting, a paint washed timber bar that stretches the entire length of the room and weathered red leather seats organized around tables made of reclaimed timber. The industrial, converted warehouse look has been overused by hipsters, but something about this building's age lends it an authentic feel.

"I'll order us some drinks. Summer, what will you have?" Daniel asks me as we find our seats.

"Just a nice robust red, thank you, Daniel." He doesn't ask Christopher, I notice, before he heads off to get our drinks.

I should have asked for a fishbowl-sized glass. I think I'm going to need it with Mr. Gorgeous-and-brooding next to me.

"How are you settling in so far, Sunshine? Do you need anything?" he asks as I look around the room, taking in the atmosphere. Is he deliberately drawing my gaze back to him or just creating small talk for the sake of it? I notice he still refuses to use my name.

I lock eyes with him. The chemistry between us is there, always, but right now it's controlled, simmering underneath that perfect facade.

"Great. It'll take me about a month to get the kinks of the job ironed out, but I'll get there." Daniel returns with our drinks and a lowball glass with amber liquid for Christopher. It's a whiskey, neat, and I bet it's expensive.

Over the next hour we alternate between making polite conversation and watching Triptych's performance.

The musical trio is entertaining, with considerable talent, and despite my limited musical knowledge I find them captivating. Daniel and Christopher must know something about music, because they spend at least twenty minutes discussing details about timing, stage presence, and key changes. It's all Greek to me, but I still thought they were very good.

We head out to the next stop in much the same way as we started, Christopher in the back seat brooding in silence and me trying not to inhale his delicious scent.

Shortly after our arrival at our second stop, I watch as Christopher brings a whiskey glass to his lips, unable to avoid admiring his strong hands and moist lips. I convince myself it must be the wine and excuse myself to go clear my head in the ladies' room whilst the male and female musical duo we're scouting takes a break. Both musicians play guitar, and their harmonies are perfection—to me, anyway. I think they might be our top contenders, from what Christopher and Daniel say.

On my way back to the table, a hand at my elbow stops me. I turn to my left to see who has taken my arm.

"I have to say, you are the most beautiful creature in this bar tonight." The man in front of me is tall, and wearing casual jeans and a button-up shirt. His blue eyes are lovely, but they don't stun me like a certain other blue-eyed person. His long, brown hair is tied back in a manbun, which suits him—an impressive feat, because usually a manbun is an immediate turn-off for me. He has a short, neatly-trimmed beard that accentuates his jawline. I admit, this man is attractive, but he isn't you-know-who.

"Referring to a woman as a creature isn't exactly the best pickup line," I respond, extracting my arm from his hold.

Rather than running away in shame like I expect him to, Mr. Manbun smiles, sips his beer, and elaborates, "My apologies. I simply meant to attribute you as something incredible; unearthly."

"Such as?" I engage with him for a moment, interested in watching him try to save his dignity.

"Like… your hair reminds me of a mermaid. Legends say mermaids are the most beautiful creatures of the sea."

OK, this guy isn't as bad as I first thought. He's kind of cheesy yet flattering at the same time.

I laugh. "Nice save. But, next time, try something more personal." I find myself enjoying this exchange as I try to forget a certain brooding lump over on the other side of the room.

"Such as?" he asks, just like I did to him moments ago.

"Hm… Compliment a woman on her perfume, saying she smells unique. Praise her outfit, saying she wears it better than anyone else. Tell her she radiates happiness and has the most beautiful smile you've ever seen." I smile at him now; the wine has loosened me up.

"She has the most beautiful smile I've ever seen," he teases, taking a step closer. I'm certain he's about to continue when I feel someone press themselves against my back. A hard male body is right up on me, my back to his front, claiming the limited personal space I have in this already crowded bar. Mr. Manbun notices and stands up taller, no longer laughing. Annoyance is on his face clear as day as he looks over my shoulder.

"Sunshine, you're needed back at the table." I roll my eyes at Christopher acting like a bodyguard.

"Thank you for the chat. I'm on work duty tonight," I explain apologetically to Mr. Manbun. He gives me a curt nod and starts walking away.

I spin around, ready to give Christopher a piece of my mind, but he's not looking at me. He's staring murderously at Mr. Manbun. This angry version of Christopher is new to me. I've only seen him in work-mode or playful-smart-ass-mode. I place my hand firmly on his chest to get his attention, and he releases Mr. Manbun from his intense glare.

"Christopher?" I push him back gently, not sure what's going on in his head right now; maybe he knows this man? I can't think of any reason he'd act so hostile towards a stranger.

Christopher looks at me and the anger fades from his eyes. "Come on." He takes my hand and leads me back to the table.

Daniel is deep in conversation with the bar manager, and I shake my head as I sit down, wondering without words what the hell just happened. He ignores me, swallows his entire glass of single malt scotch and sits back as the duo starts their second set.

For the rest of the night, Christopher barely speaks two words to me. Even watching a truly talented singer/songwriter at a fantastic tapas restaurant on Hackney Road—our third stop of the night—isn't enough to return him to his regular self. Daniel doesn't comment on Christopher's behavior, so I follow his example and ignore my… *colleague* like he's a sulking child.

Geoffrey delivers us back to the hotel just before midnight. It's been a long night, but I think we've found at least one unique and entertaining act that will do very well at The Wave.

Daniel departs at the front doors of The Houston, and Christopher and I walk silently to the staff elevator. We enter the elevator and I decide I can't stand the silence any longer. "What crawled up your ass?" I ask from my little corner of the elevator. Christopher is standing on the opposite side, as far from me as possible, arms crossed and pouting. His eyes look darker than usual, but they're glued to the floor.

"Nothing," he says simply, but he doesn't look at me.

We arrive at our floor, and he's about to walk in the other direction like a petulant child, but I grab his arm and hold him in place.

"Christopher!" I exclaim in frustration. We have to work this out; how will we work together otherwise?

"Sunshine, I'm on edge. Don't push it," he growls right in my face, leaving almost no space between us.

"Why are you mad at me?" I lower my tone, hoping to diffuse the tension. I know I should just go back to my apartment and leave him be, but I'm worried he'll stay mad at me.

Next thing I know, I'm being shoved up against the wall, his hand in my hair, his body pressed against mine. He's so close, so hot, so furious—

"I'm mad at myself!" His voice is rough and angry. "I'm fucking mad because I can't stop thinking about you. I'm mad I have to see you all the fucking time, and I'm mad that you can just ignore me and chat up some other guy at the bar!"

He's practically seething, and his grip in my hair is so tight that I couldn't pull my head away even if I wanted to. My heart rate is through the roof, and I can't even form an answer.

How can two people that just met feel such palpable lust, frustration… fierce attraction.

I don't know what to say, and I'm still in a state of shock when his mouth crashes onto mine. Logical Summer is yelling at me to stop. Stop feeling so warm, stop liking it, stop kissing him back!

I know this is all kinds of wrong, but my traitorous body is softening for him, letting him kiss me like the world is about to end.

He moans, and my knees turn to jelly as I feel the sound vibrate through my open mouth. I barely register his hand taking my leg and wrapping it around his hip, letting his body fit in even closer to mine. One of his hands is behind my head, making sure he doesn't crush me against the wall, but his other one grips my thigh hard enough to leave a bruise.

He's a contradiction of gentleness and punishment. And he is punishing me right now, with his whole body.

I can't stop. My hands are in his hair, holding on, maybe gripping too hard, but this kiss is next level. It's the perfect balance of lips and tongues and pressure and pain, nothing like a first kiss should be.

Christopher is not tentative or humble; he is a take-what-he-wants no-holds-barred kind of first kisser… And *fuck*, it's the best damn kiss I've ever experienced. He finally settles down, gently releasing my leg from his grip, and his other hand comes up, smoothing my hair back from my face.

He touches me with reverence, with softness. Completely at odds with the power and fervency of a second ago. His forehead touches mine. His breathing is ragged, like he just sprinted five kilometers on a treadmill. No words can describe what just happened.

"You all right, Sunshine?" His voice is barely a whisper.

"God, no," I practically pant between his warm body and the cold wall. I could escape if I really wanted to. But I don't want to.

He smooths my hair back again, lifting my chin just enough for me to meet his eyes, and we stare at each other. I wonder where we go from here.

Christopher leans in, keeping those vivid blue eyes on me, and kisses my lips twice softly, soothingly, before he lets me go. He steps back, his eyes never leaving mine, and then after a beat, a really fluttery beat of my heart, he walks away, down that long hallway and into his apartment.

No words, no apologies, no explanation.

He doesn't even look back before he closes the door.

I'm left with a strange feeling—one I've never felt before. The only word I can use to describe how I feel right now is ambivalent. I'm stuck choosing between what's good for me and what I want.

And what I want is very, very bad.

CHAPTER NINE

IT'S A LOVE-HATE THING

I run my fingers over my lips. I didn't sleep well. I still can't get the kiss out of my head—if I can even call it a kiss. It was more like an out-of-body experience. It feels surreal, like that moment just before you wake up from an incredible dream. I might've thought it *was* a dream if it wasn't for the evidence Christopher left on my body.

I have a set of bruises on my thigh in the shape of his fingers, pale yellow around the edges and deep blue around the fingertips. I trace the bruises, imagining his hands on my skin again. It's like he marked me. Like I'm his.

"Get a grip, Summer," I tell myself, letting go of my leg. Christopher isn't mine, and I most certainly am *not* his.

But my mind wanders back to the thought of his hands, gripping my thigh firmly with one to hold me in place, while his other cradled my head as if I were made of glass. Christopher is a contradiction. Rough and gentle. Mine and not mine.

As much as my body relished the agony of his kiss—and it was torturous—in the morning light, logic is telling me to run. I can't let anything like this happen again. What would Bee and Jarrod think? What would Mr. and Mrs. Houston think? I have a reputation to keep and people to protect from my terrible lapses in judgment. I won't let his beautiful fucking face ruin everything.

I decide the best way to communicate my decision is via text message. Gutless, I know, but this way I don't have to say it while looking into his eyes.

Christopher,

Last night got a little out of hand. Can we ignore what happened and focus on work?

Regards, Summer

I press send.

My stomach instantly feels queasy, like I just drank raw eggs and protein powder. Today is going to suck; I just know it.

I'm still in bed when I get an early text message from Bee that instantly lifts my spirits. Apparently her best friend Anton is taking me out this Friday night, or so she explains with a myriad of cocktail and chili pepper emojis. Does that mean the drinks will be spicy, or the company?

I've heard a lot about Anton from Bee, and I have a feeling I'm going to need several buckets of Tylenol when I wake up on Saturday morning. His and Bee's 'Margharita Mondays' sound legendary.

Surprisingly, my day is Christopher-free. I know he's incredibly busy with Christmas preparations and organizing IT system upgrades right now, but he didn't have to leave me on read. It's just a typical guy thing, isn't it? He probably assumes I've been waiting all day for his response.

Well, no such luck. I couldn't care less. I repeat that to myself throughout the day, just waiting for it to sink in.

I'm almost done with my last meeting for the afternoon: a Zoom call with our wine supplier and sommelier, a friend of Eléa's. Claude is a true French gentleman, right down to his waxed mustache. He's eccentric and brilliant, and his wine knowledge is legendary in the industry.

"Thank you, Claude. It was nice chatting with you, and I look forward to the wine exhibition next week. It will be my first time in France," I reveal with an excited grin. Eléa usually attends them, but she has insisted I go this year, as she won't be leaving New York for the moment.

"Summer, it will be my pleasure to host you this year, *mon petit oiseau*." He claps his hands together. "It will be *fantastique... bon après-midi*."

I say farewell and end the call with both Claude and Eléa. It's six p.m., almost time to call it quits for the day. I just have a couple of emails to send before I can relax.

My phone sits on my desk, as silent as it's been all day. I resist the urge to check again if Christopher has replied.

It was my idea to concentrate on work, and I want to make sure I keep that focus strong, but every time I close my eyes I feel his lips on mine, his body fused to mine. Not an inch of space between us.

Summer! Get over it already. It can't happen again.

I pack up my laptop and head back towards my suite, where I have a nice bottle of 'forget the beautiful asshole' waiting for me.

I exit the elevator and head towards my apartment, and as I do I hear a high-pitched, musical laugh coming from behind me. I turn around and see Christopher standing outside his door with an absolutely stunning woman. When I say woman, I really mean supermodel.

She's tall and willowy, with killer legs—I can see her legs because she's wearing a tiny black halter-neck dress that clings to her slim frame. Her hair is a brown bob that bounces on her shoulders, perfectly straight and glossy. Her skin is a golden olive color, and her lips are stained a gorgeous burgundy red, like an expensive wine. If my stomach didn't drop the second I saw her standing beside Christopher, saw how *perfect* they look together, I would be in awe. She's a vision of elegance.

I feel stupid just standing here and staring at them. The woman adjusts Christopher's tie with a giggle, and then he spots me across the hall. The intensity of his gaze travels the length of the hallway and hits me like a punch to the chest. How can he affect me from that distance when he has another woman less than five inches away from him?

I've just decided to turn away and ignore them when the woman—the supermodel, the lover, the girlfriend, whatever she is—sees me. I grit my teeth, ready for a jealous stare, but she smiles, radiating friendliness. My chest still feels constricted, and I struggle to draw a breath without hearing how shaky it is. Fucking feelings. They get you at the worst moments.

"Summer!" she squeals, and trots over to me, like a model on the catwalk. With her sky-high gold stilettos, she is picture-perfect.

I knew he'd have beautiful women falling at his feet. I wouldn't even be surprised if he has a new one just like this every weekend.

As she reaches me, I freeze, and suddenly I'm engulfed in a warm embrace amidst a cloud of feminine energy and expensive perfume. I tentatively hug her back, one hand still clutching my laptop bag like it's my lifeline.

My eyes collide with Christopher's over the woman's shoulder, but his expression doesn't offer any explanation.

"Um, hi…" I say uncertainly, as she finally releases me.

"Oh, my God, I'm so sorry. You don't know who I am!" she exclaims, and turns to yell at Christopher. "Chris, you tosser! You didn't tell her I was coming over?" She obviously knows him well enough to call him names—although, she could have called him something worse, like *asshole*. Asshole.

"I was busy," is his lame reply. He hasn't even moved; he's just standing casually by his door, eyeing me with interest.

"I apologize for the ambush, Summer. I'm Vivian." She offers me another genuine smile. "Bee's told me so much about you, and I was hoping to pop in and introduce myself."

I mentally run through the catalog of things Bee's told me about Vivian: she's in her late twenties, stunningly beautiful—obviously—a makeup artist—which explains the perfectly made-up face and exquisite lip color—and a personal stylist—she dressed and styled Bee during her stay at The Houston. I also recall Bee telling me Vivian sends designer clothing over to Mr. and Mrs. Houston for their events and charity galas.

Even though my secondhand knowledge of Vivian tells me that she's a wonderful person and a genuine friend to Bee and Jarrod, my stupid brain still wants to know if she's sleeping with Mr. Asshole over there.

I shouldn't care, I know that, but I can't help the tiny bit of jealousy that's lodged itself in my throat. I wish I could vomit it up. I feel pathetic, but I'm human.

With effort, I manage a real smile. "I'm happy to meet you, Vivian. Bee has told me so much about you." Her eyes light up when I mention our mutual friend.

"I miss my girl! Don't you get me started, or I'll mess up my face. I have a hot date tonight." Suddenly I like her even more.

"A hot date? Well then, how about I offer you a drink, and you can give me some hair and makeup tips for when I have my own hot date?" My eyes wander over to see Christopher's reaction. His eyes narrow, and his nostrils flare, but he doesn't say a word.

"Christopher," I greet him, and then I pull Vivian towards my suite.

"Summer." My name is on his lips at last, but it's neither casual nor sweet. It's exasperation, frustration, and maybe even a warning.

Vivian and I hang out for about an hour, and contrary to my first impression we hit it off like PB&J. I'm not surprised, considering the way Bee talks about her. It might be nice to have a female friend here in the UK.

Vivian and I discuss everything: clothes, wine, shoes, men. She starts telling me all about Christopher like he's her little brother, singing his praises, telling me how wonderful he is, and admitting to occasionally wanting to smack him over the head and send him to the naughty corner.

"I'm telling you, Summer, if he even upsets one hair on your head, I'll stomp on his bare toes with my sharpest stilettos!" she warns, and we laugh together, her cheeks rosy from the wine.

"I can handle him just fine, but I'll let you know if I need to borrow those shoes for myself!"

I was reluctant to let her go, but Vivian assured me she would see me tomorrow night for Anton's welcome dinner in my honor. I'm nervous at the thought of meeting Bee's group, but also excited to be thrust into such a warm and inviting sanctuary. I work long hours, so it's difficult to meet people I don't work with.

My plan for the rest of the night is to do some more work on my laptop while watching reruns of The Vampire Diaries. What a party animal I am, I laugh to myself.

Christopher's probably out with some beautiful birdy, enjoying himself, not even sparing me a second thought. I clench my jaw, trying hard not to visualize beautiful women like Vivian falling all over him. It would be a nightmare for me to be constantly ogled and objectified, but the Asshole probably enjoys every second!

I'm in the gym Friday morning before work when I feel the hairs on the back of my neck rise like there's danger nearby, but I see nothing. Turning my head to the side, I see Christopher step onto the treadmill beside me. Again, a whole workout room, yet he chooses to invade my space.

Silent and unmoving, he stares down at my legs like they're the most fascinating thing he's ever seen. It's unnerving. I gaze down, wondering what he's looking at, thinking he's about to make some kind of remark about my shorts being too short, but then I see it: the faint handprint he left behind, still visible on my skin.

I look up, expecting him to say something, but he doesn't. I'm pretending it didn't happen, so I say nothing.

"Morning, Sunshine." He finally speaks, gracing me with his pretty accent that American women love. But I'm immune because I'm half Australian, so a foreign accent can't sway me— or so I tell myself.

"Good morning, Christopher. I hope you are well," I say politely, like we're nothing more than work colleagues.

It sounds stupid even to my ears, especially after our kiss, but I'm trying desperately to keep things professional.

I try to avoid looking too closely at him, but for the first time I see a glimpse of a thigh tattoo peeking out under the cuff of his gym shorts as he starts his workout. God, a thigh tattoo. If that doesn't spell 'fuckboy' then I don't know what does.

I don't want him to know I saw, so I avert my eyes. I wish I knew what the tattoo is. I love tattoos—not necessarily being covered in them, but the right placement can make them hot. I'd like to get something for my mother one day, something special just for me, to remind me she's always with me.

"Just grand… And you?" he volleys back.

"I'm great. We've a lot to do this weekend, with the Christmas decorations going up and the new rosters implemented. Your mother said my belongings will arrive this afternoon too, so I'm excited to spend the weekend unpacking, " I babble. My goal is to keep the conversation away from anything intimate, and so far I'm succeeding.

"Oh, and I have to give you the dates I'll be in France next week for the wine convention." I start puffing as my fast walk on the treadmill gets my heart pumping. A thin sheet of sweat glistens on my skin.

"You're a busy little bee, aren't you, Sunshine?" he remarks in that smart-ass manner of his. I smirk as I realize I've definitely pissed him off. There's nothing like a little healthy rivalry to stir the blood.

"More like exceptionally organized and competent, but I'll take that comparison—bees are hard workers. The world wouldn't exist without them," I boast, keeping pace with his large strides.

"Well, I'm allergic. I get this hideous rash all over my body for like a week, so I'm not exactly a fan of the little fuckers. The only bee I'm not allergic to is Brooklyn." That naughty boy smile appears on his face, and I relax a little. The Christopher I first met is back, and I have a much better chance of handling him than the hot, brooding, intense beast I glimpsed the other night.

"I'm going to get ready for work," I say, switching off my machine. "I'm starting early because I have a dinner to attend tonight, so I'll be leaving work early to get ready."

His baby blues are on me. They shift to my lips for a split second, then his mask returns. He looks straight ahead at the T.V. on the wall and nods. "I'll see you later, Sunshine."

"Asshole," I mumble as I walk away, wiping my face with my towel and taking a sip of water. I hear a faint chuckle behind me telling me he heard, and this time I don't care.

My day flies by in a blink. Christmastime is going to be hectic, and there's a lot to prepare. Christopher is doing his fair share of the work, so we have most things well under way by the time I decide to call it quits for the evening.

I hear a gentle knock on my office door just as I close my laptop. "Come in!"

Alex, one of the hotel security guards, opens the door and steps inside. "Sorry to bother you, Ms. Hart, but your shipment from America has arrived."

I stand up and stretch, realizing I haven't stepped away from my desk for a while. "I'll come upstairs and open my suite. I was just packing up anyway."

Alex nods. "Okay, Miss. The concierge are already waiting to take everything up now."

He gives me a thumbs up.

After fifteen short minutes of hotel staff traipsing in and out of my apartment, my precious belongings are finally here. Even though I don't have time to unpack tonight because of my dinner plans, I can't wait for this weekend so I can just relax with a glass of wine, put on some music, and unpack my entire life from a stack of boxes sent to me across the Atlantic.

My phone buzzes with a voice message from Bee.

"Have a smoking time tonight, girlfriend! Wear the yellow number—you'll be unforgettable in it. Relax, have fun, and get a little wasted." She takes a breath, and then she starts singing *Single Ladies* by Beyonce as a way of telling me to cut loose. When she finishes, she pauses for a second, like she's weighing her words before she speaks.

"I know you're on the other side of the world, babe, but you're not alone. You have us now: you have the Houston family, you have me, and soon, you'll have more of my crazy little bunch. If that's enough, then that's great. *But* if you find something over there that makes your heart beat faster, makes your tummy flutter, makes your breath catch in the scariest fucking way... don't ignore it, Summer. I know your work is number one, but don't let it get in the way of love." My eyes are unfocused as I watch the world outside through my window, realizing Bee knows me too damn well. "Don't be afraid to take chances. What's the worst that can happen? Mad-hot sex, remember! Have fun along the way." She laughs, which makes me smile, and the message ends.

I take a moment to absorb her words. She's right, I know, but opening up isn't my strong suit. I'm a vault that rarely gets unlocked.

Tonight, just for Bee, I'll wear the yellow number. I'll drink margaritas and I'll act my age. I'm a single girl and I want to have some fun. I'll never completely rid myself of my love for black and grey, order and control, but adding a little pop of color and excitement into my life now and then can't hurt.

Before showering, I pull my clothes out of my closet. Like an evening primrose that only blooms at night, I'll come alive as the sun sets and the moon rises.

This is where I belong now—this new apartment, this new hotel, this new continent. It's time to stop grieving and move forward.

Summer is coming back to life.

CHAPTER TEN

RED LIPSTICK

My phone buzzes, and I unlock it to read a message from Vivian.

I'm here!

Vivian organized to meet me in the lobby so we can travel together to dinner with all of Bee's 'inner sanctum'—or so she calls it. I'm nervous, but very much looking forward to meeting Anton and the others and having a night off to enjoy myself without the pressure of work—and one particularly hot co-worker.

I react to Vivian's message with a thumbs-up emoji and grab my coat and purse from the bed.

I can't help admiring my reflection as I walk past the mirror. The yellow dress is stunning, with a color somewhere between lemon and whipped butter. I'm not used to wearing clothes this bright, but the dress complements my skin tone. The dress is strapless with a gingham check pattern and features crocheted lace panels that frame the fitted bodice. It flares out at the waist into a full skirt that barely brushes the top of my knee, with a layer of tulle underneath for extra shape. It's cold out, but I've completed the outfit with a black trench coat to keep me warm until I reach the restaurant. My feet are clad in a pair of strappy, black three-inch stiletto sandals, and my lips are accentuated with bold, matte-red lipstick. The red is adventurous, but Bee has unlocked a new me.

I head out of my suite and press the down button on the elevator's wall panel. As I'm getting my access card out to scan it inside the elevator, I hear the click of a door closing. I tilt my head just slightly, expecting to see Christopher outside his apartment.

As I turn away, I do a double-take, unable to stop myself from staring. I thought business Christopher was beautiful, but this version of him is remarkably stunning. Clearing my throat, I try to talk, but I can't seem to get the words out.

He's wearing fitted—more like sculpted, actually—black pants, and I can see the shape of his muscular thighs through the fabric. A black V-neck sweater hugs his chest like someone sewed it right onto his body. A thin gold chain rests against the sliver of smooth skin visible on his chest. I don't know why, but men who wear chain necklaces just do it for me. As he approaches, I inhale his scent deeply. I close my eyes, praying that he's not coming tonight, because I don't think my fun, relaxing night will be so relaxing when he's around me looking like this.

"You're coming, aren't you?" I ask with a sigh. He can totally feel my frustration, because he smirks a little, side-eyeing me as the elevator doors open. He gestures for me to enter first.

"Not yet, but hopefully soon." It takes a moment for me to catch his innuendo, but when I do I lean back against the wall, as far from the Adonis-in-black as possible, and shake my head. He truly does test me. I need wine so badly right now. Fuck it, I need to get laid. *That's* what I need.

"I meant, are you coming to dinner, smartass, but you knew that." I look away. As much as it sounds like it, I'm not angry with him; I'm annoyed at myself for not being able to ignore him. I should be treating him like any other co-worker, but he makes it impossible.

"What's under that coat, Sunshine?" His murmured question prompts me to look at him across the elevator.

His eyes travel from my silky ponytail to my pointed high heels, finally landing on my blood-red lips. He has no visible reaction, but his voice is a little deeper and huskier than usual. Is he just playing with me like a lion plays with its food? He's a total fuckboy for sure, but is there even a smidgen of real desire in there? I'm not sure yet.

Christopher's a contradiction. Everyone keeps telling me he's a happy-go-lucky, fun-loving guy, but so far he seems more like a moody, contentious mountain of testosterone.

"A dress," I answer simply as we arrive on the ground floor. I walk off, and thankfully Christopher remains closed-lipped for now.

I spot Vivian across the lobby and head over to her, weaving through crowds of chattering guests. All the restaurants are jam-packed tonight, and The Wave is quickly filling with after-work crowds. It's good to see mine and Christopher's hard work paying off.

"Summer, you look like a high-end escort in that trench coat and heels." Vivian air kisses my cheeks. "I'm dying to see what's underneath, baby girl." I flush at the comment.

"Well, I'm wearing more than just lingerie, I can tell you that much. I just wanted to cover up until dinner because it's bloody freezing outside." As though to affirm my words, the front doors open to admit another group of guests, and a rush of cold night air hits me.

Vivian's wearing a retro-style jumpsuit in the boldest, baddest red I've ever seen, with a deep V almost down to her navel. It's backless, held up with a tie around her swan-like neck.

Her skin glows with translucent sparkles from a shimmering, pearlescent body cream, and her super-long legs are accentuated by the wide leg flare. Tonight, her hair is down, with her perfectly blunt bangs framing her eyes. She is a vision of yesteryear, like Wonder Woman crossed with a seventies movie star.

"Hey, babe," Vivian greets Christopher, giving him air kisses as well, whilst making sure not to smudge her perfect makeup. She doesn't seem surprised to see him, so I assume she knew he was coming.

"You look stunning tonight, Viv. The lads will be tucking themselves under their belts, no doubt." He sends a devilish grin her way.

"You're a pig. Do you know that?" she shoots back at him. Christopher lets out a natural laugh, clearly amused, and swings to face me. Those luscious lips transform his face when they curve up into a smile.

I'm confused. Tucking under their belts? "What does that mean?" I ask, and Vivian just rolls her eyes, taking my hand to lead me outside to our car.

"Believe me, Summer, you don't want to understand Chris's humor—it's nasty."

As we get into the car, it hits me. *Tucking themselves under their belt.* Meaning they would have to be sporting a boner to do that, and a big one, too, if it's going to reach up that high.

I slide in next to Vivian, and Christopher follows behind me. I'm sandwiched between them, but at least it's warm.

Christopher laughs at me, and I realize my disgust at the meaning of his joke must be all over my face.

"Took you long enough, Sunshine." I give him an annoyed glance.

"Your accent throws me sometimes," I retort. "I'm not slow." His sparkling eyes are so close I can see the graduation from the darker rim to the clear blue center. They land on my lips, and I hold my breath. I'm stuck.

"Red suits you."

"I'm not wearing red," I respond, and his eyes drop again to my mouth, reminding me of the lipstick I'm wearing. I feel a little self-conscious, and I nervously suck on my bottom lip. I feel him exhale against my cheek, making goosebumps explode all over my body. His gaze drifts out the window, prompting me to look at Vivian while I fight to control my pounding heart.

"So, Vivian, where are we going for dinner?" I turn my body towards her to prevent my eyes sliding back over to Christopher.

"We thought we'd show you some local hospitality and produce, so Anton booked this fabulous place called 20 Berkeley. It's set across multiple floors and styled after an English manor house. The menu is modern and unique and there's a great cocktail bar in the basement. After dinner we'll hit the clubs and dance our asses off. I can't wait!" she exclaims excitedly, putting her hands together.

"It sounds amazing. Thank you again. You didn't have to go to all this trouble." I give her hand a squeeze.

"Naturally, we did. Bee and Jarrod have explicitly instructed me to ensure you have a fantastic time, and an even better one later in the night if the opportunity arises." I blush at her words as she winks at me. Is it that obvious I'm painfully single?

Christopher clears his throat, eyes snapping to Vivian. They share a glance, and I feel like a kid stuck between feuding siblings right now, but I have no idea what it's about.

"What?" she asks with a smirk.

"Don't start," he answers back.

"I'm sure we'll have a great time," I say, trying to break up their quarrel. "Vivian, there's no need to find me any… *entertainment*. I promise I can find my own." She nods. It's just teasing, I know that.

"I know you can, babe. Look at you: smart, accomplished, the cutest freckles." For a second, her eyes dart to Christopher silently seated next to me. "Your accent is to die for. It's not completely American, but not quite Australian either. The British men are going to love you no matter what." She laughs now. "And when you're ready, you can have all the *entertainment* you want. We don't judge on this side of the world." I smile at her words.

"We're here," Christopher tells us, ending the conversation abruptly.

The car pulls up out front of a gorgeous red-brick building with cute canvas awnings over the front entrance. Christopher exits the car first and offers me his hand. I don't mind when a man opens the door; I like a little chivalry now and then. Besides, I'm in heels, and I don't want to risk injury on these old pavements. I thank him as I step aside, and he assists Vivian out of the car next, eyes still on me.

We barely take one step inside the restaurant before I'm ambushed by a tall, immaculately dressed man with perfect glowing skin the color of coffee beans. I know, instantly and without a doubt, this is Anton.

Bee told me he came to England from the Caribbean as a young teen to perform as a professional dancer, and I can see the elegance in his posture and the way he moves.

Anton embraces me like a long-lost cousin, and when he finally releases me, still holding my arms in both of his hands, he states, "Well, fuck-a-duck, Summer, you are just adorable." With a smile in his dark eyes, he scrutinizes me. "Of course, Bee told me all about you, but now I can finally meet you in person and see for myself." His eyes roam my flushed face; I'm not used to this kind of attention like Bee. "Trey! Get over here and look at these strawberry shortcake freckles, would you?" I blush awkwardly under the weight of everyone's gaze.

"Anton, it's nice to finally meet you." Bee told me he has no filter, that whatever he thinks, he says, and I'm starting to understand what she meant.

"The pleasure is ours, Summer." He kisses my hand like a proper gentleman.

"Anton, mate, give her some breathing room, would you?" Christopher exclaims with a huff. Anton gives him the middle finger and smiles. "You get her all week, pretty boy. Tonight, she's ours." He gives me a wink, taking my hand again and walking me over to introduce me to the rest of the group waiting beside a large oval table in our private dining area.

I meet Mel, Bee's manager, and her husband, Simon. They're only staying for dinner, because they have a two-year-old baby at home with a sitter. Mel is petite, in her mid-thirties, with straight, auburn hair. I can't believe this seemingly harmless person is the same woman Bee says could defeat entire armies with just a glance! Her husband is sweet, perhaps a little shy or just introverted, with glasses and thick, blond hair. Next is Trey, Anton's partner, a lawyer. He's the opposite of Anton with his muted colors. His plain blue shirt, nice pants, and shiny polished shoes give him a very corporate look, where Anton wears a vivid green, pinstripe shirt, matching green designer glasses, and ripped denim jeans—very *Vogue*. He could be on a magazine cover tomorrow and I wouldn't question it.

Once we're all acquainted, a server comes over to introduce himself and take my coat. It's warm in here, and with all of us together I'm feeling flushed, even though I haven't had a sip of wine yet.

As I gratefully hand my coat over, I fidget a little with my dress as I feel everyone's eyes on me. Beside me, Anton gasps. Taking my hand, he leads me in a slow twirl, absorbing me in my yellow strapless dress. "Summer, wow! You shine like a lighthouse on a dark winter's night." I smile. His description is lovely and totally unnecessary, but I thank him anyway.

"Thank you, Anton. Bee took me shopping—I normally wear black, but she insisted I try some color now and again." He smiles, letting go of my hand.

"Our girl can shop, I know that much, and she has an eye for color, too. It's perfection."

Anton pulls a chair out for me, and as I move to sit I look up and find a set of sky-blue eyes staring at me. Christopher is standing, intently watching me. I break the connection before the entire table notices him staring; I don't want them to think we have a problem.

Though Vivian and Anton are on either side of me, the round table allows for easy conversation between all seven of us, and I spend the next two hours talking about myself at the others' request. They—mostly Anton and Vivian—ask me question after question about my life in Australia.

I choose to leave out my mom and I's experience of domestic violence and barely escaping with our lives, deciding it's a little much for polite dinner conversation. Instead, everyone thinks we returned to America after my dad passed away. I tell them about working for Mr. and Mrs. Houston, New York, my photography.

Several fantastic dishes and many glasses of sparkling wine later, I feel a pleasant buzz in my limbs. I'm not drunk, not by a long shot, but I'm comfortable, and the nervousness I felt earlier is gone. These are great people. Bee might have brought them all together, but they're really like a family, and I can see how their dynamic works.

I glance at my wine, taking a sip as I catch Christopher looking at me again. He's said little to me during dinner, but he's been keeping conversation with the others. I've noticed he's good with people and has no problem conversing with them. He's charming when he wants to be, but lately that easy-going nature seems to elude him. Maybe I rub him the wrong way? I put the thought out of my mind.

Dessert is a decadent Cambridgeshire strawberry and elderflower cheesecake with a sprinkling of fresh mint. It looks like edible art but tastes like heaven.

"Well, thank you all for a lovely dinner," Mel says, effectively ending all other conversations at the table. "Summer, it was so good to meet you, but Simon and I must escape home. Our sitter doubles her fee after ten p.m.!" I nod in understanding. Getting a sitter on a Friday night is probably very costly. "Don't be a stranger; we expect you at our monthly family dinners."

I stand as Mel and Simon come over to my side of the table to embrace me one at a time in a big hug. I'm still not used to this type of physical affection, but the wine has given me enough liquid courage to feel comfortable.

"So nice to meet you both. Take care."

They do the rounds of the table and head out into the night.

"Well, bitches, it's party time!" Anton announces, and Vivian holds up her wine, joining him in a toast. "To Summer: may your move to London bring you happiness, health, and most of all a place to call home." Her eyes shine under the vintage chandeliers.

I thank them all for such an unforgettable dinner, and we stand, preparing to leave for the next location. I don't know where they're taking me, but everyone looks ready to party. Well, Anton, Trey, and Vivian do. Christopher's a little more reserved. Bee told me he loves to drink and party, but I'm not seeing that side tonight.

"I'll just use the ladies' room… Be back in five," I say, as the others finish the last of their drinks and motion to the server for the check.

I find the ladies' room and freshen up, washing my hands and checking on my makeup. My lipstick has held up well; maybe this expensive matte color was worth the hype. You can never really believe what they say in advertising these days, but the proof is staring me in the face. My cheeks are flushed and I'm starting to like this yellow dress, both presumably from the wine.

As I head out the door, I almost collide with Christopher, who's casually leaning against the wall, looking at his phone. Surprise makes my steps falter. Was he waiting for me?

He returns his phone to his pocket but his posture remains relaxed. Well, as relaxed as a lion stalking its prey. He takes another look at me, from my shoes, up my legs, to my dress, and finally my face. His own face gives nothing away.

"Is something the matter?" I ask, perplexed at his up-and-down behavior lately.

"Yes… You look good enough to eat, Sunshine… Too good." He touches my shoulder with just one finger, so lightly, running it over my collarbone and up my neck. I close my eyes. The wine hasn't completely affected my better judgment yet, but it's slowed my reactions enough to give him time.

"Christopher, we can't," I whisper when I open my eyes.

"Why? I know you're attracted to me; you can't hide it from me, Sunshine." He takes my chin, forcing me to look at his face. There's no armor, no poker face, just open emotions.

"I don't deny being attracted to you," I respond, trying to maintain eye contact with him. Still holding my chin, he moves his thumb over my red lips.

"We work together. What would your parents think?" I grasp desperately for a reason, for logic, even as I feel myself melting. "They trust me. I can't mess up my career over a casual fling."

He takes a moment to digest my concerns, not denying or affirming my words, just thinking. I'd love to know what he's thinking about, because his face gives me nothing. Well, I shouldn't say nothing; it's like a classified document that I don't have the code to decipher.

"I don't know what this is, Sunshine, but I know it's no one else's business. What you and I do in our personal time is *ours*." I shake my head to disagree with him, to argue the point even though it's not the time and place, but his next words stop me. One sentence throws me into a storm of confusion and astonishment.

"I refuse to continue doing what others expect. I want something for myself."

He moves in closer, leaving me no room to protest. One hand shifts behind my back, pressing me against him, and the other moves from my chin, sliding around the back of my neck. He grabs my ponytail, tugging it down so my neck arches and my face angles up towards his. He brushes his lips on mine, just the lightest of touches.

"What I want is you, Summer." Then his lips take mine in what I have come to understand as The Christopher Houston Kiss. A kiss that radiates so much heat, a hunger that just won't subside. He isn't gentle, but he doesn't hurt me either. I hear a sound, like a desperate hum, and it wakes me from my daze. Was that me or him?

Reality comes crashing back. We're in the dim hallway outside the ladies' room, and the others are waiting… His kiss somehow scrambles my mind and makes me forget my surroundings. How does he do that?

I push against him, placing my hands on his chest to get him to stop, to give me some breathing room, and he finally obliges and stops trying to devour my soul through my mouth.

I feel mystified. "Christopher, I need some space; the others are waiting," I plead.

He pauses a moment to catch his breath. I can see he's not unaffected himself. His pupils are dilated; his chest rises quickly with each heaving breath. Stepping back, he runs a hand through his hair to create distance between us.

I take a few deep breaths, smoothing down my hair and dress because I probably have that 'I just got mauled' look about me. Christopher's kisses are passionate. He touches me in ways that make it seem like we just had sex, even though it was simply kissing. I can't deny it feels different with him.

"This is madness," I say, running my finger under my lips to see if lipstick has smudged over my chin, but it's clean. Thank fuck for that. "We have to go." I step around him to walk back to the table. As we make our way through the restaurant, I hear him murmur behind me.

"I had no choice, Sunshine. You wield those red lips like a weapon." Even though I don't turn around, I can feel his unabated hunger still lurking between us. The beast is still hungry after his meal—or maybe that was just the appetizer. Either way, it didn't satisfy him at all. And to be honest, the dinner I had was delicious, but it didn't compare to tasting Christopher's lips again. He's the most mouthwatering, intensely satisfying dessert.

CHAPTER ELEVEN

TOO MANY TOMMYS

We take a Maxi Taxi to a club called Koko. Vivian describes it on the way as an iconic indie club that's hosted everyone from Madonna and the Sex Pistols to Prince. It's a heritage building that recently had a massive seventy-million-pound makeover, and tonight it's hosting a famous Spanish DJ who plays house and disco music.

I need to work off the calories I had at dinner. The meal was exceptional, and I shouldn't have eaten dessert, but it was too good to refuse. I can dance the food off tonight instead of hitting the gym early tomorrow, as I have a feeling the number of drinks we're about to consume will prevent my usual six a.m. wake-up.

"We're going to dance our feet off tonight!" Anton grasps Trey's hand, grinning and doing a little shake of his toned dancer's ass. I smile at his antics. He's going to slaughter us on the dance floor tonight.

"Are you ready, baby girl?" Vivian takes my arm, and we walk towards the entry together. Christopher is a step behind; still silent, but I feel his presence.

"I am. You know, I really haven't gone out in forever," I say as we're motioned through the entryway. I don't admit that after my mother's death, I now spend all my time working or taking pictures of inanimate objects, not socializing or going out to dinners and clubs other than the occasional outing with Eléa. I live like a hermit. This is uncharted territory for me.

We hand our items into the cloakroom and follow Anton into the crowded, noisy room filled with pumping music and flashing strobe lights. I'm trailing behind Vivian when a hand captures mine from behind.

I turn around to find Christopher holding my hand. It's dark, but I can see the colored lights reflecting in his eyes.

"Sunshine, if you need me, just give me a look. There can be some real dickheads in this place." He smooths the skin on my hand with his thumb. I just nod. I appreciate the offer, but I know I'll be fine. I'm going to be dancing, that's all. Dancing and forgetting about how good he tastes.

We head in to search for the others, who we've already lost in the crowd. I spot them at the bar, drinks in hand, and we push our way through to them. Anton hands me a glass of something, and I take a sniff. "It's a Tommy's," he tells me, and I check the drinks menu placed on the bar. A Tommy's is a take on the classic margarita, which combines Tequila Exotico Blanco, agave syrup, and lime. I take a sip and release a sound of pleasant surprise. It's sharp and delicious. I give Anton the thumbs up, and he grins.

"I knew you'd be a margarita girl. My Honeybee has good taste in friends." He winks before taking off to dance with Trey.

Vivian and I gulp down two—no, three—Tommy's in quick succession, and suddenly I'm feeling amazing. We leave Christopher at the bar chatting with some of his friends that spotted him not long after we arrived. He's not exactly hard to miss when he's so tall and striking.

The music's strong beat pulses from the maxed-out speakers as we find Anton and Trey in the fray. We let loose, our bodies shifting with the vibrations pounding the floor under my heels. Such freedom is completely new to me, and it's exhilarating.

Trey brings over four shots of an unidentifiable pink liquid, and we knock them back like water to keep the buzz going.

Vivian looks like a goddess in red as she dances her butt off, and a little fan club of groupies forms behind her. She must spot someone she likes, because she allows a tall, muscular man to dance with her putting his hands on her hips. She looks over at me, laughing, and winks. I smile and give her a nod because, shit, he looks like a mirror image of Michael B. Jordan. I'll be disappointed if she doesn't take that hunk home tonight.

We dance for around two hours, and thanks to the magic of the drinks, we're all feeling pretty relaxed. I'm enjoying living in the moment. Christopher's kiss from earlier is still on my lips, but the alcohol haze is helping blur it from my memory.

I feel a set of hands slide around my waist from behind. What I thought might be Anton or Trey is a total stranger. He's attractive, with hazel eyes, light brown hair, and dimples. I mean, come on, how do they breed so many beautiful men on this side of the world? I twist my face towards him.

"I've been watching you for an hour," he says, leaning in close to my ear so I can hear him. "I can't take my eyes off you in this dress." It might be the alcohol, or just that I want to make myself forget my growing feelings for Christopher, but I don't immediately shove him away. I've been trying to forget about my brooding, walking-fantasy co-worker, but my heart and body aren't listening. Opening myself to experiences with others may help me conquer this infatuation and lust.

I smile at him over my shoulder and let him pull me in and press his body to mine. I close my eyes and try to enjoy the feeling of his hands, his breath on my neck. But the minute I close them, I picture Christopher. I picture his hands on me, touching me, his lips on my neck, kissing me.

And then I feel nothing. He's gone. Turning, I open my eyes to see Christopher standing behind me, the dimpled hottie I was just dancing with sprawled out on the sticky dance floor. The other guy's face is a mix of confusion and anger, and I worry things will escalate unless I get Christopher out of here. I grab him by the arm, but he doesn't budge. He's still standing in front of me protectively, like a bodyguard. I inwardly cringe.

"Christopher!" I shout over the music. He turns around, blue eyes like a Bunsen burner blazing on full power. I wonder if he drank as much as us, because I've never seen him so fired up.

"Come on, Peach, time to go home." Anton steps in, taking my hand and jabbing Christopher in the back as a signal to follow. I check to make sure Vivian and Trey are with us, then we pick up our belongings from coat check before heading out into the crisp night air.

After pushing through the throng of people standing around the exit, most of them smoking or vaping, I turn and jab my finger into Christopher's chest.

"What the hell was that? You could have started a massive fight in there!" The pitch of my voice is high, but I lower my volume to avoid garnering attention from the revelers out the front.

"Way to ruin our fun, Chris." Vivian pouts and comes over to hug me, rubbing my back in a sympathetic gesture.

"I have a client tomorrow, anyway. I'll see you during the week when I pop in for work." She kisses my cheek and turns around to say goodbye to the guys. Patting Christopher on the arm, she mumbles something to him. I think it sounds like 'love-sick fool', but I can't be certain.

"We'll take Viv home in a taxi," Anton says, and I nod, thankful she isn't leaving on her own.

Christopher is still silent. He's not angry, but he's simmering like a pot of water that will soon get to boiling point and overflow. I can't wait, I think sarcastically, with a mental eye roll.

I give Anton and Trey a kiss goodbye. "Thank you for an amazing evening. I really appreciate it."

"No thank you necessary. You're ours now, Summer. We get to keep you and your freckles." He taps my nose. "I'll call you for mid-week lunch."

"Sounds perfect."

"Chris, you big dumb idiot, cool off in a cold shower." Anton gives him a one-armed shoulder hug and Christopher simply nods, his eyes following my every move. We wave the others off as they leave in a taxi, then suddenly we're alone. It's been a big night.

"Come on, Sunshine. Let's go home." He takes my hand and leads me to the next available taxi lined up on the street.

We spend the entire ride home in silence, me trying to figure out what happened and him ignoring what happened. I've got a good buzz going still. I lost count of how much I drank, but I'm not so far gone that I don't know my surroundings.

We're about to enter the private hotel elevator when my stiletto catches on the gap in the door join. I almost pitch forward when powerful hands grip my waist and save me from falling headfirst. I laugh, because for some reason it's funny that I almost faceplanted.

"Easy there, Sunshine. You've had a bit to drink." The humor is back in Christopher's voice for the first time tonight.

"I have not." I beam up at him. His hands remain around my waist, holding me up.

"Have too." His grin is so pretty. Why didn't he smile when we were out?

We reach our floor and walk towards my room. I enter the code, inputting it wrong on my first attempt, then the door opens. He walks me right to my bedroom, halting in the doorway.

"I can manage. I'm not drunk," I say, but he keeps his hands on my waist, making sure I don't faceplant almost for the second time.

"Sunshine, you are definitely *not* sober, I can assure you of that." I observe him. I did a lot of dancing, but I didn't see what he was doing earlier.

"Are you drunk?" I ask.

He smiles down at me, moving a strand of hair out of my eyes. A few locks escaped in the last couple of hours while I was dancing and jumping around with the others. I had a great time before the ending fell flat.

"No, not drunk," he answers quietly. I wonder why.

My inhibitions are lowered, so I blurt out the question. "Why didn't you drink?"

He takes a moment to look at me, one hand still on my hip holding me up, the other hand smoothing my hair back. I'm sure I look like a mess right now. I wonder if my red lipstick lasted the whole night, like it said it would on the box.

"Because I wanted to make sure someone was looking after you. I can't drink and take care of you at the same time."

I take in a gasping breath, my lungs suddenly devoid of oxygen. He's admitting I'm his reason for staying sober. He was thinking about me, watching me, caring for me.

My heart races a mile a minute, and I can't help my next statement. My brain and mouth are not working in sync because of the stupid Tommy's I downed tonight, so the next words out of my mouth come as a shock, even to me.

"I pretended he was you. I closed my eyes, and I pictured you behind me, not him," I whisper. Christopher's arm is still around me. We're so close, and then, unexpectedly, I'm falling, collapsing onto the bed, a heavy weight pressing down on me. He holds my face with both hands, his chest moving up and down as he breathes, hitting me with each exhale, and then after a brief pause he kisses me. He holds me while his mouth devours mine, like he's been starving for a taste.

I can't believe I told him that. I can't believe I said that out loud. I can't believe I'm kissing him back like a maniac on crack. He's so addictive. I'm hooked after just one taste.

We are like two horny teenagers who can't get enough. I suck on his tongue as he kisses me again, and I feel him hardening. I feel it straining against my leg as my dress bunches up to my thighs. I feel his desire, his need, his body heat through my thin dress, and I can't stop. Maybe it's a little to do with alcohol, maybe it's a lot to do with my feelings for him, or maybe it's just a desperate-mess-who-moved-to-the-other-side-of-the-world, mid-life-crisis kind of reason. Right now, I just want to feel this. With him.

"Sunshine." He attempts to pull away, but I grab his face, make him look me in the eye.

"Don't stop," I say firmly, giving him permission.

"Summer…" My name on his lips sounds so beautiful when he says it with need, with desire.

"I want to." I lean in to kiss him again. He moans into my mouth. He wants this. I know it.

"I'm not doing this with you now. I want you completely sober when I have you. Do you understand?"

I hear what he's saying but my body isn't listening. I kiss him again. I kiss him with my whole body, wrapping my legs around him to lock him to me. "Please," I whisper between kisses. "Please give me something."

He pulls back and stares at me for a second with those blue eyes, those kiss-swollen, luscious lips. I trace his lips with my finger. I've wanted to touch them since the very first day. I know this won't last, and I want to have one night of freedom before work and responsibility hit me like a truck tomorrow morning.

I just want a little taste, then I'll give him back. I'll forget it happened. I can do that, I'm sure I can.

His hand moves my dress. It slides up my thigh, gently, softly, like he is debating going further. I observe his expression, noting his increasingly rapid, shallow breaths, and I close my eyes once they reach that spot. Yes!

I now notice the dampness in my underwear. I feel the warmth of his fingers moving them aside, and then I feel his skin on my skin. I moan again. It's exactly what I need. He kisses me again. I don't open my eyes. I want to experience this with all my other senses switched off. I only want to feel him touch me there, and fuck, he does it so well.

We kiss the whole time, his mouth consuming me, and when he slips a finger inside me, pushing into me, I break. I gasp, and my mouth opens wide, but my eyes remain shut. My body moves with him, my hips lifting with every stroke. I feel him stretching me further with another finger, and suddenly he kisses me like I have all the air he'll ever need. Rougher, more aggressive, more possessive.

His mouth moves to my neck. I sense him losing control as his teeth scrape my skin and the tempo of his fingers increases. His fingers… fuck me, thumb pressing on my clit, his mouth sucking on my neck, and I shatter. I arch my back, my hips rising as I tighten around his fingers. I know he feels it, feels everything.

My heart pounds as I finally come back to my senses. The orgasm he gave me is still rippling through my body. He must realize I'm sensitive, because he withdraws his hand slowly, and gently moves my underwear back into place, kissing my cheek softly.

I turn my head sideways to look at him, and his mind-melding stare makes me nervous.

"You're so beautiful when you let go, Sunshine." He kisses me again, just a soft brush of his lips on mine. I feel like he's ending this after taking just a small fragment of what he really wants, even though I was offering him more.

"Are we stopping?" I ask, relaxing as the post-orgasm release renders me weak. I run my hand through his hair, and he closes his eyes for a moment, his erection still pressing on my thigh as evidence of his desire.

"Yes, Sunshine, we're stopping." He moves off me. His body was heavy, and I feel a slight chill as my bare legs are exposed to air. He smooths down my dress, covering me up again, and leans on his hand watching me as we lay on my bed. "Trust me, I want to, but you're slightly inebriated, and I will not fuck you when you'll more than likely change your mind tomorrow."

"You know we can't do this for real, don't you? We have responsibilities here. What would the staff say? What would your family say?" I ask, looking up towards the ceiling, thinking about the situation I got myself into. I'm fucked. Well, not literally, but it's a goddamn mess for sure.

"Summer, when are you going to realize I don't give a fuck what people think? I can't live my life pandering to everyone else's expectations. My parents will understand. My mother is French, remember?" He smiles, playing with my hair as he speaks. "She understands passion. They're an amorous bunch." I laugh at his words. The French do have a reputation for being romantic.

"What do you want from me? You have nothing to lose; I do." I look away. A fling could ruin my career, and that worries me. I have no home, no security, no family to fall back on. He has all that in spades. I have to consider my future.

"Look at me." He tilts my chin back towards him. Direct eye contact with his crystal eyes, darker now in the low-lit bedroom.

"I want you to stop pushing me away, stop ignoring this." He waves his hand between us. "I don't know how to label it, and honestly, you frustrate me to no end, Sunshine." I smile at his frowning expression. Clearly, I've gotten under his skin somehow. "I don't date. I don't do girlfriends. What I do is work, drink, fuck, and then do it all again." I open my mouth, about to snap a few harsh words at him, but he covers my mouth with his hand. I'm pretty sure it's the hand that just provided me with an amazing orgasm, but at least it's my own juices and not some nasty birdy that he touched tonight.

"But," he continues after a pause, "you have clearly bewitched me with your strange American ways, your smart mouth and these cute as fuck Australian freckles." Then he leans over with his hand still covering my mouth and kisses the tip of my nose while I watch him silently. "So, let's just allow things to happen naturally. Who knows, we might even like each other." He takes his hand off my face and I suck in some air.

"*Like* you?" I ask him with a smile. "You'll have to try really hard. I don't like many people."

"I'll make sure to try really hard, especially when I'm fucking your brains out, Sunshine, because when I do… you'll not only like me, you'll *love* me." He smirks. I know it's a joke, but his use of the 'L' word petrifies me. I don't think he meant it in that way, but damn. I could fall for him, I know it.

"One condition," I negotiate, and he eyes me with caution.

"What?" he speaks with hesitation and suspicion. I lean up on my arm to match him so we're on the same level, facing each other on the bed.

"I want this to be a secret. We can't go parading this in front of the staff or other people." I observe his face for a reaction. "Otherwise, the deal is off and there'll be no fucking my brains out."

"Summer, we're adults, not in nursery school," he answers with a huff, clearly a little annoyed.

"That's my condition. I don't want my position here mocked or questioned." He can see that I'm serious. Work is my focus until I pay off my student loans and can save enough to invest in my own property and create a nest egg for myself. It's a circumstance of being brought up by a single mother who struggled financially. We never relied on anyone, and now my future is in my own hands. As much as I want *his* hands all over me, I need job protection foremost.

"You're obstinate, do you know that?" he asks, kissing me. "For now, I'll comply with your condition. But I'm warning you, I won't lie to my family. If they ask me outright, I'll have to tell them." I nod. I wouldn't ask him to lie to his parents or to Jarrod.

"You'll just have to be stealthy. Ignore me at work, then sneak in during the middle of the night and make me come."

"Fuck, Sunshine, you have no idea." He takes my hand, linking our fingers together. "Your dirty talk is getting me hard again." I look down; he isn't lying.

"On that note, I'm going to let you sleep off the Tommy's and hopefully remember our conversation tomorrow, so when I sneak into your room at night you won't call security and have me arrested."

It's funny now, but it's a scary thought to wake up and find someone in your room in the middle of the night. I smile, remembering finding Christopher passed out at my door in the middle of the night. He wasn't so scary then.

Christopher pulls me off the bed. The edge between us before is gone, and now being with him feels amiable.

"Sleep tight, Sunshine. I'll see you tomorrow." He kisses me again, that melting heat and passion he seems to radiate every time we kiss.

When he leaves, I debate taking a shower and cleaning myself up, but I decide to fall asleep as I am, with his touch still on me, his kisses still on my lips. I don't want to wash them off just yet.

I hope I've made the right decision, because it's going to be a big deal, concealing our relationship—or whatever we call it—from the world I've only just entered.

I hope Christopher Houston is worth the risk.

CHAPTER TWELVE

GREEN-EYED MONSTER

Unpacking my boxes takes up all of Saturday. Reunited with my belongings, I celebrate by turning up the music and decorating my small space.

Every moment I allow myself to think, Christopher and our agreement consume my thoughts. Anticipating being intimate with him isn't too hard for me since I've already seen him in just a towel. He's fucking beautiful…

I can't concentrate on what I'm supposed to be doing. How will I do my job *after* we have sex? What if I can't even be in the same room with him after that without thinking about all the dirty stuff?

See? This is the exact reason I want to keep my personal and work lives as separate as Brad and Angelina at Christmas time.

My phone buzzes.

Ms. Hart,

The Christmas decorations are up. I know it's your day off, but I wanted you to know it went smoothly. Enjoy your weekend.

Jenny

I read Jenny's message and type a quick reply of thanks. She's our weekend manager, and probably the same age my mother would be now—mid-forties. Jenny is the epitome of a working mom. She has teenagers at home and her husband is a paramedic, so they coordinate around his shifts.

Jenny told me Christmas is her favorite time of year. The city streets have had their festive decorations up since I arrived, which I noticed on our drive last night. The whole of London is a sea of magical lights and color.

Eléa's style is more sophisticated. She prefers her hotels decorated in just sage green and gold, with no red in sight other than a touch of blush in the flowers and ribbons. It's much like the lady herself: polished, tasteful, and chic.

I have another message from Bee:

Summer, I hope you enjoyed last night! I hear Anton wants to adopt you, and Christopher misbehaved! Fair warning, girlfriend, he can be a handful. Look after him for us... He needs a female to keep him grounded. Don't be afraid to tell him to 'suck a fat one', as Jarrod suggests. We hope he isn't too insufferable, but I'm sure you have it all under control.

I laugh out loud, partly because of her dirty vocabulary and partly because things are definitely not under my control.

When he puts his hands on me, or in me like last night, my control is about as strong as a marshmallow over a flame. He melts my insides.

I send a reply to Bee with hearts and flowers. I don't want to lie to her, so I write nothing about last night other than that I loved her friends and had a great time.

I spend the next few hours hanging up the rest of my clothing and putting my rolled-up photographs into the frames around my suite that Eléa had waiting for me. I pack my mother's items into the closet. I've kept some of her jewelry that I wear from time to time, dresses, and sweaters that remind me of her.

My little box of seashells goes on my bedside table so I can see it every day and remember both of my parents who departed this world far too early.

My heart pings, just enough to feel a prick of sadness, but I know they'd be proud that I'm working for an amazing company and finishing my master's degree in business.

There's a knock on my door. Checking the time, I notice it's later than expected. The day has flown by so quickly I didn't even realize my headache from last night's drinking went away.

When I open the door, Christopher stands there in his dangerously snug jeans and a blue button-up shirt with the sleeves rolled up, looking casual and relaxed. I notice he's styled his hair and he's wearing his spiced rum and vintage leather aftershave and smells like a sexy pirate. I don't know what fragrance he wears, but it's enough to induce excitement in the vicinity of my underwear.

I clear my throat. He's standing there waiting for me to speak, and I must have been too obvious in my inspection because his smirk is a little knowing.

"Hi."

I lean on the door jamb and wait for him to begin.

He takes his time looking me over just as I did him, even though I don't look as nice in my casual leggings, oversized t-shirt, and messy bun. This is my standard 'at home' look that I don for maximum comfort; the effortlessly cool homeless-chic-slash-off-duty-nineties-supermodel aesthetic.

"You look good for someone who drank a gallon of margaritas last night," he comments. "Can I come in?" I nod and step aside to let him enter my little abode—one he invades frequently, I might add.

"I feel well. I had a slight headache this morning, but I drank two bottles of water, so I'm good now."

"And do you remember everything, Sunshine? No missing parts of the evening?" He watches my face.

I smile at him, realizing he's checking to see if I remember everything that happened, or perhaps he's worried I'll change my mind and blame it on the alcohol.

I might just mess with him a bit.

I look up to the ceiling and rub my temples for effect. "Um… Some parts are a little fuzzy. I remember dancing, and us leaving in the taxi, but everything after that is a blur. I hope I wasn't any trouble for you. Although… I can't remember getting into bed. Did you put me to bed, Christopher?"

His expression is pure shock. I try hard not to laugh, but something in my eyes gives me away, because next second he's on me, pulling me to him. He slides one hand to the back of my neck, and my pulse races at the contact.

"You're fucking with me, Sunshine. That's not nice." He kisses my laughing mouth, stealing my breath, and suddenly I'm not laughing. I'm practically moaning with how good he kisses me. He just seems to do everything with such exertion, such enthusiasm. It's hard to stop. Christopher is like a bullet train, accelerating from zero to two hundred miles per hour.

He lifts me up, and I wrap my legs around his waist. We don't even come up for air. He carries me to the sofa and sits down with me in his lap. His hands are all over me. The tie in my hair has disappeared, and it's hanging down like a curtain around us.

As usual, the heady scent of his aftershave reminds me of a seductive pirate, and his hands explore my body as if it were the most valuable treasure, his for the taking. I'm not complaining; his touch is provocative.

His roaming hands move to my face and gently pry our lips apart. I take a much-needed breath and smooth my hair back from my face. Lost in the moment has a whole new meaning. I was lost in him.

"As much as I want to continue this with you, Sunshine, I have to run." I search for any pretense in his face, but there's none. He looks truly remorseful. His hands are still smoothing over me, over my hair, my shoulders and down my arms, where he takes my hands in his.

"I have dinner plans tonight. I would cancel, but it's my mate's stag night. I have to attend." He kisses me on the lips, softly.

"Stag night?" I query.

"You know, bachelor party, he's getting married soon." It clicks.

"Oh, of course, wow. That's going to be a fun evening for you." I'm reluctant to let him go, but I understand he has a prior commitment. I remove myself from his lap, and he stands and smooths the creases I caused from his shirt.

"I'll see you tomorrow." I nod, walking him to the door and opening it for him. He takes another look at me, just a few seconds of his eyes roaming my face, and he decides one more kiss is essential. Christopher takes my jaw in his hand and brings me to him, kissing me like I'm his last breath. I grab his neck so I don't crease his shirt again, careful not to mess up his hair. I scrape my nails over the back of his head, unable to kiss him and not hold on.

The heated contact makes his eyes look glassy when he pulls away. I know I must do something to him—I feel it in the way he responds—but I don't know if he feels what I feel to the same extent.

"Have a good night," I whisper. He watches me step back, and as I close the door I hear his parting words: "It's not the night I really want, Sunshine."

My lips are still tingling, and my hair is a mess. I look like I have sex hair again. He can't kiss me politely; it has to be an explosive event.

I'm not complaining, but I have to be mindful to never kiss him in public, because I'll look like a ravaged mess. It would be embarrassing for people to see me in that state, especially co-workers. I have to keep his hands off me in public.

But in private, gosh... he can mess me up as much as he wants. I lose all control when he touches me, and it's partly my fault, I know that, but the way he takes control and devours me is crazy. It completely messes with my insides.

"Get yourself together, Summer," I coach myself, and try to focus on cleaning up the last of the boxes.

Once I finish, I place the empty boxes outside my door and call the staff to take them to the waste bins. I play some more music and pour myself another glass of red wine, managing to finish everything about two hours later.

Finally, I crash in bed to scroll through social media and stalk Christopher's profiles. I rarely use social media. I don't like putting my private life out there for all the world to see, probably because my mother always worried that Steven would find us and track us down. It was possible—he was so obsessive and controlling it would have been a hit to his ego to have her escape like she did—but we don't know if he even tried. We moved around constantly. Mom had no social media or publicly listed numbers. I shudder to think about what would have happened if he found us.

Christopher's social media profiles are filled with pictures of him having fun with friends. His mates seem like they're a big part of his life. There are photos of him partying, drinking, and with girls. I haven't seen any of them around here, so I'm not sure if they're just friends or past hook-ups. There are photos of him and Jarrod on stage somewhere, Christopher on drums and Jarrod playing guitar. In one beautiful family photo, Eléa's eyes are bright, and she has a radiant smile on her face. No doubt she's happy to have both her boys in the picture with her.

As I'm scrolling, I see a set of new photos pop up that someone has just tagged Christopher in, and my stomach drops. They're pictures of *half-naked* women, all over Christopher and his mates. I've heard enough about bachelor parties to know they can get rowdy, but seeing pictures of it in real time, knowing that right now he's surrounded by stunning, lingerie-clad beauties, makes my stomach turn over. The photos are pretty raunchy, and I'm surprised social media allows them. I flick through quickly, before they get taken down. All the men are fairly drunk, I'm sure, but one picture makes me feel sick immediately.

Christopher's on a sofa in what looks like a penthouse apartment or hotel room, and there's a blond in a white bikini seated beside him. She has her hand on his thigh, her face turned to him while he laughs at something, not looking at the camera. She's leaning into him with a familiar look in her eyes; the same look I had a few hours ago. The 'I want to fuck you' look. I couldn't help it, and by the look of it, neither can she. Her unbound hair is tousled. Definitely sex hair—I know the look.

"Fuck!" I throw my phone on the bed. Getting jealous won't help me. I have no claim on him. We aren't even dating!

I don't know *what* we are, but I know that I won't just be a side piece that he can have at home and still go out to play when he feels like it. I have too much self-respect for that. My mom made me self-sufficient and independent for a reason. She didn't want me to repeat her past mistakes. I know what my heart wants, but my head is ultimately the best decision maker.

I decide to take a hot shower, scrub away my thoughts and those images from my mind. Tomorrow, I'll take my frustrations out in the gym and maybe get some clarity on what I should do about Christopher and his playboy ways. I don't know if I can trust him yet, that's the problem. I don't trust easily, and now I'm wondering if I should even continue this thing. This… *affair*. Are we even friends?

I huff and turn the shower to the hottest setting, because I can't do lukewarm showers. I'm not in cheap student accommodation with tepid water anymore. I've worked hard for the life I have, and I don't want to lose it. Especially over a sexy, blue-eyed pirate.

As I toss and turn for what seems like hours, my brain won't be quiet. My home is perfect, all unpacked. I'm surrounded by my belongings, my photographs, my memories, yet I still feel unsettled. Like I'm on a ship out at sea and can't remember what solid ground feels like. The swaying back-and-forth makes me feel anxious.

Or maybe, if I'm honest with myself, it's my gut telling me I *should* be uneasy. That I'm going to get hurt, and we should stop now before things get more intense.

But I haven't felt like this in ages, not since I fell for Cody Peterson in my accounting classes at college. He was so pretty to look at, with dirty blond hair, rich coffee eyes, and a physique akin to an NHL star.

I remember he used to train at the college gym, and I obsessed over him for months. Eventually, I got the courage to talk to him, and we hit it off immediately. He was into health and fitness and a seriously smart numbers man. I even visualized our future together after graduation.

What I didn't realize was there were three or four other girls also envisioning their futures with Cody at the same time. Or, rather, Cody was spreading himself thin by hooking up with us all simultaneously.

It was my first real heartbreak, but I soon got over it when my mother died. That snapped me out of my heartbreak real fast. From then on, I decided I was just going to concentrate on work and securing my future before thinking about dating.

Christopher is a bolt of lightning that I didn't expect. It hit me hard and fast, just like his first kiss. It was instant lust and passion and something else… A *charge*.

I drift into a fitful sleep, but an hour later I hear a loud banging on my door, waking me from my already disturbed sleep.

This feels like déjà vu. It's close to four, and once again I'm dressed in a t-shirt and underwear, answering my door after not enough sleep and too many emotions.

I swing the door open, annoyed and unsurprised to see Christopher yet again standing there, looking less-than-perfectly groomed and very drunk. He's holding himself up with one hand on the door frame, and the other holds a mostly empty bottle of whiskey. If he gets sick or passes out again, I'm not helping him. He can sleep on the floor this time.

"What do you want, Christopher? It's four a.m." He looks at me with a flushed face, glassy eyes, and a smile, as if I'm his next drink.

That smile falters a little at my 'I'm tired and can't do this shit now' tone.

"What's wrong, Sunshine? Are you upset?" He leans forward like he's about to keel over, but catches himself again and straightens up. Gosh, he is flat-out hammered.

"It's late. Why don't you go to bed? I'll see you tomorrow." I make to close the door, but he stops me, pushing his hand on the door and stepping in closer. I can still smell his aftershave, the essence of him, but I can also smell top-shelf liquor; nutty, buttery, with a hint of caramel.

"Can I come in?" he asks, sounding confused. He has no idea why I'm suddenly cold and annoyed, and I doubt he'll be able to work it out in his current state.

"I think it's best you go home," I answer, trying to remove his hand from my door, but the drunk idiot is too strong. I sigh and rub my hand over my face.

"Christopher, please, can we talk tomorrow? I can't do this right now." And maybe my tone, or something in my face, sobers him up a little. He realizes this isn't a game. I'm serious, and I'm tired.

He takes my chin, and I try to turn away from him, but he forces me back by turning my head towards him, with gentle pressure on my face. I look up into those baby-blue eyes, seeing confusion and worry. I attempt to avert my gaze once more, aware

I'm losing the battle to stay cold, because every time he touches me I heat up like a furnace.

"Summer, what happened? Have I upset you?" His gentle whisper unsettles me even more. If he was an arrogant asshole, I could deal with that, but this side of him, the softer side, just kills me.

He runs his thumb over my lips, his glassy eyes following the movement, and I shut my eyes. I can't stand him looking at me so deeply, so intensely. He's trying to read my mind again; I can feel it.

"Can we *please* do this tomorrow?" I beg. I open my eyes, and he sees what I've been trying to hide behind since I opened the door. He sees hurt and anxiety, and maybe he can see my pathetic jealousy. I'm more upset with myself than I am with him. I have no right to feel like this, but I can't help it.

He releases me. Stepping back, he pauses for a minute. We stare at each other, and then he breaks eye contact, running a hand through his brown locks.

"I'll see you tomorrow, Sunshine."

And with that, he walks away. It's not the steady, solid gait he usually has when he walks, but at least he's not tripping over, considering how much he drank tonight. I wait to ensure he makes it to the other end of the hallway. Once he opens his door, he turns back, taking a last look my way, then disappears inside. The quiet click of his door is muffled by the sound of my heart, which is beating so loud I think it'll leap out of my chest.

I close my door and head back to bed. I have to get up in two hours, but I don't think sleep is going to comfort me tonight when all I can see is the image of Christopher with an almost-naked woman draped all over him.

I'm jealous; I've never been jealous. This emotion is new to me, and I'm resenting myself for even allowing it. Perhaps Shakespeare's depiction of jealousy in Iago's warning to Othello was accurate.

If I dwell on this, I'll go insane.

CHAPTER THIRTEEN

FRENCH WINE

The weekend is over in a flash. I worked out so hard on Sunday that I ended up taking an afternoon nap, just to catch up on sleep and recuperate. After waking up from my nap, I packed my camera and went on an afternoon photography journey. It was the first free time I had to just breathe and take in the city since my arrival.

The local architecture riveted me. I took so many photos, and I look forward to spending the next couple of weeks going through them and deciding what to print. My first selection of artwork for my new home excites me.

I spent the rest of my time avoiding Christopher. He sent numerous messages saying he wants to see me, but I still haven't had the guts to answer. I've spent all of Monday concealed in the hotel maintenance staff's office. I have, of course, still done my job, only in hiding. I feel a little pathetic, but it's self-preservation, because the beautiful man that helps me run this hotel is far too potent a specimen to risk going up against face-to-face.

If I stayed in my room, I know Christopher would have found me and cornered me to talk about what happened on Saturday night. I realize I was being irrational, but I need some alone time to clear my head. I can't think when he's right there, looking at me… touching me.

At six thirty, I finish sending out final work emails and shut down my laptop. Tomorrow I leave for the wine exhibition in France, where I'll finally get a breather from the hotel, from *him*, for three whole days. I have a car arranged in the morning to take me to the train station where I'll catch the Eurostar to Paris. Claude has arranged for a car to chauffeur me from there to the winery, which should only take about thirty minutes.

Clos Du Pas Saint-Maurice in Suresnes is one of the oldest wineries outside of Paris, and they're hosting this year's event. There, hoteliers and sommeliers from around the world will mingle, and sample some of the finest bespoke wines produced. I can't wait.

Anxious, I head back to my suite, hoping to avoid bumping into the gorgeous jerk, and thankfully I reach my room without incident.

I start packing a small suitcase for the trip, and as I'm packing, I hear my phone beep with a message. I debate whether to check it, but decide to look in case it's work.

We need to talk.

I know this, but I want a few more days before I have to see him, so I try delay tactics in the hopes it will work.

I know. Sorry, I've been busy. I'll be back late Thursday night. Can we talk on Friday?

Hopefully it's enough to placate him for the time being. I continue packing and hear another message ping my phone.

No, it's not suitable, Sunshine.

He doesn't elaborate, just sends the one line. I decide to leave it at that, and hopefully when I'm back at the end of the week he'll be more amenable. I doubt it, though; Christopher doesn't seem the type to give up easily.

But at least I have three days to think about what my next move is, because right now I desperately need that space and time to help me decide.

Ten minutes later, my phone rings. My heart does a little flip, but it's not Christopher, it's Bee.

"Hello," I answer.

"Girlfriend, you are a hard one to track down!" Bee's musical voice graces me from the other end of the phone.

"I know! Sorry, I had a busy weekend unpacking, and I finally got out and did an impromptu photography session on Sunday afternoon. I'm packing a case for France. I can't wait to just have a couple of days away from work—well, the hotel—and just chill out, you know? It's been a big transition here." I take a deep breath. It feels good to talk to her, but terrible not telling her the absolute truth.

"I know, babe. It's difficult moving to another country, without the familiar sights, sounds, and not to mention *people*. Trust me, Summer, I get it. I just wanted to check in and see how you are?"

I'm unsure what Christopher has shared, if anything, so I need to be cautious. I don't want to lie, but I'm not ready to reveal everything yet. I'm not ready to come clean with admitting that I had my tongue in her soon-to-be brother-in-law's mouth. Or that I let him do more than that—and really enjoyed it, too.

Just the thought of him touching me brings flashbacks of that night. At the time I wanted more, and now I'm so relieved that he stopped it when he did. Seeing those pictures the following night would have been even more devastating if we'd slept together. A sudden pain stabs my chest, which I soothe by rubbing it.

"How are you both? Are the shows going well? I bet there's not even standing room on the nights you sing." I change the subject—hopefully it's not too obvious a shutdown.

"Ha, yes, it's bloody incredible, Summer. Jarrod and I are having a ball writing and singing together. We have one more meeting with the record producer, and I think we'll finally cut a deal. Jarrod has been a little overprotective in making sure the contract is exactly what I want. I mean, I'm glad to have his support through all this, but he can be a little overbearing when it comes to my wellbeing." She laughs.

"Oh, really? I would never have guessed!" I laugh too. I know he's totally obsessed with her, and if anyone tried to hurt her, Jarrod would be a formidable force indeed.

"Right! I mean, I love him for it. He knows my past, he knows what made me leave the industry when I was young." She's divulged to me some of what happened to her as a child star—the male-dominated industry, the sleazy producers, the sexual assault she endured. It's amazing she's so strong and, well… *normal*, considering her past.

I love that about Bee: she's claiming her place back in an industry that almost destroyed her, and doing it with strength, confidence, and the man of her dreams by her side.

"I have faith in both of you," I say sincerely.

"Thanks, babe. Your support means the world to me. I'll let you go because you have an early morning, but Summer…" She pauses. "Things will settle. Take a couple of days to relax, and I'll check in with you on the weekend."

I thank Bee and tell her I'll chat with her soon. I promise to give her all the details about my first trip to Paris. She was there recently with Jarrod, and she loved it. I'd love to go back one day, with a man of my own, to experience it as a couple just like she did. But for now, I'm destined to concentrate on work, drink a ton of expensive wine, and hopefully forget about the blue-eyed Adonis I work with—for three days, at least.

The next morning, I dress in casual jeans, a red wool wrap sweater, and black stiletto ankle boots. Warm enough to travel in, but smart enough to look presentable when I arrive. I don't bother to page the reception for help with my bag, as I only have a small case to travel with. I just extend the handle and roll it in and out of the elevator myself.

It's right on seven a.m., making me punctual as usual, so my car should arrive in ten minutes. I can't remember a time when I was late for something without good reason. Though it once caused me anxiety, my undiagnosed obsession with punctuality now calms me.

I make my way over to Alice at the reception desk once I arrive in the lobby. "Good morning, Ms. Hart. Peter will take you to your car. Have a wonderful time in Paris."

"Thank you, Alice, I will. See you when I get back," I respond, as she waves Peter over from the front entry where he's greeting our incoming and outgoing clientele.

"I'll take that for you, Miss. How are you this morning?" Peter greets me, as he collapses the extendable handle of my small suitcase and picks it up by the side handle. He leads me away from the front doors, towards the private service elevator for staff and management.

"Good, thank you, Peter. Is the car not waiting out front?" I ask.

He takes his card out to scan it on the elevator access panel. "No, Miss, we have a car for you in the basement."

When the elevator dings its arrival at the basement level, I follow Peter into the underground parking lot. We run all our services down here—garbage removal, hotel linen—and any deliveries come via the basement dock. We need to keep the front of the hotel pristine for guests, so it stays free of service workers.

I quickly scan through the emails on my phone, making sure I'm not leaving behind any unfinished work, as I follow Peter to the car.

"Here we are, Miss. Have a glorious trip."

I look up from my phone, and suddenly all the chilly morning air is sucked from my lungs, and I stop dead in my tracks.

Christopher is leaning against a shiny black car, arms crossed over his winter coat, eyes on me with such intensity it feels like a punch to the gut.

I can't manage any words. I just watch as Christopher takes my case from Peter and shakes his hand in thanks, while Peter nods at us and returns the way we came. I watch Christopher put my case in the trunk and walk casually over to the passenger side door. He opens it and waits expectantly, opening it and standing there waiting for me. Expecting me to just jump in.

"Come on, Sunshine. You don't want to make us late, now, do you?" His tone mocks me, but he has a point. Being late for the train is a distressing thought, especially knowing Claude has planned for my arrival.

"What's going on? Are you driving me to the station?" I ask, hopeful that he'll just drop me off and I'll be on my way. He looks so good in those black jeans and black winter coat—the kind you see in stores like Bergdorf Goodman—that it'll be hard to concentrate until I'm far away. He's so tall and handsome, and he's wearing my favorite color. Christopher doesn't play fair.

"No, Sunshine, I'm not driving you to the train station," he answers with a smirk. I relax for less than a second, because his next words crush any hope I have left. "I'm driving *us* to the station."

My stomach drops. It's the only part of my body that moves, like I'm stuck on a roller coaster, with all my insides the wrong way up.

I attempt to say something, but then he tilts his head at me again and taps the roof of the car impatiently.

"Let's go. We have about three hours' travel time ahead of us. Do you have your passport?" I nod. I walk towards the car and stop, turning to look up at him for a moment. What I see in his eyes scares me. It's determination mixed with satisfaction.

I mumble, "Asshole," as I take a seat in the car, and he closes the door behind me. If he heard me, he doesn't comment, but his smile when he takes his own seat on the driver's side indicates he did. He turns the heating on and the radio down, and we depart.

As we leave the safety of the Houston Hotel, where I could hide from him in all the little nooks and crannies, I realize that there will be no hiding over the next few days. He's going to be in my face the whole time, not giving me an inch of space. He likes to stand too close, so close I'm sure all my freckles blur together.

We travel in silence for a short while as I watch him expertly navigate the city traffic. I never got my license because, as a city girl with no commute to work other than taking an elevator down a few floors, it wasn't necessary. I can't imagine driving in New York. It'd stress me out so much I'd probably have an accident.

Watching the way Christopher handles such a sleek machine, so easily, with one hand on the wheel and the other on the gearshift, does something to me. He catches me staring and gives me a little once-over. I look out the window at people making their way to work in the early morning traffic, and the Christmas decorations that make the city feel magical. London rivals New York with their stunning display of color.

"We need to talk, Sunshine." I look back at him, his eyes glancing at me every so often while still maintaining his attention on the road.

"We could have done that after I returned," I answer curtly, not bothering to disguise my frustration.

"We could have, but I don't like to wait for things. You've avoided me long enough."

I huff out a breath, realizing now he forced my hand. I have no way out. I'm stuck with him for the next three days—not to mention the nights… Damn, this is going to be difficult.

"Can we talk about it later, when we arrive? The first event is tonight, and right now we have somewhere to be. The train leaves St. Pancras at exactly eight fifteen whether or not we're on board." I pause in thought. "We'll have a few hours to relax and unpack, then we can talk before the welcome dinner at seven." I think my request is reasonable, and I gather he doesn't want to miss the train either, so we settle on this compromise.

"Sure, Sunshine, I'll wait till then, but not a second longer— or you won't make the seven p.m. dinner," he says, like a warning. I don't know what he'd actually do if I refused to open my hotel door for him. Part of me wants to defy him, just to find out. The other part, the mature part, is telling me to get it over with so I don't have to play hide and seek around The Houston anymore.

I go back to looking out the window. I'll have the entire train ride to debate with myself about what I'm going to say. I'm not looking forward to this impending face-off, but I know it's going to happen regardless, so I put my big girl pants on, prepare a speech in my head, and hope to God it comes out sounding believable. I don't want him seeing the truth behind my eyes, the eyes that want him so badly every time they see him, yet turn green when a beautiful woman is next to him.

Over the next few hours, I experience a mix of wonder and awe as we travel from one country to the next in the comfort of the first-class cabin on the Eurostar. The train is incredibly quick, and it cuts the six hours of driving time from London to Paris in half. We enjoy smoked salmon and corn fritters with silky hollandaise sauce for breakfast, and then make small talk over *pain au chocolat* and steaming hot coffee. Christopher describes Paris and the sights I should make time to visit next time I'm there and not having to work.

When we finally arrive at Gare du Nord in Paris, the driver that Claude arranged for us is waiting, holding a sign, to drive us to our hotel. We'll be staying nearby the winery where the convention is being held.

I experience the entire drive with Christopher's eyes on me rather than on the outside scenery, and it's a little unnerving. He doesn't look away when I catch his eyes on me, like most people would. Unabashedly, he stares, baby-blues studying me with such curiosity, and I feel like I'm on display yet again.

For the most part, I ignore him, preferring to keep my eyes on the beautiful, magical city of Paris. The historical architecture is so charming, and I feel like I've stepped into another time altogether. I spot a familiar shape outside my window, and my breath catches in my throat. The Eiffel Tower. The photographer in me instantly feels desperate to capture it, uniquely, different from other images of the iconic structure.

We finally make it to Suresnes, a commune in Hauts-de-Seine in the western suburbs of Paris, and we pull up at our hotel. After we exit the car, our driver unloads mine and Christopher's suitcases, and Christopher carries them both with ease into the quaint little hotel. Because this hotel is just a short walk from the vineyard, the place is booked solid, and it shows in the number of international guests milling around the lobby. I think many of the hotels in the area would be full, not only due to the event, but it's also right before Christmas.

We approach the counter to check in, joining a short queue of three solo travelers. Listening to the hotel staff conversing with the people before us, I'm a little relieved Christopher's here to handle things. My French is nonexistent, and Google Translate probably wouldn't cut it here. What if they spit in my food out of spite? I've heard some French people can be quite rude, especially to tourists who only speak English.

It's kind of mesmerizing and a little hot listening to Christopher so comfortably transition to French. I won't ever admit that to his face, but it's doing all kinds of things to my system. Because it's his mother's native language, he speaks it better than anyone else I've heard.

The concierge hands a key over to Christopher, and he signs some paperwork. I step up next to him, ready to receive my own key, but he turns around, collecting our bags, and starts walking away.

"Christopher, I need to sign for my key. I don't speak French, remember?" Did he forget I'm here too?

"There is no other key, Sunshine, just this." He holds up his room key—yes, they use real, old-fashioned keys here; there are no modern plastic cards like other hotels have. I think it's cute, but my key admiration fades when I realize what he just said.

"What do you mean? I have a room booked for myself separately." I cross my arms over my chest, because if he thinks he is taking one room, then I'm going to lose my shit.

"Well, unless you can argue with them in French, we have no choice. There are no more rooms. This place is fully booked, and so are the five other hotels in the area. There are three hundred guests here for the convention, *and* it's the peak Christmas season. It's one room or nothing, Sunshine." My jaw is still on the floor.

I look over at the concierge, who gives me a fake smile and looks away. He understands English, I can tell by the arrogant smirk on his face. I move forward to communicate with him, but he just holds up his hand and shoos me away like a bug. Some hospitality. I'll be emailing the manager about this.

"*Aucune chambre disponible,*" he states, and goes back to staring at his computer screen. I feel my face heating with anger, and maybe a little feminine rage, as more guests arrive behind us.

"What did he say?" I ask Christopher with a huff, who doesn't even seem perturbed in the slightest at our situation.

"He said there are no more rooms, Sunshine. Now can we please just make it to our room already? I have to take a leak." He picks up the cases again and starts walking, like it's totally no big deal that we have to spend the next three days and nights. I just hope the room is bigger than my closet back at The Houston.

We find our room, and surprisingly it's a decent-sized suite, thank goodness.

It has two queen beds, a small seating area with a desk, and a large en-suite bathroom with a full-size tub and walk-in shower.

They've clearly updated the space within the last few years, so as much as I'm annoyed at the situation, I'm happy we at least have space to move around each other. I almost had a heart attack picturing a tiny single-size bed and miniature bathroom.

Christopher walks into the bathroom, and I place my bag on the bed closest to the window. The view is gorgeous: green vineyards in the distance, and buildings dotted around reminding me we're just a stone's throw from the busy city.

I take a deep breath in, because I know Christopher won't wait any longer. He's been patient so far, not asking me a single thing the entire trip, but my time is up.

Not even a second later, I hear him exit the bathroom, and as I turn around he takes a seat on his bed. Calm, hands together, as he leans on his knees in a casual pose. He doesn't need to say a thing; I know what he wants from me.

I take a nervous breath and look back outside. I don't think I can speak and look at him at the same time. "It's not going to work," I start.

"Are we back to that? I thought we agreed to see where this went. I said I would be discreet, even though I don't think it's necessary," he cuts in as I turn around, watching him as he speaks, observing his face for any hint of a lie.

"I know. But I had time to think, and I feel like it's too much. It'll be too difficult to maintain a professional relationship and a personal one in the same space. I'm sorry," I say, my heart beating so loudly in my chest I can feel my breath catch. The lie I'm spewing makes me feel sick.

"What happened? I left Saturday night. We were fine Sunshine—more than fine—then you ghosted me… Why? I want the truth. Don't give me the 'we work together' bullshit. You know there's something happening between us."

I turn back towards the window, avoiding his stare. His eyes possess the uncanny ability to uncover my hidden truths, regardless of how fiercely I attempt to mask them.

As I'm thinking up my next words, he's suddenly there, spinning me around, seizing my face. I try to move away, but it's no use. This is why I didn't want to speak in person. He gives me no room to back away, to collect myself. He just takes up all my space, and I don't have the self-control to stop him. Or I just don't want to.

"Summer, fucking tell me! What is wrong?" My eyes glass over, the threat of tears brimming my lashes. I try to blink them away, but it's no use. I have to say it, because otherwise he won't leave me alone.

I stare at him, my stormy gray eyes locking onto his sky blue, and let it out. I'm honest for the first time in a long time, and even though it's embarrassing as hell, it feels good to get it out of my system.

"I saw the photos," I answer. I blink the tears away as I feel one falling onto my cheek.

"What photos?" he asks, confused.

"The ones from the bachelor party Saturday night. Someone tagged you online—with those women. I know I have no right to tell you how to live your life, but I won't be played, Christopher. I can't be a side piece sitting at The Houston waiting for you, while you go out and fuck your way around London." I take a deep breath, my lungs burning, my eyes blurry with tears, but it's finally out. Roaming my face, he assesses the seriousness of my expression, the pink flush in my cheeks for admitting I was jealous. He refuses to let go, however. His grip is firm but tender.

"Summer… *Jesus*." The pad of his thumb rubs my tears away, and he hesitates for just a second before kissing me—the barest of touches on my lips—and I let him, because all I can do right now is stand there and let him have a little piece of me.

He lets me go after a minute and walks over to the desk, where a serving tray with wine and whiskey glasses sits. He picks up two wine glasses, takes a bottle of white wine from the minibar, and pours two glasses. He's still not speaking, not denying anything, not answering me yet. My heart beats so hard I feel it against my rib cage.

"Have a drink." He hands me a glass, and I take a sip of the chilled wine. It's fruity and smooth, and it soothes the tears at the back of my throat. I watch him also take a sip, preparing to tell me about the Saturday night fun he had. I brace for it.

"Whatever you are thinking happened, didn't," he says. "I know the photos probably looked like we had some gigantic orgy." He smiles. The asshole actually smiles at me, like it's so hilarious. "I know how it looks. The women wore some pretty revealing attire."

I interrupt him. "Lingerie," I state.

"Yes, lingerie," he says with a shake of his head, like this is amusing him to no end. "They were just hired performers. They did their usual show, made some money and left." I eye him over my wineglass, not one hundred percent convinced it was that simple.

"Summer, Jack's whole family were there. The men. I mean. His father, his pop, uncle, mates. We hired the dancers to do a performance. Yes, they are *strippers*, but they are not prostitutes, Sunshine. They do their job, get paid, and leave." He pauses, smiling at me. "We played poker the rest of the night. I lost two thousand to those fuckers," he admits, and I investigate his face for any untruths. I think he's honest.

"I saw a photo of you with a woman, it looked…" I don't get to finish because he takes my chin in his free hand and runs his thumb over my lips, cool now after the chilled wine I just drank.

"I admit it probably looked seedy as hell, but I promise I have no interest in banging strippers—or banging anyone else, for that matter. I was enjoying the night. It was my mate's last night of freedom." Smiling again, he caresses my face and down the side of my neck, slowly, softly. I take another sip, the wine helping to calm my nerves. I want to believe him. I want to trust him.

"Sunshine, if it isn't already clear, I'm completely captivated by you. I'll gladly demonstrate it until you're convinced." He takes my glass, placing them both on the side table, before he does that thing again. The thing that makes me forget to breathe.

He kisses me like I'm the best thing he's ever tasted, like I'm the most expensive wine in all of France, a five hundred thousand dollar bottle of nineteen-forty-five Romanée Conti.

The French… They know how to make wine, and they *certainly* know how to kiss.

CHAPTER FOURTEEN

JUGGLING ACT

I'm putting the last touches on my hair and makeup when Christopher knocks on the bathroom door.

"The car will be here in ten minutes, Sunshine," he tells me, as I confirm by glancing at my watch. It's six forty p.m., and we're about to head out for the opening night dinner. Christopher's words calmed my nerves, but it was his actions that really showed me—or rather, proved to me—his investment and desire to give our relationship a chance. I'm out of excuses, I'm out of resistance, I want this too. I remind myself that I deserve to have some personal happiness. It takes a while for that to sink in, but I'm ready to believe it.

Earlier, I cleaned up my face, and we explored the local area for a while. We had a beautiful lunch at a small bistro. There was no menu, because they just serve whatever produce they source on the day. The beef bourguignon was probably the best I've ever tasted. I've been privy to French cuisine since working at The Houston in New York, but it just tastes different here, more authentic. We went easy on the wine, because tonight we'll partake in plenty of exquisite fermented grape juice from all over the world.

Christopher held my hand while we walked the streets and looked around the local shops. So many quaint little buildings.

We don't have to hide here, which is great, but I know it will be a juggling act when we get back to London, back to our hotel home.

"I'll just be a minute," I respond, checking my handiwork in the mirror. My safe, comforting black is back. Tonight, I'm one hundred percent me.

My dress is an A-line with long bishop-style sleeves, an elegantly contrasted transparent lace top and flared skirt. I've finished it off with black strappy stilettos and red lips—I know how much Christopher liked them last time. I've styled my hair in a messy up-do, leaving the lace back of the dress uncovered for maximum effect.

I open the door and exit the bathroom. Christopher is standing at the window, watching the passers-by on the street outside. He is, of course, beautiful. He's in a black tailored suit that fits him like a glove. It's definitely not an off-the-rack purchase. I like that he makes an effort to look good. His hair, his clothes, and his smell call me like the most succulent of desserts.

"I'm ready," I whisper. I don't want to startle him when he's so fixated on the outside world he didn't hear me come out of the bathroom.

As he turns, I'm instantly drawn to his captivating gaze. The eyes I fell for take me in, from my hair to my shoes, and then slowly back up to my blood-red lips. I stand there, waiting, while he takes his time, drinking me in like a delicious and full-bodied burgundy wine.

"Summer." He pauses, before he swallows his words. He says nothing else, but his eyes flash fire and I can tell the moment the beast takes over, because he stalks towards me like I'm about to be his next meal. Intense, purposeful, and hungry. I hold up my hand to stop whatever he is about to do.

"No." I take a step back. I need a little space, because if he gets his hands on me now, we won't make it to the event. I can't lie, his passion excites me, but I have a job to do, and I can't go looking like I was just fucked within an inch of my life.

"We have to go, please." His eyes close for the briefest of seconds. He takes a deep breath to compose himself.

"Fine, but I'm warning you, Sunshine. Tonight, when we get back to this room, I will shred that dress."

I don't doubt his words, but I think he's going to do more than shred my dress. He's going to shred my heart into tiny little pieces.

Christopher takes my hand, giving me one last look, and we head out to do what we came to do: mingle, make connections, represent his family's hotel professionally, and, of course, taste some really bloody delicious wine.

The night goes fantastically. Claude is such a character in person. It's a pleasure to meet him and the rest of his staff.

These events attract many international wine makers and buyers, and Christopher takes his work seriously, introducing me to the connections he knows, translating to English when necessary, and subtly fending off a couple of businessmen—who noticed my lack of a wedding ring and asked me to breakfast, and lunch, respectively.

I'm apparently too busy to accommodate them, or so Christopher told them, because I didn't even have time to decline. He hasn't left my side for a minute.

We were supposed to be seated separately at dinner—they like guests to mix outside their work associates and meet new potential affiliates—but again, I'm drawn back into the Christopher Houston orbit when he sneakily switches his name card with the person who was *supposed* to be sitting next to me—sorry, André Moreau from Hôtel Château Frontenac. My half-British, half-French companion is not playing fair. He plays to win, and I'm his prize.

Christopher makes no apologies for monopolizing my personal space. The very air I breathe is a mix of oxygen and him. I only get a short reprieve when I visit the ladies' room. I've noticed the looks he garners, the women who walk past him in the hopes he will turn those baby-blues in their direction, but he doesn't even bat an eye at them. I wonder if he's purposely avoiding looking at all, knowing I spilled my guts—my jealous guts—to him this afternoon. Perhaps he's attempting to reassure me he's not a player, at least not at the moment.

The night has concluded. The wine was amazing. Christopher and I have compiled a catalog of potential new wines for the London and New York hotels, and we'll fine-tune the list over the next couple of days.

I fix my hair and touch up my perfume in the ladies' room mirror and prepare to head back out.

"You are with *Monsieur Christophe, oui?*" Turning, I see a stunning blond woman washing her hands at the basin. She must be in her late twenties or early thirties, and she's dripping with diamonds. I assume they're the real deal because they, along with her floor-length gold dress, shine under the lights like exploding stars.

"Christopher? I work with him," I answer, extending my hand. She must be a client or business partner. I represent the hotel, so naturally, I give her my best professional smile.

"I'm Summer Hart, from The Houston Hotel New York. I'm based in London at the moment."

She dries her hands and takes mine briefly. Her eyes scan my outfit like a chef would inspect a dish his apprentice offered. I can't tell if it's outright revulsion, or if her face is just permanently fixed with a look of disgust. I'd like to think my outfit—my look—isn't the reason she looks ready to spit out whatever she swallowed tonight.

"Sorry, and you are?" I enquire, while she makes a show of washing her hands again. *Seriously!* Do I come across as having the Ebola virus? Or am I filthy because I'm American?

"Brigitte," she responds while she touches up her makeup in the mirror. I decide not to ask any more questions. She clearly has the personality of a wet rag and either hates me personally or hates Americans. I can't tell which, but I don't really care.

"Nice to meet you, Brigitte," I throw over my shoulder as I exit the ladies' room. She mumbles something unintelligible in French as I go.

I find Christopher chatting with some hotel tycoons; they own multiple hotels but don't actively work in them, not like Mr. and Mrs. Houston. These are the type of owners who live half the year on yachts in the Mediterranean and the other half attending parties and social events. They probably only come here for the status. They have no idea about grape cultivation or wine education.

"Here she is." Christopher guides me with a hand on my back and introduces me to the men. I dutifully shake hands and nod when I'm expected to, but they don't switch to English for my benefit. They continue in French and only speak to Christopher. Is this a European thing or a female thing? I'm yet to work out why some people here are so offended by my accent.

Christopher, yet again, compensates by translating when he can, and I appreciate him trying to include me. I may need to take some classes. Speaking another language will help me be a better manager, as we have many European clients who frequent London.

We are just about to take our leave when Brigitte arrives. *"Christophe… mon amour, comment vas-tu."*

She saunters right up to Christopher and kisses his cheeks three times. Her eyes slide to me before snapping back at him with a bright, flirty smile.

"Brigitte… Je vais bien merci." He pulls me back into the circle, placing a hand on my back, despite my inability to understand their conversation. However, I heard her use the word 'amour', meaning love, implying some familiarity with him. I suspect she wants to be more than an acquaintance, because she is practically drooling all over him. It's as obvious as a snake in a henhouse.

"Have you had the pleasure of meeting Summer? She just moved here from New York, where she was General Manager and my mother's protégé." His eyes sparkle.

"Bonne soirée." She nods to me, then proceeds to ignore me for the next ten minutes while she claws at Christopher with her sparkly talon-like nails and over-filled lips. If she ever fell overboard, those lips, along with the twin flotation devices surgically attached to her chest, would probably save her. I'm jealous again, but it's not like she can hear my thoughts—although I'm guessing Christopher can read my face, because he detaches

her with expert handling and takes my hand, clarifying that we are here together.

He squeezes my fingers gently, and his eyes match his gesture by telling me it's almost over and we can leave the function to finish what we started earlier. My heartbeat increases just thinking about taking that next step. The step, or leap, that's been slowly revealing itself since I arrived in London with just a suitcase and a few belongings. I've been standing on that precipice since we met, and tonight I'm going to dive off the edge.

We finally make it out, saying our goodbyes, and find our car ready at the entrance to the estate. Christopher must have messaged the driver to pull the car around, and I'm glad we don't have to wait too long.

Once we settle in for the short drive back to the hotel, the air changes. Christopher has transitioned back from work mode to personal mode, to the Christopher I know in private. The one that sets my pulse racing with just a look.

"Brigitte is unique," I state. I don't know how well they know each other.

"She's just an old friend; not someone you need to worry about, Sunshine." He takes my hand in his warm one, kissing the back of mine and rubbing his lips over my skin. I get tingles all the way to my toes.

It looks like it's snowing outside. Minuscule, itty-bitty white flakes begin to fall around the car.

"I'm not worried, but she wants you, that much I can tell." I run my hand over my hair, checking to make sure it's all still in place, a little nervous gesture that his eyes follow. He's so calm, not fidgeting at all.

"Her parents own a large international hotel franchise. She's a nepo baby, and when she doesn't get what she wants she throws a tantrum. Jarrod slept with her years ago, just once, and she thinks I'm next in line because he didn't want her." He shrugs like it's just an annoying thing he has to put up with.

"So, you didn't—" I don't get to finish my question, because he grabs my face in both his hands and shuts me up with a kiss. Not just any kiss, but a Christopher-special, core-melting, all-lips-and-tongue kiss.

As we arrive at the front of the hotel, he detaches his luscious mouth from mine. Cool air floats between us again.

"No, and I never will." I guess that answers my question.

I smile to myself as he thanks the driver in French, and we head into the hotel. I'm suddenly really nervous. I mean, I know I'm ready—we've been dancing around the sexual tension for weeks—but now it's really happening.

Internal heating has kept our hotel room comfortably warm despite the frosty weather outside. I set my bag down and take off my shoes as Christopher pours us more wine, not that I need it after tonight. I was careful at the event because I didn't want to overdo it, but now the alcohol may help to slow my racing heart and calm my nerves.

"Thank you," I say as he hands me the glass.

"Don't be nervous, Sunshine. I don't bite." His flirtatious smirk is back.

"I might," I reply. He stares at me while he takes a gulp of his wine. The eye contact is fierce enough to make me look away first. That was a bold statement for me to make, and he liked it. The way he looks at me is more than just lust.

It's like he's been holding himself back this whole time, and that tether is going to snap at any moment.

"Enough talking," he murmurs in a gravelly tone, and I can't tell if it's the chilled wine affecting his voice or the desire I see in his eyes.

He steps closer, setting his empty glass down on the desk next to me. I hardly turn and place my glass down before he's on me, lifting me up as he kisses me hotly, and I wrap my legs around his waist, just like I did last weekend. The carnality of his kiss is even more hungry and desperate than before. Every time we kiss, I feel electrical charges shooting through my veins. I wonder if he feels it too.

We devour each other, my hands running through his hair. I don't care if I mess it up. He has nowhere to be, so I'm able to ruin it, just like he's ruining me.

With my dress hitched to my waist and my legs around him, his fingers move through my hair, scattering the pins holding it in place. I have full confidence he won't drop me, even though his entire focus is on kissing the absolute life out of me.

My back lands against the wall with a thump, but I barely feel it. All the pent-up frustration and the sizzling sexual chemistry between us since my arrival erupts. There's no more caution, no more thinking, no more worrying about workplace professionalism, because Christopher and I chase a common goal. We need to get this out of our systems before we explode. Damn, I want him to make me explode so badly.

I'm so wet already, just from his kisses. I don't even need foreplay, I just need to ease this rising pressure, or I'll come right now, like this. His arousal rests, hard, against my damp underwear, and I can feel it through his taut pants, pressing into my core. If he doesn't do something to me right now I just might die.

"Christopher," I mumble around his lips. It's hard to talk like this, but I try and pull away. He keeps chasing me, capturing my mouth for more. "Please, I can't wait anymore," I beg.

Something inside him hears me, because I feel a tight pull around my hips, then my underwear snaps off my body. I blink, trance temporarily broken, as I pull my face away. "Did you just rip my expensive La Perla panties?" I ask, shocked.

His answering smirk is all the confirmation I need. The asshole just ruined my really nice underwear without even seeing them!

"I'll buy you some more, Sunshine." Once again, his mouth shuts me up. He meant it when he said enough talking. He isn't stopping for words, and his demand for action is completely agreeable to me.

His hand easily finds my wet heat, ready and waiting for him, and I moan. It feels so good to feel him touching me, finally, skin on skin. His firm, confident movements make me suck in a breath. I gasp, my back arching off the wall, when he enters me with two fingers.

I needed this so badly. I ride his fingers for less than one minute, because it takes a record low amount of time for his fingers flexing inside me to make me explode. It's never been so fast, so hard, not like this. He captures my moans and drinks them in, his own chest rumbling while I grind against his hand, riding out the most exciting orgasm I've had in a long time.

Just as I'm coming down from that shockingly fast detonation, he leans back, maintaining our kiss, and removes his leather belt, ripping his pants open to unleash the weapon he's been keeping hidden down there. There's no chance of us even making it to the bed. I just know he's going to take me up against the wall in the next five milliseconds it takes him to push his clothing out of the way. With his pants open, I barely have time to look down before he grips the back of my neck with one hand, simultaneously moving my dress aside with the other.

"Eyes on me, Sunshine." He tilts my head just enough so I'm staring into his face, into his eyes, as he pushes inside me. I close my eyes, my body ready. Even so, the sensation of him stretching me surprises me. All at once, it's both too much and not enough.

"Summer." His voice is stronger, more commanding, forcing me to open my eyes again. I watch him as he pushes all the way in, taking up all my space, and we stay like that, locked together, with my legs around his hips, my hands gripping his hair, him staring into my eyes while he holds us up.

Finally, we're connected.

"Fuck, you feel good, do you know that?" he says. "Like the warmest, wettest heaven I've ever felt."

A tender kiss, barely brushing my lips, speaks more than words as his gaze holds mine.

"Right now, I need to take you hard, Summer. I'll take it slow next time." I barely manage a nod of my head before he's moving. He wasn't exaggerating. He's pounding into me like it's the last time he will ever have sex. Like a death row prisoner who knows it's the last time he'll ever be inside a woman. I lose all train of thought, and all I can do is hold on because this crazy, 'mad-hot sex'—thanks, Bee—is actually happening. And I fucking love every second.

Christopher can't even kiss me because the motion of our bodies is so violent that we practically dent the dry wall.

Both his hands are on my ass now, holding me up while gripping me enough to give himself leverage. I lean forward, my gasps and his heavy breathing so loud they can probably hear us in the next room, but I'm too far gone to care. I'm chasing the next orgasm like a drug addict; that's the only way to describe the feeling. I need that hit only he can give me.

"I'm coming," I pant, as I bite his shoulder through his shirt. I wasn't lying before—it's this or the whole hotel hears what he's doing to me.

"Fuck!" He grits out, trying to keep his voice low, but the sensations are too much for both of us. I convulse around him, my teeth locking onto his shoulder, and he sucks in a breath before he joins me and comes with a heavy moan. Trying to remain quiet didn't go according to plan, but at least we tried. He buries his face in my neck as he fills me.

We remain like this for a few minutes, breathing into each other, the wall of the hotel room holding us both up.

"Shit. Sorry, Sunshine, we didn't make it to the bed," he pants.

A breathy laugh escapes me, and he pushes my hair back from my face, so sweetly, before kissing me again. Now that he can, he takes his time. Ripples still zap me like little electric shocks, and I tighten around him. He's still inside me, and I can feel his hot, sticky wetness on my thighs.

"If you keep doing that, round two will be against this wall again." He smiles wickedly. I feel him grind into me and I moan into another kiss. Our hard and fast session took the edge off but hasn't completely abated the need for more.

"We didn't use a condom," I state, realizing just now.

"I know." We lock eyes. It was stupid, but the moment was so crazy, we both lost our senses.

"I'm on birth control," I assure him. "I'm healthy. I got tested a few months ago, and I haven't been with anyone else since," I explain. I don't want him to think I'm reckless with my safety.

"I'm clean. I had a physical recently, but just so you don't panic, I want you to know I *never* go bare. I always use protection. This is a first for me." Relief must show in my eyes. I believe him. I don't think he would lie about an important issue like this, to my face, especially while he's still inside me.

He's not as hard as he was when he was pounding the life out of me, but he's definitely not soft yet either.

"My legs are going numb," I say. He chuckles, and the movement pushes him inside me even more. We both suck in a gasping breath in response.

Christopher watches me again as he gently pulls out. The slickness all over my thighs runs down my legs as he helps me stand, holding me up by my hips. Both of us are a total mess, and I push my dress down and smooth my hair. I bet I have that just-fucked hair, for real now. No one could see me in this state and believe I was doing anything else. It's clear as day I just had outrageous hotel sex with this hottie in front of me.

"We need a shower, then I'm going to fuck you slowly, in bed, where it's comfortable. All right, Sunshine?"

And that dazzling smile, with those luscious lips I've become obsessed with, makes my heart sprint faster than Usain Bolt running the hundred meters at the Olympics. If I thought he affected me *before* having sex, then I'm in big trouble. I'm already craving my next hit, and my drug of choice is a six-foot-three walking contradiction who found his way into my life—*crashed* into it, if I'm honest.

Now I just have to work out how to juggle work and Christopher without losing my head.

CHAPTER FIFTEEN

WORK HARD PLAY HARD

My phone wakes me up when it starts buzzing from somewhere in the hotel room.

I'm surrounded by soft fabric and hard muscles, covered by the hotel's plush linen and draped in my new favorite accessory, Christopher. I feel his naked chest to my back, his long, firm legs intertwined with mine, his lips practically touching my neck. Even in sleep, he doesn't give me any breathing room.

Not waking up alone feels pretty good, especially after the best night of my life. The sex was… amazing, but no words can really define the feeling of what he does to me.

After we shared a hot shower together—shower sex included because Christopher couldn't wait until we made it to an actual bed—we collapsed onto his bed, naked and definitely satisfied.

We talked for a while about the event, about the hotel, his family. It was nice. I don't think I've seen him so relaxed; I guess all the pent-up tension was keeping us at each other's throats. Now, his beastly behavior seems a little tamed.

He certainly does like it rough, though. I'm not complaining about the way he commands my body, giving me so much pleasure and the biggest, mind-blowing orgasms. It's like he just can't help himself.

I lean over the side of the bed, finding my phone on the floor. I have a missed call from Eléa. I will have to call her back soon; we chat every week, and I usually fill her in on all the happenings at the London hotel, but I can't speak to her right now, not while I'm still in bed with her son.

Christopher's hand moves as he stirs, and I stretch a little, my body sore and slightly achy just like after a big gym session.

"Don't do that, Sunshine, or we won't make it to breakfast." I smile. He can't be serious; we may have set a record last night.

"Do what?" I ask, turning to face him. Damn, he's so pretty. Even this close, the morning after an action-packed sex marathon. Those eyes are closed, but his lips are smiling. I touch his face, just with the tips of my fingers. His skin is smooth, clean-shaven. He captures my finger in his mouth, biting it, leaving a sting.

"Ouch!" I gasp, pulling my hand away. "What was that for?" I question, looking into his eyes, drinking him in. They're open now and watching me with amusement.

"You know exactly what that was for—that little movement you just did. Fuck... I don't have the energy for another extensively vigorous session without food first. I'm bloody starving, Sunshine." I laugh. I'm hungry, too, but Christopher could probably eat enough for a small village. I've seen enough of him to know that food governs his day, and he gets *hangry* if he doesn't eat regularly. Honestly, though, I don't blame him after witnessing his performance last night. I simply *came* along for the ride.

"Oh, are you hungry? Poor baby…" I pout. "You don't want to waste away or anything." I pinch his abs, the skin barely allowing me an inch of flexibility. The man is all firm sinew and muscle. I don't where he puts all the food he eats.

He takes my hand and moves it down onto something a lot more pliable, shooting me a mischievous and wickedly sexy grin. As I grip him tighter, it becomes obvious he's definitely *not* too tired for a morning session. My body responds so fast, even after the hours of exertion last night. I can go again, and apparently so can he.

"I thought you were too tired," I murmur teasingly, while I stroke him. His eyes roll upwards, closing in satisfaction, and a flush blooms on his cheeks.

"Sunshine, I'll never be too tired for you," he sighs, already sounding breathless. He opens his eyes and pushes me flat on my back, moving over the top of me.

I look up into his face, that beautiful, perfect face that intrigued me when I first found him on my doorstep. We watch each other for a few seconds, eye contact and the anticipation making me wet and ready for him so swiftly. Taking my leg, he places it around his thigh, opening me up to him as he gets ready to enter me again.

"I promised you slow, and I didn't deliver that last night," he whispers. I feel the tip of his erection pressing firmly against my clit, ready to slide down and inside me. Unable to stop myself, I twitch, making him rub on my sensitive clit, and I shudder with desperation.

"I'm going to give you that. Just nice and slow, alright, Sunshine?" I think it's a rhetorical question, because he doesn't wait for an answer. He pushes into me so gently, so slowly, that I almost want to force him to go faster, harder. He doesn't. Taking his time, he tortures me while holding himself above me, watching my face as he fucks me so languidly that sweat beads on his brow.

"Christopher," I moan, needing him to move faster, but he doesn't. He keeps his promise, so much so that I can't even say this is fucking anymore. I feel so out of my depth, so taken, so possessed. I don't think this is just sex now, the way he looks at me. The feelings I'm experiencing, it feels more like... It feels like it could be... love.

The thought shocks me, and I turn my face away, feeling too raw to let him see me like this.

"Look at me," he quietly commands, and I hesitate. "Summer." My name on his lips is enough to send me over the edge. It's a different precipice from last night. This is much higher, much scarier, and when I come crashing down, I know he understands what just happened.

He holds me through my orgasm, pushing me over the edge, before he allows himself to follow. He's on me, inside me, surrounding me, and I suck in some air as he takes my face, kissing my eyes, then my cheeks, and now my mouth. He moves his lips over me, almost with apology, like he knows he forced me to give him a little piece of myself that I'm never getting back.

"Don't hide from me." His words bring me back. I feel like I was under a spell, the moment was so intense and confusing.

Throat closed with emotion, I can't answer him. I'm afraid.

"We are in this together, understand?" I nod.

I understand, but does he? Does he even realize what he's done? Shit, I don't know how, but I think I just fell in love with Christopher Houston.

I'm saved by his phone ringing, and he withdraws from me. I'm wet, and messy, and I feel his warmth seeping out of me when he pulls out. I need another shower, so I motion towards the bathroom as he answers his phone, and he nods.

I get up and head over to the door.

"*Bonjour, maman*," he speaks to Eléa. She is obviously trying to call us and find out how last night went—the event, networking with other hotel owners, meeting the suppliers and producers.

"Yes, she's here with me now," he answers in English, and I freak out. I shake my head. I don't trust him not to give us away.

"Mm, yes, we're having breakfast right now, in fact," he replies with a smirk, just for me. He looks at me standing there, totally naked, poised at the bathroom door but too scared to go in because I want to hear the conversation.

His eyes rake over my body like a hungry predator. Damn, we *just* did it, and he's already giving me the sex eyes again!

"Just the usual, you know—tartines, croissants." He pauses, his eyes still giving me heat as I cross my arms over my chest with my most business-like expression. Unfortunately—for me, not him—I'm buck naked, so that really doesn't work in the moment.

I'm not overly shy about my body—it's something I work hard for, with all those hours in the gym and making sure I give my body the nutrients it needs without overeating—but I'm getting a tiny bit self-conscious with his intense stares.

"*Oui*, lots of cream, so sweet. I could eat it all day long."

I feel my face flame as he looks down at my bare lower half. Christopher, the asshole, is basically telling his mother that he had *me* for breakfast! I'll kill him! He starts laughing, and I motion that I'll cut his throat, running my thumb across my neck, but it just makes him laugh harder.

He continues his conversation, not embarrassed that every word is a lie and that he's actually talking about sex—to *his* mom, and *my* boss. I decide it's time to tease him back.

I run my hand over my chest, slowly, down my stomach till it reaches the place he was just staring at. I glide my fingers through the still-wet folds and throw my head back, closing my eyes. It has the desired effect. I hear him stop laughing immediately.

"Mum, I have to go. I'll call you later… No, everything is *merveilleux*, I just saw someone I need to speak to urgently." He leaps from the bed, his breathing heavy, words tumbling from his lips. I laugh and run into the bathroom before he can make it across the room, his phone flying backwards and landing on the bed.

I just get the door latched when I feel him tug on the handle.

"Sunshine, you better open this door right now." He pounds on it with his enormous hands.

"Or what?" My laugh traveling through the door as I turn on the taps for the shower, waiting for it to heat up.

"Summer, open the fucking door." His voice gets louder, more urgent, and I can't help but smile. It's about time I made him suffer, just a little. "I'm going to punish you. Do you know that?"

I step in. The hot water and steam feel so good on my skin. As much as I like sex with Christopher, it feels good to get clean, even though I don't think I'll remain spotless for long. He's going to mess me up again, and by the sound of it, sooner rather than later.

"All right, Sunshine, don't say I didn't warn you!" Then everything goes quiet.

When I emerge ten minutes later, fresh and clean, covered in a warm fluffy towel, Christopher follows through with his threat. He punishes—or, perhaps, *rewards*—me over and over with the best form of discipline. I honestly think he would have kept me locked in the room all day if it wasn't for his need for food surpassing his need to fuck me into oblivion.

Thank goodness for French pastries and excellent coffee; they pair perfectly with mind-blowing sex.

The rest of our trip is fantastic. We spend it in our own little bubble of wine, sex and food, and I can't complain. Christopher is unfatigued in everything. Somehow, he can work like a pro during the day, charming the pants off the other attendees, *and* give me his undivided attention all night.

I'm exhausted as we make our way home late Thursday night. I think I need a night in my bed alone to recover. I wonder if too much sex can be bad for you, like by causing some kind of physical condition.

Once again, we park the car in the basement parking lot, and Christopher carries our bags to the service elevator. There are a few staff are here and there, but it's the night shift now, quiet and uneventful. He takes my hand as we wait for the elevator, and I freeze, looking around to check if anyone saw.

"What?" he asks with a confused look on his face. We enter the elevator, and I wait until the doors close before replying.

"Christopher, you can't just hold my hand here. We have to be careful," I say, a little panicked.

He lets out a frustrated breath. "Summer, we aren't kids. We don't have to hide."

"I know, but nothing's changed. I mean it—I need some time to cement my position here first, before we can go public… I need to feel ready and know that people won't judge me." He doesn't understand the climb from my perspective. I know he works hard, but it's clear he's never had to work his way up. His privileged upbringing is evident right now.

"Please, just for a while?" I ask, looking back up at him.

He takes a few moments to think, obviously not happy with my request, but I think he's mulling it over for me.

"I'll give you some time, but don't take too long. I don't play games when it comes to this."

I don't know what he means by 'this', but I note the seriousness of his tone and I nod.

The lobby is busy right now because the hotel's restaurants and The Wave are open, but we bypass the public areas and head for the private elevator to our apartments.

We soon arrive at our floor.

"Do you want to come in and stay the night in my apartment?" he asks when we step out.

It's tempting, but I really need some rest. I have a full day of work tomorrow, and we have our Christmas events to prepare for shortly. It's going to be full on till after New Year's Eve with all the celebrations and functions booked here.

"No, I need to rest. *Someone* just abused my body for the last three days. I'm spent."

"Abused?" he repeats in mock horror, hand clutching his chest like it hurts. "Don't you mean awakened, aroused, pleasured—" I interrupt him, covering his mouth—the same mouth that woke me this morning by thoroughly eating me out.

His enthusiasm for oral sex is only surpassed by his enthusiasm for eating proper food. Christopher does everything with maximum effort. Afterwards, he told me I was his favorite *'petit-déjeuner'* ever—after a quick Google search, I deduced that it means 'small lunch', or breakfast. So, basically, I'm a meal he enjoys very much.

"I'd love to, but I really need sleep, and I can't get that with you." I take my hand away, and I replace it with my lips, kissing him. He takes control, like he always does, giving me that all-consuming, melting kiss I now expect. Every time we kiss, it feels like the first and last time simultaneously.

"I'll see you tomorrow, Sunshine." He swipes his thumb across my bottom lip, his eyes lingering for a second before he collects his case and heads over to his door.

As I walk in the opposite direction, we share one last look. A smirk graces his lips, and I shake my head. He thinks I'm going to be knocking on his door later tonight... I may very well think about it, but I won't let myself.

I need time to process this, he and I together. I need to have one of those girl moments where I can panic in private. I just complicated my life, and now I have to work doubly as hard to prove myself so no one questions my motives.

The next two weeks fly past. I've been so busy with holiday preparations at the hotel that Christopher and I barely have a moment to ourselves. It's the silly season, and we're both working six days a week just to get everything done on time. Some staff are working through Christmas, some are taking holidays, and rosters keep changing. With the influx of hotel guests, we've needed double our usual staff.

The city of London is alive with festive energy, and its lit-up nights are magical. I miss my New York, but here, with Christopher, it makes homesickness less raw.

I have regular dates with Anton and Vivian. They know Christopher and I are busy, but they force us to take time away from work.

I had the best Margarita Monday with Anton recently. He cooked a mouthwatering chicken curry and supplied me with so much alcohol I had to crash the night in Bee's flat next door. She told Anton to give me the key, and to pass on the message that if I ever needed time away from the Houston, I could stay at her place. Anton's been monitoring the flat for her, seeing as how he lives right across the hallway.

Their building is a stunning Victorian townhouse mansion, and they share the third floor, which has an airy open-plan design and hardwood floors. The shops and funky homes around the area are gorgeous; I need to explore more when things quiet down.

Christopher and I managed a couple of date nights—he took me to a show in Covent Garden, then later we had the best dinner at a fashionable restaurant where we both ate way too much.

We've been alternating between sleeping together one night and having a night alone the next. It's too much to have consecutive nights in each other's beds; we end up having way too much sex and not enough sleep. The only resolution was to separate so we can recover.

Right now, we're working hard and playing harder. My relationship with Christopher has progressed, and we physically can't get enough of each other, but we somehow focus during the day so we can run the hotel successfully. I think he's really trying to show me he can separate work from his private life. He hasn't been out boozing with his mates, either, aside from his friend's wedding, when he totally took advantage of the open bar and came home drunk—but I expected that.

Today is Christmas, and I wake to Christopher kissing every inch of my body, giving me his mouth, his lips, and his tongue as a present. So, I reciprocate by giving him the best blow job in my arsenal. He's so satisfied he can't speak afterwards.

I give myself a pat on the back. It's rare anyone can silence Christopher Houston. "Sunshine, that was…" he begins, slowly getting his voice back.

"Unbelievable? Extraordinary? The best you've ever had?" I laugh, running my hand down his beautiful chest, his abs flexing as I work my way further down. We're in my suite this morning.

"All the above," he answers, kissing the top of my head. I run my fingers over the tattoo on his thigh. It's a military-style tattoo with the British flag and insignia. He told me his great-grandfather was a heroic, decorated soldier who fought in World War II. I love that he has a reminder of his family's sacrifice on his body. I want that for my mom. She didn't fight in a war, but she fought a massive battle, and I want to remember her strength. I want to look at a reminder of her on me every day.

"Can you take me to get a tattoo one day?" I ask, tracing his beautiful artwork with my fingers.

"Of course, Sunshine, what do you want?" He runs his hand through my hair as I rest my head on his stomach.

"Something for my mom. I'm not sure yet, but when I decide, will you take me?" I look up. The appeal of his blue eyes never seems to fade. Even though I look at them every day, they still send shivers through me.

"I would be honored." I feel a lump of tears in the back of my throat at his response. I can't bring my mother back, and I'm in a new city with a new life, but now I feel much less alone, because he's here with me.

"I have something for you." He leans over the side of the bed, searching.

"We said no gifts!" I panic. We promised not to make a fuss because we had no time to go shopping.

"*You* said no gifts. I just nodded," he answers, and I give him my angry face. I don't like receiving gifts. It makes me feel uncomfortable, *especially* when I don't reciprocate.

"Christopher," I start, but he interrupts me.

"Summer…" A smile plays on those lush lips of his. "It's just a small thing." He hands me a little black box with a black ribbon—my color, which makes me smile.

I unravel the ribbon and open the box to find the most beautiful gold charm bracelet. It has stunning small round links with tiny little charms on it. I bring it closer so I can see them better. There's the Eiffel Tower in Paris… a love heart with diamonds… My eyes flick to his. He's watching me closely. I see a miniature Empire State building… Big Ben… a little seashell… and a ribbon crossed over a tiny pink stone.

I recognize the symbol—it's the breast cancer awareness sign. My eyes fill with tears. As much as I try to stop them, they escape through my lashes and spill down my cheeks. I don't think anyone has ever given me such a meaningful gift in my life other than my mother.

He's curated all these little pieces of me: my dad, my mom, my life in New York and now London, and our time together in Paris. The love heart must be for him.

I have no words. All I can manage is the barest whisper. "Thank you."

But he knows. He knows exactly how important this is to me; that's why he did it. And I'm terrified to admit it, because it's so fast, so intense, so risky that it hurts… but I'm in love with him. I'm in love with Christopher Houston.

CHAPTER SIXTEEN

IT'S ALL BLACK

"The property agents' convention is underway, Ms. Hart," Alice says, peeking her head around my office door.

"Thank you, Alice. I'll just finish up here and head across shortly," I reply, looking up while continuing to tap the computer keys. Alice gives me a thumbs up as she leaves.

The Houston Hotel simultaneously hosts two international property conventions in London and New York. Time Magazine dubbed last year's New York counterpart the 'largest event of the year for the world's most profitable property magnates'. Despite its comparatively smaller size, the London hotel remains highly successful. It's been nice to have a smaller hotel during the busy holiday season. I feel a little calmer and less frantic here.

Christmas was spectacular. London was a winter wonderland, freezing yet beautiful. Christopher and I had an amazing dinner hosted by Anton and Trey, with Mel, Simon, and a very adorable two-year-old Kate, and even Vivian popped in after her big family gathering. Although Mel cultivates a tough persona, she's actually quite gentle, and her and Simon arrived with a heap of presents for all of us.

Seeing Christopher give Kate a gift he purchased was so sickeningly cute that it made my ovaries feel like they would burst. I wanted to watch him play funny faces with her all night, but after the excitement of the day she desperately needed an early bedtime. Toddlers, they're all action until they crash out.

Anton worked his magic and put Bee, Jarrod, Eléa and Max on video on his T.V. so we could wish them all a merry Christmas. It would have been better to have them in the room with us, but seeing their faces, in real time, was more than a consolation.

Christopher especially looked overjoyed to see his family, and my heart felt a little sad for him. He isn't used to being alone like I am, and the longing to be with his family was evident in his eyes.

Those same eyes spent much of the day locked on mine, with too much heat, too much need. I had to work so hard at staying neutral in front of everyone, but he didn't seem to care. I worry they all noticed his gazes, his lingering touches, his attention that always seemed to find me, but no one said anything.

After Christmas, we hosted the best rooftop New Year's Eve party the hotel has ever seen. On New Year's Day I woke up next to a very warm, very naked Christopher, who spent the night making up for not being able to kiss me at midnight, much to his frustration. Afterwards, he took his time showing me his personal New Year's resolutions, in private. We had a long weekend and didn't leave his apartment once. The combination of exhaustion mixed with finally getting some alone time was enough to keep us in our own little bubble for a while.

Thankfully, room service kept us fed, while Christopher made sure I had every luxury known to man—the best French wine, hot baths with deliciously fragrant bath oils—and ample entertainment—we stayed up late watching movies. Unfortunately, he forced me to watch so many Fast and Furious films I practically had to threaten to return to my suite before he let me choose one.

I made him watch one of my favorite childhood movies, an Australian film called Red Dog. When it came out, I was missing Australia, my schoolmates, and my dad after running to the United States, and I was struggling to adjust to this new world we now called home. My mom, who grew up in the States, settled in quickly, but as a foreigner it took me longer.

I was about twelve years old, and I remember being so excited to hear the Australian accent again. I would imagine my dad in the movie, having beers with his mates and laughing at the local pub. Though the film has some sad moments, it ends on a happy note, and I must have watched it a hundred times over.

It reminds me of my first home, the happier times, when my dad was alive and my mom wasn't a punching bag for an egotistical abuser.

Christopher must have realized how much it means to me, because he curled up behind me on the sofa, his arms around me, his chin on my shoulder. It was the first time I watched the movie with someone other than mom, and this time it hurt a little less. He somehow took away the old pain and replaced it with something new. Something more secure.

I had to translate some words, which I thought was hilarious. Christopher hasn't been to Australia, and therefore thought the movie was exaggerating the way they speak, but from what I remember of the Australian 'outback', it's pretty spot on. Beer is gold, the men wear short-shorts even to work, and the sun is *hot*. It can burn your skin in the blink of an eye. Its golden rays dazzle you across the water.

When the movie finished, he let me talk for an hour about Australia. I told him how the beaches are so beautiful you think you're dreaming. I told him about the native animals. I told him just how beautiful my home country is.

When I was done, he just stared at me with those baby-blues that remind me of a clear, cloudless day, and said: "Now I know why your parents called you Summer." My face must have held a question, because he clarified by saying. "I've never experienced an Australian summer, with the scorching sun as you described, but I can't imagine anything as overwhelmingly radiant as you, Sunshine." My heart literally paused in my chest as his words seared me to my bones.

That night, I could tell it was different for both of us. We said nothing; we didn't have to. Our connection was so much stronger, and I knew I'd fallen for him hard. I knew there was no denying it anymore, that it was time to be honest with myself and everyone else in my life.

I'm madly in love with Christopher Houston, and I had absolutely no control over it whatsoever. My heart went and did that without my permission, the traitor. I know I've probably fucked up my professional life, but the regret I should feel diminishes with every kiss. Every touch.

I shake my head and close my laptop. I can't afford to sit here and let my thoughts distract me when I have work to do. I lock up my office and head out to check on the event in our function room.

After the conference concludes, the attendees will proceed to The Wave for drinks and entertainment. I know Daniel has everything under control—we have a full roster of staff and the bar is well-stocked—but I'm working a little longer tonight just to make sure everything runs smoothly.

Christopher is out at a friend's birthday dinner, so it's up to me to make sure the event goes as planned.

Christopher hasn't been drinking and partying like he did the day I arrived, and even Vivian commented that he's less 'playboy', more 'responsible business manager' lately. I had no response to her observation, because that would mean owning up to our relationship. Christopher and I need to have a conversation about how we're going to tell people, and I'm secretly dreading that conversation… I feel safe in our little bubble of wine, sex and food.

I spot Daniel at the back of the function room, and I walk over to him.

"How's it all going?" I ask. He looks so handsome tonight, in his dark burgundy three-piece suit. I don't think I'll ever tire of seeing men in suits.

I'm also dressed in a beautiful pantsuit that Vivian made me purchase. She told me it's 'my color', and I was hesitant at first, but now, wearing it, I feel confident and strong.

It's a wide-leg, cadet-blue tailored pantsuit, and the color is so out of my comfort zone, but it really does suit me. Vivian was right. Tonight, I've paired it with my comfortable black pumps and a black fitted cami, to offset the blue.

"It's going great, Summer. In about thirty minutes we'll finish here, then we'll direct them to The Wave. I think we should close the bar around two a.m." He nods at a woman walking past. She's eyeing him with interest, her smile a little flirty and a lot confident. I wonder if Daniel mixes business with pleasure. He's an attractive man, but from what I've seen he's a consummate professional.

I'd wager he knows how to keep his private life separate from work, a thought that makes me feel a little ill, because who am I to talk?

I shake off my discomfort. As far as I'm aware, no one, including Daniel, knows yet, so I have a little more time up my sleeve before I have to endure the whispers and workplace gossip.

"Wonderful, I'll do a walk around the room to introduce myself, then meet you at The Wave in thirty minutes. Let's get this done so we can go home and put our feet up. Thankfully, it's the last major event for a while, and we can go back to our normal routine," I say.

"You can say that again. The holiday season has been bonkers," he agrees, and I nod in acknowledgment. It certainly has.

I spend the next thirty minutes socializing with property investors, developers, and real estate agents from all over the world. I'm glad to see some women who've made it to the top of their game, holding their own in a male-dominated industry.

There are two women on the experts' panel, and they impressed me not only with their achievements but their ability to answer every question with speed, intelligence, and poise. I must tell Eléa about it when I speak to her tomorrow.

She calls me every week. I feel terrible telling her everything about the hotel, yet nothing about what I'm doing with her son. I don't know what her reaction will be, and I don't want to disappoint her. Will she regret sending me here, and trusting me with her life's work and a piece of herself? Parents can be very protective of their children, and I wonder if I'll measure up to her hopes for Christopher.

I know I'm getting ahead of myself. We're barely dating, and as much as my heart is involved, I know it's still early. We haven't even mentioned the 'L' word yet, but I feel it every time he touches me, every time he kisses me. Or maybe I'm delusional and he treats all the women he sleeps with the same way… I want to slap myself for thinking about him with other women.

I can't help but wonder if he's out having an amazing night and not even thinking about me.

The room is suddenly noisy, and I'm pulled abruptly from my thoughts. The panel has finished, and the guests are cheerily making their way out of the conference room across to the open doors of The Wave. Work is complete, and now they can let their hair down, mingle, and enjoy the best wine and liquor we have on offer.

I breathe a sigh of relief. It's been a huge few months since my arrival, and I finally feel like I've demonstrated my professionalism and reliability. Christopher and I have pulled off some monumental events while keeping the hotel running like clockwork, and after tonight, we can all take a breather and relax. I may even have time to rent a darkroom nearby and print some of my photographs soon.

I generally use a digital camera, but recently I had a chance to shoot some film photography. I want to create something pure, not filtered through an image sensor or computer. I'll have to ask Vivian if she knows where to find a dark room in the city. She knows lots of artsy people.

I spent the next two hours caught between boring property chit chat and drunk, flirty men with wedding bands on their ring fingers. Despite my fatigue, I perform at my best to foster new connections. The Houston has an excellent international reputation, and I'm a face of the brand. I need to wine and dine the big guns like a pro, and I think I do very well tonight.

Just before one thirty a.m., I head over to Daniel, and rather than interrupt his conversation, I motion that I'm done for the night. He gives me a nod and a gentle raise of his glass in response. I know what he means: we did well, and now it's time to rest. Making my way through a dense crowd of suits, I head for The Wave's door.

Christopher still hasn't returned, even though he said he'd be back by now. His friend's party must have held him up longer than expected. I look down to see if I have any missed calls or text messages from Christopher.

Because I'm not looking where I'm going, I collide with someone, hard enough that my phone crashes to the ground. This person appeared so suddenly it's almost like they stepped in front of me deliberately, but I'm sure that's not the case. I bend down to pick up my phone, apologizing profusely. That felt jarring.

"I'm so sorry!" I say, checking my phone to make sure it's not broken. Thankfully, it seems perfectly fine. "Totally my fault. I wasn't…" All the air leaves my lungs in a sharp gasp. My body freezes immediately, like a deer caught in headlights that can sense danger but is completely petrified.

Part of my mind is telling me it's not him, it's not possible, but the other part will never forget his face, his dead eyes. He looks older now, but just as threatening as the last time I saw him.

"No harm done. I'm sure it was an accident." His accent confirms my worst suspicions. His voice is rougher, more mature, than I remember. His eyes scan my face, like he too has seen a ghost from the past.

He's an attractive man even though he must be close to fifty, but that's what people don't realize: real monsters aren't always ugly. They can be tall, blond, and handsome, or accomplished business executives who seem outwardly harmless. But behind closed doors… they become the worst kind of threat.

My legs shake. I need to get away before he recognizes me. I was only ten years old; surely he has no idea who I am, even if he thinks I look familiar. I need to get my body under control. I take a deep breath and step back, then I give him my best professional face under the circumstances.

"My apologies. I'm a little tired. It's been a long day. Excuse me." I force myself to step around him, walking to the elevator on legs that feel like rubber. My lungs burn with every breath. Where the fuck is Christopher? I need him so badly.

I make it to the elevator and press the button. I notice my hand shaking, and I smooth it down my pants, trying to appear normal in case he's still watching. I shoot a quick text to Christopher, letting him know I need to see him as soon as he gets in. Hopefully he's already on the way.

The elevator pings and the doors open. My relief is tangible. As I take a step forward, I turn my head one last time to find him still standing there, still staring at me. His blond hair is still thick but streaked with gray. His suit is expensive. His sharp jaw and angular features give him an authoritarian air.

The expression he wears freaks me out, because I remember that smile. It's the same one he gave me right after I bit him to stop him hurting my mother, the same smile that says he's going to make me sorry I challenged him. It's like he's a predator, baring his teeth to warn me that running is futile.

Right now, I see that same smile the ten-year-old me saw, and I want to run so far and so fast that he can never look at me or touch me again.

I take the last step into the elevator, repeatedly pressing the door close button as fast as I can. I need to get to my room, where I'll be safe, and wait for Christopher. He'll know what to do.

I can't cause a scene without ruining our pristine reputation. I won't risk any public backlash for the hotel.

I make it to my room, slamming the door shut, and finally gulp in a lungful of air. I feel like I'm going to be sick. Visions flash before my eyes of my mother's pain, the humiliation of having to run, the fear of him finding us.

All the memories come rushing back with vivid clarity, things I don't want to remember, to relive. I dealt with that shit years ago, and I thought I would never have to feel that kind of dread again.

I force my legs to walk over to the wine cabinet, and I open a bottle of red. I gulp down two glasses, and my hands finally stop shaking. I check my phone, but there's still no response from Christopher. I send him another message.

"Fuck." I take a few deep, long breaths. The convention is over. He'll leave the hotel, and I can call security in the morning to make sure he doesn't come back.

I decide to take a shower to help relax my tense muscles. The wine is doing a decent job of keeping my nerves at bay, and once Christopher gets home I'll make him stay with me the entire night. It's not our night to be together, which probably explains why he is out later than usual, but tonight I need him next to me. I need his strong arms around me. I need to feel safe. He makes me feel safe.

I take the hottest shower I can tolerate in an attempt to clear my mind, and wrap my hair in a fluffy white towel while I dress in my usual black t-shirt and underwear. Deciding one more glass of wine is necessary, I start heading back towards my living area.

Suddenly, I feel it. That dark, oppressive air, like right before a terrible storm hits. The hair on the back of my neck instinctually stands on end, and I stop on the threshold of my bedroom.

There he stands, casually sipping my wine, the worst nightmare I could ever conjure. He's real.

"Did you think I wouldn't recognize you, Summer?" His accent, his voice, take me back to a time I don't want to think about. A time and place I loved until he ruined it, ruined my mother.

"How did you get in here?" I try and sound confident, but my voice shakes on the last word.

He laughs, taking another sip of wine, drawing out a response like he has all the time in the world.

He holds up a staff access card. I have no idea how he got it, but that must be how he got access to this floor. It doesn't explain how he got into my room, though.

"How did you get in here?" I ask again, more firmly this time.

He doesn't like that, and his smirk drops as he places the wineglass back on the counter. "You look like her, do you know that? *Exactly* like her." He takes a menacing step towards me.

I have nowhere to go. My eyes flash towards the door, my only exit, and he smiles again. That creepy, sinister 'I want to scare you' smirk. Fucking psychopath!

"Her birthday. I never forget dates, Summer... It wasn't very original of you, was it?"

His mocking tone wants me to know how intelligent he is. He got past security; he guessed my room code and got into my private space.

The realization hits me that no one will know he's in here. I can't count on anyone to come to my rescue. I'm in this situation alone, and whatever happens from here, I have to fight my way out of it.

"Where is it?" he asks, taking another step towards me. My mind is trying to think of a million ways to get out of this situation. The front door, my phone, the distance to the bathroom where I could lock myself in… but he's too close. I wouldn't make it.

"Where is what?" I ask, my eyes scanning the room for any kind of weapon I can use against him.

"DON'T FUCK WITH ME!" His scream stops me cold. I turn back towards him. His face is dark, angry. All humor is gone now, and I realize I'm in even more trouble than I thought.

He's had years to think about us, hate us—who knows, maybe he even did worse to someone else after us… *Because* of us.

"I'm not. I have no idea what you're taking about," I reply with my hands outstretched, trying to placate him.

"Where's the stone, Summer?" He vibrates with barely controlled anger, those eyes getting darker and darker every time he speaks. I'm less than five feet from him now, and my legs are getting ready to push off and run the second he charges.

"I don't know what you mean. What stone?" I keep him talking, but also because I have no fucking clue what he is on, or what he's talking about.

"Amelia took something precious from me—a rare diamond. I want it back." I'm not sure if this is bullshit to confuse me and mess with my head or not. I take a step back, putting me in my bedroom with no real exit, but giving me more space from him. I desperately need the space.

My heart beats so hard I feel like my chest will explode, my mouth dryer than a five-dollar steak.

"She's dead; she died a few years ago. I don't know why you think she took it, but I don't have it." I try to stay calm, my voice filled with fear I know he can hear. Hopefully he can also hear my honesty too.

"Fucking liars! Both of you!" he spits, advancing on me, as I leap to make it to the bathroom.

I don't bother answering him. I don't think he's even listening to me anymore. His rage is taking over, like a volcano spewing molten lava, volatile and angry.

I make a break for it, but he grabs my hair, yanking me back. My neck feels like it's being crushed in a vice, my lungs burning with the need for air. I fight as much as I can: I scratch his face, leaving gashes with my nails; I claw at his arm, the one holding my neck to the mattress; my legs kick at his back; but his solid weight is on top of me. I think about my mom, experiencing this very fear, the same absolute panic and terror, her life flashing before her eyes. Now *my* life is flashing before my eyes.

"Tell me where it is, you fucking bitch!" he yells, his fingers squeezing my neck harder, the other hand holding my clawing hands away from his face. Adrenalin helps me, but the lack of air brings darkness into the edges of my vision. The pain lessens as black dots dance in front of my eyes. His angry face flashes in and out, and distantly I hear a loud bang, but my eyes won't stay open.

I feel him release me, finally, but my eyes won't open. I hear loud noises, crunching noises, someone yelling, then nothing. It all fades to black.

CHAPTER SEVENTEEN

RECOVERY

Beep… Beep… Beep… Pain, lights, voices… Then, black.

I'm dreaming. I feel her touching my hair and my face. She's smiling at me. I want to speak, but no sound comes out.

Mom.

She caresses my hair and holds my hand. Hers is so warm, yet I feel so cold. Bright light is all around me; my eyes are closed, but I can make out shapes through my translucent eyelids, shadows creeping towards me.

I'm not ready to leave yet. She looks so beautiful with her wavy, dark hair just like mine, and her sun-kissed olive skin. She isn't speaking; just smiling at me. Why won't she talk to me? I try again to speak, but there's a sharp pain in my throat, as though I've just swallowed a thousand razor blades.

"*L'été*, don't try to speak, *chère.*"

Mom?

In a loving gesture, she pats my hand. I try again to force open my eyelids that feel like solid lead. I manage to crack them open slightly, but it's not my mother. It's Eléa.

Am I still dreaming? She's in New York, isn't she?

Where am *I*? I'm in a state of utter confusion. I can barely move; only my arms respond, and only a little.

"*L'été*, please don't move. Just relax. You are in the hospital." Her accent makes it sound like she's saying *op-ee-tahl*.

I turn to my right, and see her worried face, just a short distance away. Slowly, my eyes focus on a room that's somehow dim even though there are bright incandescent lights above me and the blinds are open. We're alone.

I see vases full of colorful flowers resting on every surface. An upholstered loveseat opposite my bed has a hospital-issue pillow and blanket on it, like someone's been sleeping there. Was it Eléa? How did she get here so fast?

My foggy brain is gradually coming back to the land of the living. I remember being at the hotel, the function, finishing work for the night, and then… The trauma comes flooding back.

His dark eyes above me, his hands around my neck, squeezing, fighting as hard as I could to breathe. Pain shoots through my throat as I remember everything. I bring a hand up to my neck. There are so many cords and tubes attached to my body, which I struggle to navigate in my sluggish state, but I have to check.

My neck feels normal on the outside, if a little tender, but inside it burns with a fire like nothing I've ever felt.

Eléa must see the horror in my eyes and realize I'm recalling what happened, because her eyes water. Mine well up too, matching hers. She's all blurry now, as the tears spill over my lashes.

"*L'été*, please… please," she begs. "You are strong, you are safe, it's over now." She smooths my hair back gently, like she's worried I'll break if she touches me. It reminds me of my mother; it comforts me.

The tears continue to flow; I can't help it. I know I can't speak, but she's ready, knowing what I need like it's her motherly instincts kicking in.

"No speaking, just listen, *chère*." I nod slightly to acknowledge her gentle request.

She dabs at my eyes even as they continue to leak. From the jug beside the bed, she pours some chilled water into a glass with a paper straw. She positions the straw against my lips, and I open my mouth, desperate for something cold to help relieve the pain.

I take a small sip, but it still hurts as I swallow. I grimace, and Eléa comments, "Slowly, *L'été, un peu...*" I take another small sip, and she removes the straw.

"So, let me tell you how it is." I nod for her to go ahead. I'm slightly more comfortable now, even though swallowing feels worse than getting throat-punched by a two hundred pound MMA fighter.

"That wicked man—I won't say his name—he was at the hotel. We checked the security cameras. He saw you in The Wave." She eyes me a little warily, but I nod for her to go on. I want to know everything.

"He followed you for a while, then when you were leaving, he caused a collision. You walked into him." I remember. It feels like a year ago, but it just happened. It *was* deliberate, then—he knew who I was.

I nod again for her to continue. "He saw you take the lift. He found one of the staff members—Cathy, in housekeeping. You know her?" I nod in assent. Poor Cathy. She's a single mom to a nine-year-old girl; I hope he didn't hurt her. My worry must show in my frown, because Eléa quickly adds, "Cathy is fine, *chère*. He charmed her, distracted her, and when she turned around, he stole her staff card from the cleaning cart. She was part of the clean-up shift after the conference, remember?"

I nod again. I feel like a bobblehead, but considering I can't speak and can barely manage these slight head movements, this is my only method of communication.

"She feels awful, *L'été*, but I assured her it wasn't her fault, that dangerous man is very cunning." Her face turns hard as she looks out the window. Anger simmers under the surface of her usually composed features.

"He got access to your room, but we don't know how. Did he guess the code?" I nod yes, he did. I could never have imagined that this would happen, let alone that my past would come back to haunt me, to *hurt* me, by using my mother's date of birth. It's inconceivable.

"You know what happened after that. He attacked you." I nod again, my tears threatening to fall yet again. Only he and I know what happened in there.

Now, the part I don't understand—did they find me unconscious? Where is he? Did they arrest him? I have a hundred questions flying around my head, but I can't put the pieces of the puzzle together.

"I'm so sorry, my beautiful girl, that this happened to you. *L'été,* you were supposed to be safe in our home."

I know she feels responsible, but I won't let her; this isn't her fault. I shake my head no, and tears roll down my cheeks. I wish I could tell her that, I wish I could speak so badly.

"Christopher…" She tries to speak herself, but the emotion is too much and she has to pause.

For a second, I panic. I can't remember seeing him that night. I remember sending him messages, but he never responded.

What happened? I hope he's alright. I beg her with my eyes to finish the story.

"He hasn't left your side since it happened. I made him go home earlier to shower. He'll be back soon, and you can see him yourself. My son found you in your room with that man." I shake my head. I don't understand.

"Christopher said he came home to hear you screaming. He almost broke the door down to get inside, and he made it just in time." I cry noiselessly, unable to produce any sounds, just silent agony. I can't imagine him finding me like that, but if he didn't, I may not be here now.

Eléa continues, her voice emotional and raw. "Christopher stopped him. That's all that matters now." This is the heavily edited version of events, I'm sure. I remember the few times Christopher saw other men talking to me, and how he reacted. 'Christopher stopped him' must be the understatement of the century.

"You are going to be well again soon. The doctors will be here later this afternoon to speak to you. They tell me some things because I am on your medical insurance documents, but they were waiting for you to wake up before they say anything more."

I nod. I listed Eléa as my next of kin in case of emergencies—like this, I suppose. I squeeze her hand, trying to show her how much I appreciate her flying all this way for me.

"Everyone is here, *L'été*, in the family waiting room down the hall," she tells me while she strokes my hair again. Who is 'everyone'?

"Did you think it was just me, *chère*?" She shakes her head. "No. Max, Jarrod, Brooklyn, we all took the first flight over. Vivian and Anton are here, too."

I'm so shocked I can hardly believe they're all here, in the hospital, for *me*, but the one person I want to see most—the one my heart needs to see—is Christopher.

She points to the sofa with the rumpled blanket and pillow. "Christopher, he slept here." I can't imagine he got much sleep on that tiny piece of furniture; he's far too large a man for it.

My eyes float back to hers; we are both emotional and exhausted. I must look like a wreck. I lift my hand to touch my face, feeling for anything broken, for damage.

"Don't, darling, you will heal. It's nothing permanent," she assures me. Fuck. I feel some swelling on my cheek, and it hurts to touch. I bet I'm bruised. I cry again, not sure what I'm going to do. This is too much information to wake up to suddenly.

I was just settling in at the London hotel. I was just admitting my feelings for Christopher. Then, suddenly, like a nightmare come true, I was almost dead—no, *murdered*. I feel sick just thinking about it.

"Please, *L'été*, don't cry. We're here. You're not alone." As she gently touches my swollen cheek with the back of her soft hand, the door opens, and Christopher walks in. His hair is wet, like he rushed out of the shower so fast he didn't towel it off at all. He stands there, frozen for a minute, maybe in shock that I'm awake. Those beautiful eyes, the ones that follow me whenever we are together, now look anguished, tortured even.

We stare at each other for a minute. Eléa is forgotten in the space of a heartbeat when he murmurs softly. "*Mère, donne-nous un moment.* I need a moment with Summer," he translates for me. His eyes flick to her, then straight back to me, intensely, fiercely.

"Of course, *mon fils*," she answers, then gives me a little tap to get my attention. "I'll be back soon, *L'été*. I'll let everyone know you're awake." She heads out of the room, the door quietly clicking shut behind her.

Christopher stands there across the room, looking at me like he can't believe I'm awake. He hasn't moved since he entered. Was it really that touch and go? His eyes tell me as much.

I attempt to wipe the lingering tears clouding my vision from my eyes.

"Don't," he whispers as he starts to walk slowly towards me. I feel like I'm in some crazy dream. "I'll do it." The bed dips under his weight as he sits by my hip. The hospital bed is elevated, with my torso up at a forty-five-degree angle, so I don't have to lift my head to look at him.

Christopher is gentle as he touches my face, his thumbs wiping under my eyes so softly, with so much care, my heart breaks. He takes a huge breath, breathing in like it's the first real breath he's taken in days. His eyes roam my face and neck intensely, like when I woke up on my first night in London to find him up close and personal, counting every freckle I have. But now the smile is gone. Now, he's counting every bruise, every wound, cataloging them one by one.

I close my eyes. I don't want him to look at me like this. I can't imagine how horrible I look right now. I can't leave, or move, so I try to avoid his scrutiny by covering my face with my hands.

"Please, Sunshine, don't hide from me. I can't handle it." His beseeching tone shatters me. Christopher is normally so self-assured, so assertive. My eyes start leaking saltwater again, against my will. My emotions are all over the place. I can't speak, I can't communicate, I just have to lie here silently, hoping he can do that mind telepathy shit he does and understand me.

He takes my hand. I look down and surprise makes me gasp, sending a sharp pain shooting through my throat. Cuts and bruises cover his hands, like they were split open and barely held together. Blue, purple and green patches mar his hands, the ones that I always thought were so attractive, so beautiful and smooth for a man. Now they look like a boxer's that went ten rounds with a wooden post. My eyes fly to his. I hope he can see my confusion.

I take my hand and trace it over his cuts. He doesn't even flinch. "It's nothing, Sunshine. We can talk about it later. Just concentrate on recovering for now." He tries to downplay it, but I know you don't get cuts on your bare knuckles like that unless you've hit something *really fucking hard.*

I shake my head no. I want to know what happened. He lets out a frustrated sound, a small smile flashing on those beautiful lips. "Still stubborn, I see, even after putting me through hell for four days." I'm taken aback a little. Four days?

"Four days, Sunshine, that's how long you've been asleep for; five thousand, seven hundred and sixty minutes—I know, because I counted every single minute here with you." The pain in his eyes scares me. I may never remember everything, not the parts when I was unconscious, and not like he will, but the anguish I see in his usually untroubled face tells me everything. Christopher was really fearful. Panicked even.

I tap his hand again, touching the crusted cuts on his knuckles.

"I'm not ready to talk about it yet. I need some time." He exhales a breath, running his hand through his hair, the way he does when he gets frustrated. I nod for him to continue.

"My phone battery was dead. I can't tell you how fast I drove to get to you once I got in my car and charged my phone.

I knew something was wrong. " He looks away for a moment and I stare at his profile. He sucks his bottom lip into this mouth, like he's thinking, remembering, before he returns that blue stare back to me.

"Fuck… Sunshine, I heard you scream." He's trying to get the words out. I appreciate the effort he's making. It's obviously difficult for him.

My heart is pounding, making the machine next to me beep faster, so he can literally hear how anxious I am. I didn't know I screamed or even made a sound while I was being strangled by that maniac.

"I wanted to kill him so badly… I almost did." His soft touch on my cheek makes me emotional again, my eyes blurring for the hundredth time with tears. Christopher leans forward, slowly touching his forehead to mine, careful not to hurt any part of my face.

"I thought you were dead. I thought I lost you." His whispered words affect me like nothing else. I feel the salty tears glide down the back of my throat, burning like acid. I close my eyes just for a moment, to get myself under control.

"Please, baby, look at me." His soft words bring me back from the darkness. "I love you, Summer, you have to know that." His words are so fierce, yet his tone is so gentle. It's that Christopher-Houston-contradiction again. He can be two things at the same time, but only for me; he saves this part of himself for me.

God, I wish I could speak, wish I could tell him, but I can't. Not yet. As we communicate with our eyes, the door opens again, and I see Eléa standing on the threshold with a puffy-eyed Bee. Their concerned eyes zero in on us and our closeness.

I forgot for a second that our relationship was under the radar, and I attempt to remove my hand from his, but he stops me. My face, as swollen as it is, flushes with embarrassment.

"No, not now. Not ever again. They know, Sunshine. I'm not hiding anymore." I can only lie there like a broken doll while he keeps my hand locked in a stronghold, and with his other hand he smooths my hair back from my damaged face, love and care on display for all to see. Fuck, I wish I was prepared for this moment, for Eléa to know the truth. I had it all planned out in my head. I don't like surprises; I like to prepare for my battles.

"*L'été*, don't worry yourself, we are family *chère*, we love you. You don't think I know my son?" she asks me with a knowing smile, the first little sign of happiness I've seen since I woke up.

"Summer, there was no way you could waltz into the hotel and not make waves... Christopher didn't stand a chance," Bee exclaims with a smile. Her eyes are puffy and tired, but she is still a killer beauty, even when exhausted. I feel terrible for making them all worry.

"Hey, I had plenty of options," Christopher replies, winking at me, and I shake my head, trying to give a small smile. His playboy ways are a thing of the past, if I have any say in the matter. "I just prefer someone who doesn't take my shit, who can challenge me at work, and has the longest, fittest legs I've ever seen in gym shorts." His face is pure innocence, but his eyes give me that sizzle, that heat that we generate together.

"*Ouch*," he exclaims, rubbing his arm where his mother just pinched, or tried to—the Houston brothers have barely any loose skin. They're so fit and muscular, it's all hard planes and ripples.

I'm not complaining; I have one brother all to myself. My absolute favorite one.

"Don't mind him, *L'été*, he is, how you say *personne délirante*." I look at Christopher and he translates. He knows just what I need without me saying anything.

"She called me delusional, Sunshine," he says, rolling his eyes, but I know it's all fun. Christopher loves his mother very much, and they're so alike it's funny. That's why they butt heads. Jarrod is a little quieter and more introspective, like his dad.

Bee comes over to push Christopher out of the way. "My turn now. Give her some space, you big bear." He reluctantly detaches himself from me, but he doesn't go far, just enough to give Bee access to my bedside.

"We were so worried, Summer." She starts tearing up. I know it's hard to control emotions in these moments. I had some tough moments when my mom was sick, and especially at the end, when she was dying. It's all so surreal. At least in my case, I'm still here. I made it through.

I nod, letting her know I understand, and take her hand to show her I'm alright.

The door opens, and three unfamiliar doctors make their way in, all of them wearing pristine white coats with name tags pinned to their breast pockets. All three of them are carrying clipboards. Two of them stand by the end of my hospital bed, making notes of some kind. The third, an older man around sixty, with white hair and round glasses, approaches me. Bee steps back to give him and his colleagues some room.

"Summer, it's great to see you awake." I nod, my eyes traveling to Christopher, who watches everything with an anxious expression. He's trying to hide it, but I can tell.

"I know you can't speak right now, so just nod your head to let me know you understand. If you have any questions at the end, we can get a notepad and pen for you." I nod in response.

"I'm Dr. Silver, and this is Drs. Amari and Richards." I nod to them, holding up my hand in a little wave.

"How are you feeling, Summer? I'm glad to say you look much better than you did a few days ago." He smiles at me, checking his watch and marking something on his clipboard. I give him a thumbs up to indicate I'm as well as I can be.

"Good. You'll stay here a few more days, just for observation and to run some tests, but we expect you to make a full recovery." I gently exhale, trying not to hurt my chest and throat; it's such a relief. I see that relief when I look at Christopher again, too. His shoulders have dropped, and he looks significantly less tense than he was a few minutes ago.

"You will need some time to recover fully, so don't expect a miracle immediately. You were in pretty terrible shape when they brought you in." I nod again. I gathered from what I've been told so far that it was bad.

"The injuries you sustained were quite severe," he continues. I keep my eyes on Dr. Silver while he speaks, because otherwise the worry on the faces of the others will make me emotional again. "You have fractures to the cartilage structures of the larynx and trachea, neck trauma, bruising to your right zygomatic bone—your cheekbone," he clarifies. That's the swelling I can feel on my face. I don't remember it, but I must have taken some punches to the face during the attack.

Dr. Silver continues when I nod again, "You were lucky the pressure ceased when it did. It saved your larynx from permanent damage and prevented potential asphyxia, rapid neuronal death and neurological injury."

Just hearing that if I had been under that monster for any longer I would be a vegetable, or dead, fills me with such pain, such horror, I'm astonished I made it. My eyes find Christopher's once more. I know he saved me. He's the only reason I'm awake here right now. He must see the emotion in my eyes, because he pushes past everyone to stand next to me, taking my hand in a firm grasp of strength and support.

"We have performed extensive tests, X-rays, MRIs and C.T. scans. You will recover well, Summer. You just need to give it time. I don't want you to stress your voice box right now, so no talking for two weeks." He pushes his glasses up on his head, putting his clipboard down on my legs, which are warm under the hospital blankets.

"You may experience some hoarseness, dysphagia, anterior neck pain, and difficulty swallowing for a while." I nod again so he knows I understand. Fuck, two weeks and no talking. This is going to be interesting.

"I want you to rest up. The more you do now to look after yourself, the better your recovery will be. So…" He looks around at everyone—Eléa, Bee, and Christopher. "Summer needs rest and no stress. Liquid foods only for two weeks, like soups—warm, not hot—and smoothies." I nod. It won't be fun, but I can do it.

"And no physical activity whatsoever." Dr. Silver looks directly at Christopher holding my hand. Oh God! He means *sex*. in front of Eléa—I'm so embarrassed! My face must look like a tomato.

"What?" Christopher looks around at all the faces currently eyeballing him. "I won't touch her, I promise."

He looks down at me with that playboy smirk, like he can't help being the asshole I know him to be. *My* asshole.

I cover my eyes with my free hand. I'm sure it doesn't help, but I can't look at them while they think about me and Christopher fucking. I'm going to die of embarrassment—at least, it feels that way.

"Don't be embarrassed, Sunshine; I'm not. You need to get well so we can do lots of physical *activities* when you're healthy." The chuckle that follows his words makes me so mad I want to murder him myself.

Bee bursts out laughing, and Eléa looks like she wants to hit him this time. I shake my head, but the beautiful asshole holding my hand smiles roguishly, surely thinking all manner of dirty thoughts.

"Right, well, that's everything. Do you have any questions, Summer?" Dr. Silver asks, saving me from further embarrassment. I shake my head. It's pretty straightforward: rest, no solid food, no talking, and hopefully in a couple of weeks I'll feel more like myself.

"Before you go home I'll write up a list of instructions and give you some pain medication." I nod again. "I want to see you for a checkup in two weeks, before you start using your voice again, and we can take it from there. All the best, Summer. It looks like you'll be in good hands." I nod, while the other two doctors say goodbye and head out for the rest of their afternoon rounds.

"Alright, let the others in, but you get ten minutes, then I'm locking you all out. Summer needs rest." Christopher takes charge, and even though I'm so grateful to see them and know everyone is here for me, he's right. I'm losing steam; the emotional ride so far has drained me, and I feel like I could sleep for another four days.

My room resembles a family reunion with Max and Eléa, Jarrod and Bee, and Vivian and Anton practically pushing each other through the door to get to me. I try to keep my emotions in check; their concern and love for me awes me.

I finally get to look around at all the flowers in my room filled with the most beautiful blooms. From the London hotel, from New York, from Mel and Simon, a bunch from Anton's partner Trey. I feel like I'm in a florist. The most beautiful bouquet of all is from Christopher, which I know without even looking at the card, because they're black roses with black silk ribbons. My eyes mist up; he knows me so well in such a short time. I've never seen black roses in real life before now, but they're just as stunning and unique as I thought they'd be. He probably paid a small fortune for them.

After Christopher threatens everyone with physical harm to force them to leave, we finally have a moment alone. Sitting on the bed again, he strokes my face with such tenderness my heart hurts.

He offers me a sip of water. It's not as cold as before, but it's soothing, nonetheless.

Our eyes connect. We just watch each other, no words necessary. I know what he wants to say; I can feel it. Hopefully, he feels the same from me. My eyes close. I try to fight it, just for a little longer so I can look at him, but the pain medication must be kicking in.

"Sleep, Sunshine. I'll be here when you wake. I'm not going anywhere."

I fall asleep to his whispered words, knowing I can sleep without fear. I'm safe now.

CHAPTER EIGHTEEN

BIRTHDAY SURPRISE

I can do it myself, I type on my iPad, shaking my head.

I've been back home at The Houston for a week. Christopher has basically moved in with me, while the rest of the family is in the main apartment at the end of the hallway. He allows others to make brief visits throughout the day, but he's turned into some kind of bossy minder, dictating to his family when they can and can't spend time with me. Bee is going to rip his ears off any second. She almost called Jarrod to intervene, but Christopher relented and let us have some girl time alone while he went to the gym to work off some of that pent-up energy.

I'm bored as hell; I haven't left my room in a week. The beautiful asshole has appointed himself my nurse, my chef, my caretaker, and won't let me lift a finger! I want to slap him and kiss him at the same time. God, I wish I could kiss him. He won't even let me do that. He's taking Dr. Silver's instructions seriously, to the letter.

"I don't care if you can, Sunshine. I'm doing it for you," he says, proceeding to chop the bananas and strawberries for my lunchtime protein smoothie.

I'm surprisingly not too hungry, considering I can't eat solid food yet. I'm living off protein powder smoothies with fresh fruit, vegetables, and my all-time favorite, a salted caramel and chocolate one that Christopher adds ice-cream to.

It tastes like the most delicious dessert I've ever had. I don't even want to think about the calories in that one.

At night, I have soup prepared by one of our restaurants. Eléa and Christopher have arranged a nightly meal plan with the chefs to create thick and hearty soups that are still smooth enough for me to swallow without issue.

So far, aside from some pain at night when I lie down, I've been feeling much better. I'm only taking the pain medication for sleep now, and hopefully in another week I'll be off them for good. I'm bursting to go to the gym, but my very pretty, very frustrating personal warden won't even let me walk on a treadmill. I huff as I walk over to the sofa to sit down for the millionth time this week and pick up the magazine Vivian brought yesterday.

I feel guilty. Christopher's been doing early morning hotel work while I sleep. He takes emails and phone calls throughout the day, and the others have helped share the load. Jarrod and Daniel especially have been stepping in to lend a hand and help run things. I don't want them to give up their busy lives just to babysit me. I'll be fine, especially seeing as the police expect Steven to be in the hospital for another few weeks.

He's under arrest and recovering from multiple broken ribs, a broken collarbone, and several facial fractures. I don't feel sorry for him; I feel relieved that he got some of his own medicine back.

Christopher had to answer so many questions, and I was worried about him getting in trouble; however, given the severity of my injuries and my mother's detailed reports of past abuse in Australia, investigators here were able to verify the information with Australian authorities. To no one's surprise, Steven has a detailed history of past violence against women. They don't know how he got a passport—that's something the Australian government will have to investigate. After sentencing, he'll serve time in prison before most likely being deported back to Sydney.

Part of me wishes Steven didn't survive. I know Christopher still thinks about it. Some nights, I catch him rubbing his healing knuckles, lost in thought. I haven't asked him about that night again; I know he'll tell me when he's ready. I'm not alone in experiencing trauma, his version just differs from mine.

The blender stops, and he pours the smoothie into a large glass. I never tire of looking at him, as much as he's suffocating me right now. I think maybe his lack of space where I'm concerned has a little to do with his invisible wounds, so I'll allow him to smother me for a while longer if it makes him feel better.

"Your lunch, Sunshine." He hands me the glass, his baby-blue eyes glinting in the afternoon light. I can't believe tomorrow is my birthday already—January fifteen. I'm a summer baby in Australia where I was born, but winter everywhere else. My twenty-fifth birthday feels special this year, like a milestone of sorts.

Christopher takes a seat beside me, never away for more than a moment—at least until his mother kicks him out to give me a break. I sip my delicious drink, and a small sound comes from my throat, a little breathy moan of sorts. It's the first time I've heard a sound, and it shocks me. His azure eyes meet mine, studying my face, every freckle and fading purple bruise.

"Have I told you how proud I am of you, Sunshine?" he says in a low voice, barely loud enough for me to hear him. I cock my head to the side, waiting for him to continue. He takes my hair in his fingers, running them gently through the strands.

"You fought so hard. You did everything you could. You never gave up." It's the first time he's mentioned that night.

I can tell it's tough to think about, let alone talk about. I look down, touching my delicate charm bracelet he gave me for Christmas, my eyes brimming with tears. I haven't cried since the hospital, but now I just might start again.

Taking my chin in his hand, he lifts it so I can give him what he loves most: my eyes, stormy gray skies meeting cloudless blue. Gently, he leans over and kisses me, far too soft and cautious for my liking, not the usual all-consuming, fiery-collision kiss. But whatever he wants to give, I'll take. He barely flutters his lips on mine, but it's enough for now. Enough for me to feel him so close, his warm mouth on mine again. That little moan is back in my throat. He smiles into the kiss, his hand holding the side of my face moving us apart.

"You can't make those noises, Sunshine. It's not good for your throat." I roll my eyes at him. It's not like I can help it; it just happened. He forces me to sip my smoothie, placing his hand over mine to bring it to my lips again. Like a toddler, I comply, but once I'm better and can unleash all the words I've been holding inside, I'll let him have it. I'll punish him with my chatter nonstop, twenty-four-seven. He'll have to kiss me all the time to get me to shut up. I fully intend on payback. It's coming, Christopher, don't doubt that for a second.

"Tomorrow night, I have a table booked for seven downstairs, a little birthday dinner. What do you say, Sunshine? Do you feel like getting out for a while?" I nod. Hell yes! I'm bursting to leave my suite, even for a medical appointment. I don't want to fuss about my birthday, but this is just what I needed.

I take the iPad and type out a reply. *FUCK YES. I need out of this room! But tell them no gifts or I'm not going.*

Christopher reads my statement and laughs. I hit him in the chest to let him know I'm serious.

"Alright, Sunshine, I'll let them know. *No gifts.*" I hope he's being truthful this time, since his Christmas 'promise' was a lie. I quickly finish my smoothie, excited to check my wardrobe and find an outfit for tomorrow night. I leap up from the sofa and suddenly feel two firm hands on my waist, holding me back.

"Not so fast; you might trip over and hurt yourself." I turn around, loving his hands on me but also exasperated that he can't let me move from one room to another without his help.

I do the eye roll thing again and shake my head. That smirk says he's fully aware of his actions. He won't know what hit him when I'm better. I smile at him. Two can play this game, but there can only be one winner.

The dinner is just what I need. Vivian and Bee come over early to help me get ready. Vivian does my hair and makeup, making me look like a fifties movie star, with soft waves, winged eye liner, and red lips. She says I look like a young Gene Tierney in Leave Her to Heaven, a nineteen-forty-five American psychological thriller film noir. I've never heard of it before, but I might have to watch it next movie night.

Vivian is gorgeous as usual in a sleek white number, short and fitted, her long legs looking catwalk ready. Bee is wearing a red strapless dress tonight, her hair piled up in a messy golden bun and sky-high silver heels with a stunning diamond choker necklace. She told me Jarrod bought it for her. They're so cute together, it's like watching a romantic movie in real time. I'm hoping Vivian will meet someone soon. Her dating life is as sad as a circus without clowns, and the dating apps are full of creeps. I think she's disappointed her and Will didn't work out, but from what she tells me, he wasn't over Bee. He was honest with her, but how can you fall in love with a man who loves another woman? She had to move on from that potential heartbreak.

We kick Christopher out for a while, and he goes over to the main apartment, pounding on the drums in his music room while Jarrod plays guitar. Bee mentions how much time Christopher and Jarrod used to spend together, both playing music and working, before her and Jarrod left for New York. I want Christopher to spend as much time with his brother and parents as he can before they fly back to the U.S.

I hope he's having a great time. He plays drums casually, for a bit of fun—he's not a serious musician like Jarrod—but it's still a release for him, something he enjoys that takes his mind off work and stress.

I come out of the walk-in robe, ready to go, and do a little twirl to show the girls. I give them my 'what do you think?' expression, and judging by the looks on their faces, they love it.

Tonight, I'm wearing a new dress. I bought it online just before Christmas, hoping to wear it out, but we got too busy. It's perfect for tonight.

It's a beautiful shade of my favorite black. It's midi length, has one shoulder with a puff sleeve, a side leg slit, and a sexy cutout on the waist, with ruffles and an invisible side zipper. It's not too revealing, but it's definitely flirtatious. The little bit of skin peeking out here and there gives it an eveningwear look; I definitely wouldn't wear this out during the day.

"Summer, it's perfect," Vivian exclaims, her fashionista's eye thrilled with my choice.

"I'll be shocked if Chris doesn't rip that off you tonight," Bee says with a cheeky expression. I'm sure she has a lot of experience knowing what a hot-blooded Houston man likes. I silently laugh. I'd love him to try, but I know he won't. He'll just lie down next to me, smelling all delicious after a shower, and pretend he doesn't notice his hard-on under the sheets, or the tiny La Perla panties I wear to bed. Just to add to the torture, I know exactly what I'm doing. I'm competitive by nature; I like to accomplish things, and it's all part of my plan.

My goal is to get back to normal life and get Christopher to treat me like he used to, when he would be rougher, firmer. I'm not a fragile doll that breaks easily. I want his fingers to leave bruises on me in a good way. We had amazing sex before. I want that back. I want that strength he saw in me back. And when it's time, I'll tell him how much I love him. Though I can't say them yet, I want him to know how much those words will mean when I finally say them out loud.

The three of us make it to dinner fashionably late—well, ten minutes late—my first time being late, ever. It was totally Bee's fault; she insisted on a girls' toast before we left. I can't have any alcohol yet, but I let them suck down a full glass each while I sipped on fruit juice. I know Bee and Vivian missed each other and are making up for the last couple of months apart.

The three of us have formed a close bond—girl code and all that. Vivian likes to joke we're the new 'Charlie's Angels', which has sent Bee into a movie quote recital on multiple occasions. She insists the early-two-thousands movie is the best, not the twenty-nineteen version. Bee is a movie freak; how she remembers all the funny lines is beyond me!

As we enter the restaurant, the staff come up to greet me, like I'm some kind of local celebrity.

The concern is heartwarming, but the attention makes me anxious because I can't answer them verbally yet.

"Alright, let her have a little room. I know you all care, but Summer is still recovering; she'll have plenty of time to chat when she's back in a few weeks." Christopher takes charge, thanking the staff for their well wishes while shepherding me over to the family table. Everyone else has already arrived, and I'm greeted with a multitude of hugs and kisses.

It's a full table tonight; even Daniel's here. The concern on his face is what I'd imagine an older brother would show. We exchanged some emails this week, so I know he took it hard as well. I let him know there was nothing he could have done, nothing anyone here could have done.

The rest of the party comprises Anton and Trey, Max and Eléa—looking stunning in an elegant black pantsuit—Mel, her husband Simon, and their daughter Kate. Kate, right now, is in a cuddle sandwich with Jarrod and Bee. I watch them for a moment; I swear Bee looks about ready to be a mother herself. I could be wrong, but damn, they make an adorable-looking trio.

As we sit, Christopher takes my hand under the table, bringing it to his knee, making sure some part of me always touches him. "You look luminous, Sunshine." His eyes scan my body, lingering on my face. Vivian did such a magical job with my makeup; you can't see the fading bruises at all. I look normal—*better* than normal.

I can't say thank you, so I squeeze his hand in response.

"It's different. *You're* different, not like my usual Sunshine. More like… Moonlight." I watch him closely; his words are so beautiful, they affect me in so many ways. A new, softer Christopher has come out since the attack.

His words hold more meaning, his touches more care. It's like he's not afraid to tell me how he feels now; he's not holding back. Maybe experiencing a traumatic event does that—changes people.

"Do you know the moon doesn't actually shine on its own? It's a reflection from the sun." I shake my head. I had no idea. I thought the moon shone under its own powers. "No matter what, Sunshine, I'm mesmerized by your light." I draw a sharp breath. My heart aches far more than my throat at this moment. I really want to kiss him, tell him how I feel, but I can't. I use my free hand to caress his face, forgetting the ten—and a half—other people at the table.

Returning from our private moment, I see Eléa watching us, eyes filled with tears. The entire table is silent, making me feel self-conscious, but I look at Eléa, and she smiles—the most beautiful, happy, radiant smile I've ever seen her wear. I don't think I have to worry about her being angry with me for dating her son. I think she's just as invested in this relationship as we are. I smile back. I hope she knows her approval means the world to me. She means the world to me.

"Let's get this party started!" Christopher stands and gives the most hilarious speech to everyone about me. He's clearly loving the fact that I can't speak up and contradict his facetious take on my arrival at The Houston and how we knocked heads over the work titles. He amuses everyone with stories of our arguments, but thankfully leaves out any reference to the attack. I want to forget about it for one night.

"Finally, to Summer. I have to say, these past few months have been wild. Some of the toughest in my life, actually." He places a large black gift bag down on the table in front of me, and

I panic. I said no presents! I knew he would trick me. "But I couldn't imagine getting through it without you. Happy birthday, Sunshine." He leans down so I can hear his whispered words privately. "I fucking love you." Christopher kisses my red lips right in front of everyone. When he pulls away, I can't help it. Life is too short to be cautious. I grasp his face and make him kiss me again. I have no voice, but even if I did, I'm not sure I'd have the words to say right now anyway. I feel choked-up with emotion, for him, for these beautiful people. I look around at all the eyes watching us—some glassy with tears, others shining with happiness for us. Damn, I'm going to lose it soon. I don't want to mess up my make-up.

"Open it, Sunshine. It's from everyone." I look down at the large gift bag, which is black with silver ribbons, of course.

When I finally get my present open, I can only shake my head and look around at everyone in awe. I wish I brought the iPad so I could communicate how fucking insane this gift is!

I'm holding a brand-new Leica SL2 camera and twin lens kit. The only way to describe Leica cameras is to say they're like the Rolls Royce of photography. They're the best in the world for performance, and their craftsmanship is unrivaled. I think I'm going to faint. This set must cost twenty, or even thirty, *thousand* American dollars. And it's in my hands.

I look up at Christopher, and he smiles like it's the best thing in the world. I mean, it is—for me—but the cost of this—a camera that felt so unattainable it's basically a unicorn—makes me want to throw up!

"I know what you're thinking, Sunshine, but we decided to get you something special because *you're* special. You deserve this. Also, the small window we had to give you this, while you couldn't argue about it, was opportunistic. We want you to take amazing photos with it. Happy twenty-fifth birthday, Summer."

I feel like I could burst into tears at any second. I try shaking my head to wake myself from this dream, but it's real—a beautiful reality I now inhabit. I can't possibly refuse this.

I thank everyone without words, going around the table for extra big hugs.

We enjoy a wonderful dinner together. I jealously watch everyone else eat really delicious looking food while I'm stuck eating soup—it's tasty, pumpkin and leek, but I admit I'm getting over the liquid diet. I can't wait to eat solid food again. What I wouldn't give for a 7th Street Burger, double cheeseburger and fries!

Dessert makes up for the lack of a robust main meal when Christopher organizes an ice-cream cake for me. It's a caramel-chocolate drip cake, and I can't stuff it into my mouth fast enough. It's chilled and sweet and creamy.

Kate is doing the same thing at the other end of the table. She and I are on softer foods than the adults, but we make up for it with extra serves of ice cream.

Bee is in her element. There's only one thing she loves more than Jarrod, and that's ice-cream. It was a good choice.

Christopher knows how to please a crowd. Tonight, I heard all about his very entertaining past karaoke performances. I must witness it in person one day, but I may have to fake a sore throat, because there is no way in hell I'm getting up in front of a crowd to sing. Not for any amount of money or fame would I embarrass myself like that. I'm not beyond milking this injury if the need arises.

Later that night, in bed with Christopher, we don't speak. I don't use the iPad to convey my thanks or chat about the night. It isn't necessary. He knows how I feel, thanks to that super power he has that seemingly allows him to read my thoughts.

He just holds me as I fall asleep. The pain medication makes me drift off so easily, but part of me thinks it's my mind allowing me to fully relax because I'm in the safest place I've ever been: his arms.

"Wake up, Sunshine…" I drift awake from the medicated abyss slowly, a little foggy. Is it morning already?

"Summer, my mum is here, she has something for you."

I open my eyes to find Christopher already dressed, with Eléa sitting on the edge of the bed. I think last night was a little more exhausting than I realized. I have to remind myself I'm still recovering.

"*Bonjour, L'été,* did you sleep well?" I nod and sit up as Christopher hands me a glass of orange juice. I take a sip; it's chilled and fresh.

"*L'été,* I have some news from New York," she begins. I notice she has a package in her hands, the size of a legal envelope.

"A lawyer came to the hotel a few days ago, looking for you with a letter to deliver; we had it sent here. You need to contact him once you read it, *chère.*" She hands me the envelope.

I shrug, looking at them both. I don't know why a lawyer would look for me. I notice the name *Smith, Blackburn & Sons* on the front, with an address in the financial district. I open the letter and start reading:

I shake my head. I don't know what's going on. I hand the letter to Christopher; he's practically crawling out of his skin to know what it says. He reads it and passes it to Eléa. They share a glance, but I'm not sure any of us truly understand.

Suddenly, all the air is expelled from my lungs. The handwriting on the front is instantly recognizable as my mother's familiar script. If I thought getting an expensive camera last night was shocking, this takes the cake.

My hands shake as I unseal the envelope. It's like I'm in the twilight zone and my mother is communicating with me from beyond the grave.

CHAPTER NINETEEN

LETTERS FROM THE GRAVE

"Are you all right, Sunshine? Would you like me to read it to you?" I shake my head no. I need to do this myself.

I carefully open the envelope. It's at least a few years old but still in pristine condition. I feel like I have to preserve it, so I try not to rip the paper. I breathe in deeply to prepare myself.

"We'll wait in the other room. Take your time." Christopher's words instantly get my attention; I almost forgot I'm not alone. I nod, and they both leave, closing the bedroom doors behind them to give me some privacy. I can hear them through the door, murmuring inaudibly in French. Christopher's voice is so beautiful when he transitions to his mother's native tongue. I exhale and unfold the letter.

To my beautiful daughter Summer,

I know this may be a little strange, really strange. I thought it over a million times before I put pen to paper. I'm writing this imagining you at twenty-five. Happy Birthday, Summer, I love you so much.

Seeing you grow into a beautiful, talented, strong woman was my dream. You can't imagine how proud I am of you, your achievements, and the work you put into your studies. You have a drive and passion I never had for the academic pursuits.

I know you will do great things with it. You're probably reading this right now from the top of the world. I imagine the last few years without having to worry about my health have given you some freedom to push forward with your career dreams. I know what you're thinking... and don't!

I would give up my life a thousand times over so you could live yours. I've fulfilled my purpose. Yes, breast cancer sucks, and yes, I'm dying. But I know I'm leaving a strong and independent daughter who's going to live a wonderful, fulfilling life for us both.

I want you to do that, Summer. I want you to move on. Don't grieve for me. Enjoy a life with adventure, with passion, with love. Do that for me, will you?

My eyes mist. Damn, she knows just how to word things—the right things. I'd give up my entire career, my dreams, to have her back in a second. I keep reading.

I was always honest with you, my beautiful daughter, about everything. I never had secrets or hid the realities of life from you. Maybe that made you a little cynical. I hope not. I only wanted you to know real life has harsh moments: death, as you know. I'm not saying that there isn't a happily ever after; there is! Just not for me. You are my happiness.

I have a confession. I kept one thing from you all these years. I apologize for not telling you sooner. This is an extraordinary way to do it—after I'm gone and on your birthday—but I needed you to grow, to experience life, so you would understand my motive and the reasons it had to be this way.

I want to say I'm sorry. Sorry for not being strong enough to leave sooner. You know what I'm referring to. I kept us in a dangerous situation out of fear; I let it rule me, and I shouldn't have. I should have fought harder; I should have protected you more. But they are my *regrets. They will never be yours to live with.*

Oh, Mom… She is breaking my heart. I have never once blamed her or thought her responsible for what that monster did to us. I continue reading, her words making my heart hurt so much. I rub my chest.

In the end, I found the courage to do what I had to. I will never forget the kindness and help the women and staff from Hands of Hope gave us. Remember Maureen? I wonder if she's still working there today. I didn't keep in touch. I was scared he might trace us through them. Ridiculous, I know, but I was a paranoid mess back then. It was just you and me, kid. I had to protect you the only way I knew how.

The other reason I was so paranoid and kept moving us around when we arrived in the States, was that I took something from him. Before we left, I took a valuable item from him. He would have been so incensed when he realized what I'd done. I smile even now, all these years later, at the thought of that bastard being so furious we left. Not only that I damaged his ego, but I took a precious diamond, something he worked hard to acquire. I know he prized status and material things over anything else.

Oh. My. God!

My hand flies to my mouth. If I could yell and scream, I would right now. Fuck. He was telling the truth; she really stole a diamond from him! Well, shit. Nicely played, Mom, but it came back to haunt me after all. Not that she would have ever expected a chance run in, a random coincidence on the other side of the world.

He probably would have attacked me anyway, even if there was no diamond; it's just his nature. He isn't a man who forgets.

I know what you must be thinking, honey: "My mother, a thief? She stole from someone?" Well, technically, yes, I did. But it was my insurance. I wanted to have something that hurt him as much as he hurt us. I wanted to ensure your future so you'd be secure even if something happened to me. Summer, some punishment was warranted for him. I had to hold him accountable.

Again, this is my *doing, not yours, so don't feel bad. I knew what I was doing, and I did it without remorse. I never used the diamond, never sold it for money, because while I'm alive I'll take care of you. But now that I know I may not be here much longer, I'm going to make sure you get it.*

You're old enough to know the truth, to have finished your studies, to have settled. I give this gift to you to help you in life and to set you up for whatever it is you need to do to make your dreams come true. That bastard can rot for all I care. I did this for you, my daughter, and I'll never be sorry for putting you first.

I can't believe what I'm reading. Part of me is shocked, and the other part is damn proud my badass mother did something illegal. She carried a stolen diamond out of Australia and kept it safe all these years, not even tempted to sell it and use it for herself.

Gosh, I'm totally floored by this. I have no idea what to do. Her last words really hit home. I miss her so much.

I wish I had more time with you, but I don't. I'm writing this from my treatment room. I have a meeting on Monday with my lawyers at Smith, Blackburn & Sons to hand this letter in.

We had the diamond valued at USD315,610. It's a 5.01-carat round diamond. All the details and authentication papers are with the diamond in their locked vault. You'll need to get a current valuation to know its worth. Hopefully, diamond prices have gone up in the last few years and it's worth even more today.

I want you to pay off your student loans, buy yourself a nice apartment if you haven't got one already, go on vacation somewhere, maybe the Canary Islands—remember I used to tell you about them? Your great grandparents were from there before they moved to Spain.

Explore, my beautiful Summer. Live for the both of us.

I love you so much, and no matter where I go after here, I will continue to love you for eternity.

Mom.

Cascading down my face are tears of pride and longing, and the little noises coming from my throat are husky and raw, but they don't hurt. It just hit me now how much I wanted to hear her voice, talk to her one more time, and it's almost like I have. I'm not ready to move on, to live a life without her, but I have to. And I know this is her last word. No more letters will arrive on future birthdays. She said everything she had to say.

The doors open, and a worried Christopher walks in, his eyes scanning the tears tracking down my cheeks, ears picking up the barely audible gasps escaping me as I cry.

"Come here." He sits on the bed next to me, encasing me in his firm embrace, my head squashed to his chest.

"Hey, it's alright. No matter what it is, we'll get through it together." He gently strokes my hair, his softness at odds with how tight he's holding me.

I'm not crying because of the letter's content; I'm crying because it feels final. It's like now I'm really on my own, and she can rest in peace. I've been clinging to her for years, but now I feel like I can truly let her go.

I pull back and hand him the letter. His eyes scan my face for assurance. "Are you sure, Sunshine? If you want to keep it private, I understand." I nod. I want him to read it.

Christopher takes a moment to kiss me, just a light meeting of our lips, then he reads. It takes a few minutes, and my heart returns to its normal rhythm. I wipe my face and take another few gulps of the orange juice he brought me earlier.

"Well, fuck." He smiles, a big, beautiful grin, and I shake my head, lifting my shoulders… Asking why he is so happy.

"Sunshine, your mother was fucking exceptional. I mean, smuggling a stolen diamond, shafting that asshole in the best way she could. Saving it for you all these years. She was one hell of a woman. I will never get to meet her, but I know, just reading this, that I would have loved her. We would have got along for sure."

His words, the pride in his voice for her guts and determination, are so captivating. I grab his face and smack our lips together. I fucking love him for what he just said, and the honesty of his response. I know she would have loved him too, no doubt in my mind.

"Mum is just about fainting out there. Can we enlighten her now? Before she loses her shit?" I laugh, a small squeak of noise coming from my throat. I motion that I'm hungry, and he nods, pulling me up from the bed and giving me a smack on the behind. I shake my head at him with a smile.

"Get dressed. I'll make you some breakfast. Do you want the salted caramel smoothie?" I nod. Hell yes.

"Coming right up, my diamond princess." If I could call him a cheesy asshole right now I would, but I think he knows exactly what I'm thinking anyway, because his laugher follows him out of the room.

I need to get dressed. The next week is going to be filled with doctors' appointments, legal paperwork, and one huge fucking diamond to deal with.

Thank you, Mom, your timing is astonishingly brilliant… Just like the diamond you left me.

"Say the vowels for me, Summer."

"A… E… I… O… U."

I speak the vowel sounds as best I can, slowly. I've been at this for half an hour, with Dr. Silver coaxing my voice back one sound at a time. I have no pain, so that's positive; I just sound like a truck stop server who smokes five packs of cigarettes a day.

"Great! By the looks of it, you're well on your way to a full recovery." I turn and smile at Christopher, who insisted on coming to my appointment with me. Next he'll insist I add him to all my insurances and medical documents as my next of kin. He's appointed himself as my keeper, my protector.

He's very attractive. I can't complain as I look at him sitting there, in his fitted blue jeans, darker than his eyes. His black hoodie is disguising his physique—those toned arms and corded neck veins—but I know what he has underneath that top. I also suspect him wearing my favorite color more often is a conscious decision.

He looks stunning in black; it makes his eyes stand out even more, if possible. I want to jump his bones every day now, but he still refuses to touch me. Waiting for the go-ahead from a medical standpoint is admirable, but come on, I'm not breakable. I wish he would do something already!

"So, I can talk again?" I return my focus to Dr. Silver with this gravelly new voice I have.

"Yes, go slow, don't overdo it. And keep up with those vocal exercises. I'll see you in four weeks' time. Here's a list of everything, so you remember what we practiced." Dr. Silver hands me a pamphlet with instructions for things like vocal cord closing exercises, straw exercises to control airflow, and nasal air pressure exercises to minimize the stress on the larynx.

"And eating? Can I resume solid food now?" I ask, with unabashed hope. I really need to eat something that doesn't fit through a straw.

"Yes, your swallowing is great. It appears to be back in its normal range." I hear a cough from the other side of the room.

Christopher, the asshole, is trying to embarrass me with dick innuendos again.

"However, don't push it; we don't want a relapse." He turns to eye Christopher over his glasses. I smirk and give him the finger while Dr. Silver is looking in his direction.

Christopher pretends to be Mr. Innocent and just shrugs and goes back to looking at his phone.

"So, to sum things up for you, Summer: you can slowly resume normal behavior, but bear in mind that if you overdo things, you risk a longer recovery. Your neck and throat are still healing. Keep up the good work, have patience for a little while longer, and you'll be good as new." He shuts off the light and puts his glasses on his head.

"Look after yourself. See you in four weeks. Just let them know at reception and they will book a date in for you."

"Thank you, Dr. Silver, and I will. See you in four weeks." Christopher takes my hand as we walk out of the doctor's office and head over to the desk to make my next appointment.

As we walk back to the car, I stop him. I've waited two weeks to say something to him. It'll take a while for me to get all the words out, to tell him everything I want to say, but for now I'll start with a thank you.

"Christopher," I start, and swallow. My throat is a little raw after the appointment and all the exercises.

"Sunshine, you don't know how good it feels to hear you say my name again." He caresses my face, my neck. The bruising is all just faint yellow blotches now. Evidence of the brutal attack is all but gone. Well, the physical evidence anyway.

"Thank you," I force out. My emotions are getting away from me again. I'm not normally an emotional person, but this experience has changed me. It's also shown me that being vulnerable, asking for help, and relying on others aren't bad things. It's what friends do for each other; I understand that now.

"You don't have to thank me for anything." I cut him off, placing my fingertips over his lips. It's my turn to speak; he can listen now.

"Yes, I do. Thank you. You saved my life. You stopped him from…" I have to swallow again as unshed tears coat my throat. "Well, you know what. But I need you to know how much you mean to me. What you've done for me since the incident, taking care of me… I feel it. I feel it and more."

I remove my fingers from his lips, touching them softly as I go. I'm about to replace them with my lips, because I really need to kiss him right now, but I have one more thing to say.

"All I've ever wanted was to have a home again, somewhere I felt safe. Somewhere people could love me again. It's been a long time since I've been on my own. But now, with you, I feel like I'm home."

His eyes shine bright despite the dull sunshine outside. The wind is not freezing, but the cool afternoon air flushes my cheeks.

"I wasn't lying in the hospital. I love you, Sunshine." His whispered words are full of emotion. I wrap my arms around his neck, running my hands through his hair.

"Now, if you don't kiss me like before, I'm going to tell Eléa it was you who broke her expensive vase on our last movie night." I smile, his eyes widening at my threat. Our sex fest was a little robust that weekend. Christopher practically threw me over the sofa with his mammoth strength, and my foot hit the table behind, causing her beautiful crystal vase to crash. I cringe at the reminder.

"Me? It was your foot that connected with the table, Sunshine." He laughs as he grabs the hair at the nape of my neck, firm but not hard enough to hurt. "Blackmailing me will get you punished," he whispers against my lips.

"I hope so," I answer, before he gives me exactly what I want. The signature Christopher Houston, rough and gentle, firm but soft, passionate kiss I desperately need. It's a contradiction of everything I thought possible. And I fucking love it.

That night, after signing what feels like a mountain of legal paperwork so the diamond can be sold at auction, I'm glad I don't have to travel back to New York. I don't need to see it. What would I do with such a large rock, anyway? *Smith, Blackburn & Sons* will take care of the sale and fetch me the best price they can.

I haven't thought about what I'm going to do with the money yet, but I know, deep inside, I have to do something for *her*. Part of the money will go to paying off my student loans, and I'll be completely debt free, which feels strange. I was expecting to be paying those off for many years to come.

I just have to think about the best way to honor my mother's memory.

"What are you thinking about?" he asks me as we lie in bed. His hair is still wet from his shower. I roll over, the beauty of his features so perfect in the moonlight they make my heart ache.

"Just trying to figure out how I can honor Mom with this money and what my options are." He pulls me in closer. It's never too close for him. He invades my personal space every second of every day, like he did that first night in London, when I woke up to him in this same position, breathing on me, staring at me. I now realize that's just him—intense, interested, almost inquisitive, like a child. He loves to notice every little detail.

"Don't stress about it. Things will happen at the right time. Just concentrate on getting yourself completely healed, and you can work on what to do later." I nod; there's no rush, I guess.

He pushes my hair behind my ear, his other hand smoothing over my hip. My body responds immediately; it's healed enough for now.

"Perhaps we should stop talking?" He gives me a smirk. I've missed that mischievous look on his face. He was far too serious and worried about me. It's good to see his playfulness back again.

"Oh, are you over me talking again already?" I ask, running my hand down his chest. As he sucks in a breath, I trace the light dusting of hair down his abdomen, reaching the spot I've been dying to touch. His eyes are so focused on me; they're like lasers. He's so hard already, like steel encased in velvet, strong and silky at the same time.

"I missed your voice, yes, but I missed your mouth on mine even more." He doesn't let me respond; he kisses me with so much passion, so much depth, I almost cry.

We forgo the foreplay tonight. The need to connect in the way we do is overwhelming. I just want to feel him inside me again, to feel alive.

We kick off our underwear. I'm surprised he doesn't tear them again, but instead he quickly pulls them down my legs before resuming his passionate kisses.

His fingers trail down my side, tingling and making me shiver before he feels if I'm ready, and I am. I've been ready for a week. The sensation of his touch, as he massages me, caresses me, and penetrates me with sure strokes, almost brings me to orgasm.

"Oh God," I moan. "I've missed this." I exhale, my voice so much deeper, huskier than usual.

He doesn't say a word. He just buries his face in my neck, kissing the lingering marks of my wounds, kissing them away as he fingers me with all the passion and desire I love. He does nothing without one hundred percent precision.

I come on a breathy moan. "There she is, my Sunshine," he whispers. Christopher enters me, not giving my body a moment of recovery; he wants to feel my response, he wants to feel me squeezing him, and it heightens my reaction. My body rolls into a second mind-blowing orgasm.

Fuck, he's so good. We're so good together.

"I want more," he demands, like a pirate stealing his treasure, and I give him everything.

We spend most of the night holding each other and making love slowly. I don't remember falling asleep, but the last thing I remember is him whispering to me, "I fucking love you, Sunshine."

CHAPTER TWENTY

THE LONG FLIGHT HOME

It's taken six weeks for me to fully recover. It's also the length of time the monster has been hospitalized. Christopher really did a number on him, apparently. He's lucky he's not dead. Christopher only stopped because I was on the bed, unresponsive.

I hear Steven was remanded to prison while awaiting his July sentencing hearing. I bet he never thought coming over to a property convention in the UK would change his life and make him an international criminal… An attempted murderer. In my mother's words, I hope he rots.

I've heard snippets of what happened, but Christopher still won't go there with me. I think—no, I know—it's not the violence he exploded with that upsets him; it's me almost being killed that haunts him. So, I let him keep that night to himself. I won't pressure him to talk about it, although I wish he would speak to someone. Maybe he's been talking to Jarrod.

I was sad when the others returned to New York last week. They stayed as long as possible, but Bee and Jarrod have a recording contract to uphold. Also, Eléa and Max have to check on the hotel and the staff that were running things while they were here. I promised to video chat them weekly, so they can see for themselves that I'm fine and well looked after. I think they're also secretly thrilled that Christopher is happy and no longer alone.

I've been back at work for a couple of weeks now, although my shadow—the one that follows me everywhere, tries to take on the bulk of the work and forces me to leave early every afternoon—is adorably overbearing. I love his concern, but I'm a big girl. Christopher has been my rock through this entire ordeal, but I can't let him put his life on hold for me any longer. I need him to go back to how he was before, not worry every second that I'll get hurt.

That's why I'm currently packing my suitcase under the pretense that I have some photography editing to do. It's a weekend, so slipping away will be easier than during a busy work week. Our weekend staff are managing with experience and ease.

I've taken the last month, since my birthday—and Mom's letter—to really think about everything. I need to do this for myself and Mom. I need to accomplish this one thing on my own, so I can put my past to rest and happily move on with my life. If I tell Christopher, he may get offended that I want to be alone for a short while, but it's just something I have to do solo. I love him, but I'll regret dragging him with me; it's been too emotional already. He's done so much for me.

The diamond payment came in yesterday—wow! No kidding, I'm sitting on just over four hundred thousand after taxes and legal fees. I felt a twinge of guilt for a second, that Mom took something that wasn't hers, but then I thought, fuck it, he ruined our lives. and almost killed us *both*. It's a dose of karma my beautiful mother dished out, and I hope he chokes on it in prison.

No matter how much I hate him, I love her more. She supersedes everything. I'm going to do something with this money, and I know she'd be proud. I'm donating part of the monster's valuable diamond to the *Hands of Hope* shelter in

Australia. Ironic, really, that the violence he used to send us there will now help many other abused women and children.

That's where I'm going. It's been a secret from Bee and Vivian, and even Eléa, because I know they would want to come with me. They have the best intentions, but I need to do this on my own. One last time. Home is where I'm headed.

I watch as the lights of Sydney come into focus. It's been a long flight, the same as when I left here with just seashells in my pocket, but this time I'm flying business class and I'm all grown up. A survivor.

I've been thinking of Dad lately. Coming home, it feels nostalgic and a little somber. I've been social media stalking, and I found Dad's sister, Casey. She must have been a teenager when I left. I vaguely remember her from when I was a kid, but because they lived further out in the country I didn't see them very much. But now, with social networking so popular, I found her.

I sent her a message before I boarded the flight, and I'm hoping she sees it and responds. I'm so nervous that she won't remember me.

"We are now approaching Sydney International Airport. Please fasten your seat belts, ladies and gentlemen. It's currently eight twenty p.m. on the twenty-second of February, and it's a comfortable twenty-three degrees Celsius. Enjoy your time in Australia, folks." The pilot switches on the fasten seatbelt sign, and I prepare for landing.

Over the next two days, I dodge messages from everyone, even Christopher. Although I assure him I'm fine, he's determined to find out what I'm doing.

Sunshine, God help me if you don't tell me where you are. Did you take the money and run? Please, I just need to know you're safe. Call me.

I feel terrible, but I needed time to process everything, to set up my plan. Now, in the back of a taxi—because there are no Uber drivers in rural country areas—I make the call.

"About fucking time, Sunshine," he answers, exasperated but relieved, I think.

"I know, and I'm sorry… I had to switch off for a few days to process everything." I take a deep breath. I'm ready to talk now.

"Are you alright? I needed to hear your voice." My heart breaks a little at his quiet words.

"Yes, I'm good. Or at least I will be soon." I see a homestead up ahead. It's so pretty. One of those white-painted weatherboard houses with a porch.

It's almost the end of summer here, but it's so warm and beautiful. I missed the sunshine, the blue sky, and the white beaches.

"I'm in Australia," I say, suddenly a little nervous. This felt like a good idea when I was on the other side of the world.

"Fuck. Alright… I thought you just went M.I.A. for a weekend, but…wow…" He's taken aback. I can tell I've shocked him. "Why?" His single-word question and tone indicate he's upset at me right now.

"Don't be mad, I had to do this on my own. I knew if I told you, you'd drop everything for me and come with me," I respond. We're almost at the end of the long road; I need to be quick.

"I'm not mad; I'm worried, baby." My heart breaks at his genuine concern.

"I know. Look, I have to go; I've arrived. This is part one of my plan, the second will be in two days, and then, when I'm done, I'll come home. I promise." I take a deep breath as the taxi pulls up out front of the house. I vaguely remember it; I think I came here a few times with dad.

"I'll send you my device location. Will that make you feel better? You can see me in real time, in case of an emergency or something… Not that anything will happen! I'm fine, really." I rush out as I take cash out of my handbag for the driver.

"I'll feel better when I can see you in person, Sunshine," he answers, sounding more mollified now.

"And you will in just a few more days, Christopher. I have to do this." I hand over the money. "Thank you," I say to the taxi driver.

"No worries at all, darlin'." I smile. Gosh, hearing that Aussie accent brings back memories.

"See you in a few days," I whisper to Christopher.

"Be safe," he answers, and I disconnect the call.

I walk up the porch steps, a little nervous. I knock, knowing Casey is expecting me. When I arrived in Sydney, her message conveyed excitement and surprise. I'm so glad she was happy to hear from me after all these years.

The door opens, and a really lovely-looking woman stands there. She's just like I pictured, only older and more seasoned. She must be about thirty-seven now. With her sandy blond hair, freckles all over her tanned face and shoulders, and no makeup, she's a natural beauty; a classic country girl with hazel eyes.

"My God, you look like your mother," she exclaims, her hands coming to her chest, over her blue sundress. She's heavily pregnant, and I take a surprised breath myself.

"I have his freckles, the same as you." We stand there for a moment, drinking each-other in.

"Yes, you do. Please come in, Summer. Don't mind the mess, the girls are little tornadoes." I smile.

It's a warm house with old timber floors that look like they had a good sand and a coat of paint recently. It's filled with rustic furniture, and children's toys are all over the floor; I step around a few on my way to the kitchen.

Casey has set out a little afternoon tea on the table for us: a teapot, sponge cake with jam, and… lamingtons! Oh my god, I *loved* lamingtons. Mom used to put them in my school lunch box.

"Thank you so much for seeing me. I know it was a shock."

She motions for me to take a seat as she fills the teapot with boiling water. "It was a shock, but a good one. I've been wanting to find you for years, but you didn't have listed phone numbers or any social media accounts," she says, sitting opposite me.

"No, we left suddenly. I'll tell you everything shortly," I say, eying her round belly, "but first, tell me: when you are due, how many children do you have—?"

Just as I ask that question, two little hellions with golden-blond hair come barreling around the corner, squealing like the hounds of hell are chasing them, but it's just a cattle dog wearing a pink tiara. I burst out laughing at the sight.

"See? Tornadoes. I told you." Casey laughs and calls the girls over for introductions.

"Summer, this is Matilda—she's seven—and this little troublemaker is Ella—she's five. Girls, this is your cousin—she came all the way from America." I smile. I don't correct her and say I came via London; I'll get to all the little details soon enough.

It's an amazing and kind of dreamlike afternoon. I unload the past fifteen years on Casey. Sitting quietly, she takes it all in, her expression darkening at my account of recent events involving Steven. She has a little cry when we talk about my dad, her brother. She tells me her new baby is a boy, due in eight weeks, and they're going to name him Peter—after Dad. That makes me emotional too.

I feel like I'm divulging a segment of 'This Is Your Life', and I wonder if I'm overwhelming her, but she wants to know everything. She wants to fill in all the blanks while the girls fill the house with laughter and noise.

Casey tells me how she met her husband, Jake; that her parents passed away some years ago now, well into their eighties; what they do for work; and how the last fifteen years have been living out here. She was on her own for a while until she met Jake, and I'm glad to see her settled and happy.

I tell her about my time in New York, moving to London, and meeting Christopher. The afternoon goes by so fast I'm reluctant to leave, but I know she has dinner to make and mouths to feed. She's probably exhausted, too, being pregnant.

I call for a taxi, but it'll be another half hour before one can arrive at this remote location.

"Girls, please stop attacking your cousin, wash up now," she commands, and they moan for a few minutes. They've been sitting on me, touching my hair, counting my freckles. The girls were amazed to find we have the same-shaped freckles, and Casey told them it's because we're family.

I almost cried hearing her say that. Her eyes got a little misty, too. I have a family. It hit me like a truck when she said that.

My heart is so full it's bursting. I took a million photos with my new Leica camera. I've had it strapped to me since I arrived, capturing as much as I can, so I never forget it. This time I'm not leaving without photos or memories.

On my way out, after promising to visit again soon—keeping in touch is a non-negotiable, or Casey said she'll push this baby out then drag them all onto a plane to track me down—even Cookie, the cattle dog with the pink tiara. I laughed at the thought; the girls thought it was the best idea ever.

"I promise. I may be in London now, but I won't run away again. I'm here to stay—figuratively speaking—if you'll have me," I say, giving her a big hug around her firm belly.

"Summer, I can't tell you how happy I am to see you. You're my brother's only child. Honestly, it's like a miracle. Oh! I have something for you. Open it after you leave; I can't handle any more hormonal breakdowns." She waddles over to the side table and picks up an envelope. I take it, placing it in my bag for later.

"Thank you, Casey, you and the girls… I needed this. I needed you." My voice breaks on the last word.

"I know… Me too, Summer."

The taxi's lights shine in the darkness. The time just flew by so fast; it's late now. I feel bad for staying so long, but it was wonderful.

"See you soon. Send me pictures of the baby, of Peter," I request.

"I will, don't worry. I'm going to send you so many photos and messages you'll regret asking." She laughs.

"No, I won't," I say, and walk over to the waiting taxi.

I started the year as a twenty-five-year-old orphan, but now I'm surrounded by a new family, by people who love me, and that's more valuable than all the diamonds in the world.

It's my last day in Australia, so I go for a morning walk on Coogee Beach, taking photos of everything I can: the birds, the water, the people. It's like no time has passed at all since I was here. Returning after a long absence to a place you called home during your childhood is an odd experience.

Yesterday I went to the cemetery and placed some flowers on Dad's grave, with red and white ribbons—the colors of his favorite footy team, the Sydney Swans.

I opened the package Casey gave me, and I lost it so hard my vision blurred. She found some old photos of me and Dad. Photos of me as a little girl, on his shoulders, laughing at something. Lots of him playing footy as a teenager, fishing out on the water. I thought I'd never see any again. We left everything behind when we ran, so it was a shock to see. Her parents—my grandparents—must have kept them.

The memories are so beautiful, and I'm going to take them home and frame them. It's like she's given Dad back to me. I had no physical evidence of him other than some little seashells, and now, it's like I found him again. He *was* real.

I check my phone for directions and see I'm not far away now. I shake the sand from my shoes, making sure I'm clean for my meeting at the *Hands of Hope* shelter. I'm a little nervous but also excited about my plan to honor my mom.

The weather is so stunning today. It's hot—certainly hotter than chilly London. The end of summer here is still roasting hot for some days. Today it's twenty-nine, clear skies and pure sunshine. I'm wearing a floral red minidress, with white flowers, ruffled little sleeves, and a belted waist. I found it in a boutique down the road when I did some shopping after visiting the cemetery. I aimed to dress nicely today, to look my best, so I paired the dress with red lipstick, neutral eye makeup, and cute strappy leather sandals.

I purchased a few gifts to take home for everyone—nothing extravagant, just enough to let them know I was thinking about them—but I still have to find something for Christopher. I want to find him a present that holds significance, though I'm not sure what.

This part of the city is busy, bursting with color and life. I follow the directions and find the place I'm looking for, only ten minutes' walk from the beach. It's a nondescript building next to a Christian pre-school.

I take a deep breath and open the doors.

It's just as I remember. Outdated but clean, with a locked mesh door requiring a security key to enter. I press the buzzer and wait.

"*Hands of Hope*," someone answers through an intercom.

"Hi, I have an appointment with Maureen. My name is Summer." I hear the buzzer sound, unlocking the door. As I turn the corner, an elderly lady in navy blue capri pants and a pale pink shirt comes to greet me. I think it's Maureen, but I can't be certain. I was so young at the time.

"Summer, come through to my office. I'm Maureen." That answers my unasked question.

"Great, thank you."

As we take a seat in her neat little office at the front of the building, I take a calming breath.

My eyes scan the room and the photos on the wall of women, hundreds of women, with Maureen, smiling; many have *Hands of Hope* logo t-shirts on. I wonder if my mom is on the wall, but maybe it's been too long.

"How can I help you today, Summer? You said something about your mother when you called?" Maureen puts her glasses on, waiting for me to divulge the reason I'm here. She knows I'm not in need of services or help. I only told her it was regarding a historical situation fifteen years ago.

"Yes, I doubt you would remember me or her. I know you help so many women and children," I begin. Somehow, I get the story out, enough so she understands the time frame, what happened, who we were…

"Oh, yes." She scratches her head, then covers her mouth for a minute, thinking. I mean, she must be in her mid-sixties now.

"The American woman, I remember now." She looks at me with fresh eyes, like she really remembers us.

"Summer, you're all grown up. The accent confused me," she says, smiling.

"Yes, I lost my Aussie accent years ago," I laugh. "The reason I'm here—" I pause for a second "—is because something happened recently. I don't want to get into all the sordid details, but the man who abused us, well, he found me." Her eyes widen. I've shocked her. "I know… It's been a really messed up set of events. But something good came out of it."

I open my bag and pull out the bank envelope, handing it to her. "Don't ask me how or why, but I came into some money recently, relating to this situation." Maureen takes the envelope, and with a frown, she opens it as I keep talking. "Your shelter saved our lives, and I know my mother would be happy that I'm using some of it to help other women and children, like us. I hope you accept this donation in memory of her, Amelia Flores."

I give her a minute to read the note, and I swear, she looks like she's about to keel over.

"Summer, how? Are you sure? My gosh, sweetheart, it's a shit-ton of money." I smile at her outburst. Her cheeks turn pink in embarrassment.

"I know, but it's the right thing to do. Thank you, Maureen. Thank you for helping to save our lives fifteen years ago. Now I can move on from the grief and sadness and know the sacrifice my mom made wasn't for nothing."

She shakes her head, looking at the bank note and back at me. "It wasn't for nothing. Money or no money, Summer, she did it for you. That's all she cared about." Hearing those words gives me strength. She was so brave, so strong.

"OK. Well, I'll leave you to your work. I know it's only a drop in the ocean, but hopefully you can do a lot of good with it." My heart feels lighter already.

"Thank you again, Summer. This kind of donation will change lives. Many lives." I nod.

I hope so. Two hundred thousand dollars is not a meager amount. I gave away half the diamond money—Mom's half.

The rest I'll use to pay off my student loans and hopefully afford a nice holiday back to Australia later in the year to introduce my aunt and cousins to Christopher. I look forward to telling him all about it.

I push through the doors with one last wave to Maureen and step outside. I close my eyes, taking a moment to release the air slowly, release all the years of pain, grief, and loneliness.

I feel the sun on my face for the first time in a long time—I mean really feel it—warming me from the outside in.

I'm ready to go home now.

"You are the most radiant thing I've ever seen, Sunshine."

That voice snaps me out of my daydream, and when I open my eyes, it's like a mirage. I see him standing there, in dark shorts and a white t-shirt, aviator sunglasses on, hands in his pockets, like he's been waiting patiently for something. Or *someone*.

My mouth opens, but no sound comes out. I'm rendered speechless. He's such a beautiful vision, I'm too scared to move in case he disappears.

He takes a few steps towards me, removing his glasses so I can see his eyes. They match the sky today. So clear, so vivid, so blue. They take me in, as if he hasn't seen me in years. He's so close now I can smell his cologne, the spicy, woody scent.

Christopher takes my chin in his hands, caressing my face gently, like he's not fully sure I'm real either.

"Did you think I wouldn't come for you?" he asks, in that deep gravelly voice he has when we get intimate. "I'll chase you to the ends of the earth if I have to." His mouth, with the soft full lips, bows upwards at the ends. Damn, he is so sickeningly pretty it hurts. "Don't you get it? I fucking love you," he whispers into my lips, before he kisses me crazy.

I'll never get over the way he does this, the way he kisses with such abandon. Even on a Sydney street, in front of everyone, he doesn't care. He kisses me with so much passion, so much love, I feel it right down to my bones. Now, I'm ready to return it. He deserves it. I kiss him like the sun on my skin, warm and sultry.

I pull away, just enough so I can speak the words I've wanted to say for a while but was too afraid to.

I've lifted the weight of the past from my shoulders, and I'm ready for the future I see with him.

"You know what? I fucking love you, too." I smile so big my face hurts, and he kisses me all over. I think he kisses every single freckle on my face.

"About bloody time, Sunshine. You made me sweat over it." Christopher takes my hand, entwining his fingers in mine. "Are you hungry?"

I know for certain that he can eat at any time of the day. He's always hungry. The man devours his food like a starved animal and constantly thinks about his next meal.

"I could go for a burger," I answer, swinging my hand in his as we walk back to the beach and the local cafes.

"Good, because we have people waiting, and they're starving." I stop walking and look at him, confused.

"People?" I ask, not sure what he means.

"Yes—Mum, Dad, Jarrod, and Bee are waiting for us at the Coogee Bay Hotel, opposite the water."

My mouth hangs open. What? They were in New York! "Christopher!" I exclaim. He smiles, that naughty boy smirk I love so much that tells me he's up to no good.

"Did you think you could run away from us, Sunshine? You belong to us. We're family." He kisses my surprised face again, and I shut my mouth. Well, fuck. He brought the cavalry to Sydney for me!

"Let's eat. Then you can tell me about your little adventures in the land down under, where people speak some weird gibberish but the beer is fucking fantastic."

I can't help but laugh. He's such an asshole… but he's mine.

EPILOGUE

Eight Months Later…

"Have you packed your passport, Sunshine?" he asks. Does he think I'd forget something like that?

"You should know me by now, Christopher. It's been almost a year," I quip back. "I'm the most organized planner, and most efficient and methodical person you've ever met." I roll my eyes as if to say, 'like, really?'

"I know, but sometimes I like to annoy you; it's my favorite thing to do," he replies, smiling.

"Asshole," I murmur under my breath, but he must have heard me, because the next minute I'm on my back, lying on the folded clothes we're supposed to be packing in our suitcases.

"Do you want to be punished for that insult, Sunshine?" he speaks into my neck as he kisses me there, soft lips trailing down my collar bone. His weight is a massive pressure on top of me, but I don't care. I know he'd never hurt me.

"Yes," I answer with a breathy exhale. I'll never get sick of his form of punishment because it always involves mad-hot sex and multiple orgasms. I can't even pretend to put up a fight.

"I might actually punish you this time; make you wait for it." Those baby-blues of his are all up in my business, looking at me, examining every detail of my face the way he loves to do.

"You'd be punishing yourself if you make me wait." I push his hair from his eyes. He's been growing it longer; it looks sexy right now. I run my fingers through it. So silky and soft. Pirate hair. *Hot* pirate hair.

"How about we finish packing and move all the crap off the bed, then I'll spend the rest of the night fucking an apology from you?" His intense eye contact never fails to turn me on. From the moment we met last year, he's been trying to take my soul from my body. He wants to connect us together, fuse us, and I wouldn't have it any other way.

"I'll never apologize, but good luck trying," I challenge with a grin, leaning up to kiss his mouth while it's so close to my face.

"I'll try very hard, Sunshine, so hard you'll fall in love with me." I remember him saying similar words to me months ago, on the night I got drunk on too many Tommy's. Petrified, I thought falling in love with him would be the world's worst mistake.

The memory flashes back in my mind: we were in this same room, on my bed. I'm not scared anymore. Now I don't have to worry, because I'm already so in love with him that my heart is bursting.

"It might be a little too late for that. I already am."

"I bloody hope so Sunshine, because I kind of bought you something." I saw a mixture of anxiety and unease in his gaze as his eyes search my face.

"Bought me what, Christopher?" I ask, about to have a full-blown panic attack.

"I was going to wait until we landed in Sydney, but the waiting is more stressful than the asking, Sunshine. I'm losing it here," he tells me, as he moves off me, and we both sit up on the bed. He goes to the nightstand on his side and gets a small black box.

Now I panic for real, because, shit… is Christopher Houston about to propose to me? Fuck.

Christopher walks back to my frozen body and sits next to me. He places the little leather box in my hand and holds his over mine. He intends to get the words out before he lets me open it.

"Summer." He begins with my name, which he only reserves for really serious talks, or work.

"Oh, shit," I whisper, which makes him laugh… It's a nervous laugh, but he finds my suspicion humorous, apparently.

"Summer," he begins again. "I've thought about this for so long. I thought about doing some big over the top theatrical gesture, but that's not you." I nod for him to continue. It's true.

"This past year has been so crazy, both the best in my life and the worst." He takes a moment to look at me, really look at me. "When I almost lost you, it changed me… I'll probably be an overbearing sod for the rest of our lives, but understand it comes from a good place. I want to protect you, I want to share a life with you, and most of all, I just want to love you."

My eyes mist at his words. I'm going to cry, I know it.

"Will you let me do that? Will you marry me, Sunshine?"

I don't even need to think about it. I know my heart wants this—to fuse myself with him forever. I moved over here to London for work, for a career, but what I found was a home. He's my home.

"Yes, Christopher, I'll marry you."

His eyes light up like Fourth of July fireworks. He leans in to kiss me—the most beautiful, passionate kiss I've ever experienced. Maybe because my heart is finally free of pain, guilt, and loss, and it's full to the brim with family, friends, happiness, and with him.

"Can I see the ring now?" I ask with a teary smile.

"Fuck, sorry, baby." He lets go of my hand, and I bring the little box up to my face and slowly open it.

My breath catches. It's a stunningly large, oval-cut pink solitaire diamond with little diamonds encrusted around the gold band. I mean, it's simple, elegant, and beautiful. It takes my breath away. It's perfect.

"It's called the Amelia diamond." I look at him, confused. "I don't know why, but many diamonds get names according to how they were discovered, how rare they are, cut, color, things like that. I have no idea why or how, but it's true, Sunshine. It shares a name with your mother."

"Maybe she's still out there somewhere, watching, and this is a sign she's happy for us," I say as a single tear falls down my cheek. I'm in awe of his gesture. It's not only beautiful, it's got a precious connection to me.

"I know she is." He pulls the ring from the box and puts it on my finger, holding my hand for a moment. I watch his eyes drink in the sight of it. It's a perfect fit, tailored just for me.

"I fucking love you, Summer."

"I fucking love you, Christopher."

THE END

292

I hope you enjoyed following Summer and Christopher's journey in *The Sun*. I enjoyed creating their story and providing a second book in the Houston Hotel Series. Thank you for continuing the ride with me. The third and final book, *The Rain*—Vivian's story—will be out shortly. Take care.

Tanya Rose.